A descant for gossips

Thea Astley was born in Brisbane and studied at the University of Queensland. Since 1958 she has published sixteen books. Her first collection of short stories, *Hunting the Wild Pineapple*, won the Townsville Literary Foundation Award in 1979, and *It's Raining in Mango* won the Steele Rudd Award and the 1988 FAW ANA Literature Award. She has won the Miles Franklin Award three times: in 1962 for *The Well Dressed Explorer*, in 1965 for *The Slow Natives* (which also won the Moomba Award), and in 1972 for *The Acolyte*. *A Kindness Cup* won the *Age* Book of the Year Award, *Beachmasters* won the Australian Literary Society Gold Medal in 1987, and *Reaching Tin River* won the New South Wales Award for fiction. Her most recent novels are *Vanishing Points, Coda* and *The Multiple Effects of Rainshadow*, which was shortlisted for the Miles Franklin Award and won the FAW Australian Unity Award for Fiction and the *Age* Book of the Year in 1997. Thea Astley lives on the New South Wales south coast and writes full time.

Also by Thea Astley

Girl With a Monkey
The Well Dressed Explorer
The Slow Natives
A Boat Load of Home Folk
The Acolyte
A Kindness Cup
Hunting the Wild Pineapple
An Item from the Late News
Beachmasters
It's Raining in Mango
Reaching Tin River
Vanishing Points
Coda
The Multiple Effects of Rainshadow
Collected Stories

THEA ASTLEY

A descant for gossips

UNIVERSITY OF QUEENSLAND PRESS

First published by Angus and Robertson
Published 1983 by University of Queensland Press
Box 42, St Lucia, Queensland 4067 Australia
Reprinted 1984, 1987, 1989, 1991, 1996, 1998

Printed in Australia by McPherson's Printing Group

Distributed in the USA and Canada by
International Specialized Book Services, Inc.,
5804 N.E. Hassalo Street, Portland, Oregon 97213–3640

Cataloguing in Publication Data
National Library of Australia

Astley, Thea, 1925– .
A descant for gossips.

First published: Sydney : Angus and Robertson, 1960

I. Title.

A823'.3

ISBN 0 7022 1843 X

One

Almost as long as Vinny Lalor could remember she had been on the fringe of things. Family and school both found her their least important member. They circled giddily without needing her. She was afraid, as she clung to the spinning edges of her world, that one day she would be flung unwanted and violently into space. Even the new season did not burst over her in a green flurry. Buds flocked along the adolescent trees, but she came, after her fourteenth winter, unmoved by the spring into the first week of the last term.

There was over everything, town and people, a dusty aridity, a breathlessness of rising temperatures and dry winds. Stolidly across the railway tracks the two pubs faced each other, roaring every evening until eleven with butterfactory hands come to cool off and to play snooker and pool in the rooms behind the bars. Spring came over the town with the poker and the beer and the starting-price betting all going on as usual, and as usual the bleary eye of the law turned in upon itself or lack-lustrely courting the youngest of the maids in the far-side pub. The clear sunlight in the daytime and at night the inspidity of starlight bathed both houses and shops with an equal uninterest, a flatness that pointed to no emotion behind the facades but made everything appear strangely two-dimensional.

Cruciform, the two main streets had as their pivotal point the school, both primary and secondary sections, and martyred along the town's four limbs were a score of shops and business premises and three times as many houses. There were other roads leading out to the mountain district around Cootharabah and there was the road that curled in across the Mary Valley, but over all the deathly stillness and quiet of that first yawn of near summer shimmered amongst the scrub box and the tallow trees. Spring paraphrased itself with shoots from sap rising in the hoop-pine forests to the west and the piccabeen palms and sand cypresses to the east; but here, centred in hills, valleyed below Bundarra, hammer-hitting the hard blue sky, there were only the new pastures, the sprawling paddocks of Rhodes and paspalum, green-squared between township and forest. What there was of spring in the lack-lyricism of the summer opening was known in seascaped detail to the black swans and cranes fifteen miles away over the water-acres of Cooroibah, but not to Gungee, and not to Vinny Lalor now moving through the motionless morning to her personal crucifixion at the town's heart.

An eight-thirty sun cut the shadows back into the hot grass. A butcher bird drew a swift and lovely arc from the crest of a red cedar into the roadside scrub. And there was nothing ahead of the girl dawdling towards the town but dust, sunlight, crimped trees, the downhill bush road and the uphill town one. She held her schoolbag in front of her, banging it one-two, one-two, with her knees as she walked, watching the wide dark blue strip at the bottom of her letdown tunic flap forward with each jerk. She hated it. And she hated the way her panama sagged and bubbled where the rain had caught it last winter. A universal spleen engaged her whole being with bitterness translated into kicks at stones, nudgings at schoolbag, and a scowl into the vibrant sun. Only one thing prevented her turning about and setting off home again with a plea of illness, and that was the fact that in her case was her special holiday essay, in planning and completing which she had felt an inexplicable delight. For days she had longed to hand it in to Mr. Moller, calculating grandly on his recognition of her genius, and subsequently her prestige (if not popularity) amongst her schoolfellows. For always, from the day when she had first attended school right up to her senior classes, she had been outside the group, position undesired but inevitable.

It seems that in the mob there is frequently the one shunned or suspect or unlovely in some very simple and irremediable way. And in this case it was Vinny. She was not a pretty child or even a particularly clever one. She was thin, pale, and red-headed. Her eyes were a peculiarly light grey and like her mouth they were nearly always unsmiling. But then she had little reason to smile. Glancing back beyond the safe family barricade of compulsory kindness, and discounting it, for she realized now its worth and its worthlessness, she saw in the uneventful years herself, when the skipping season was at its height, left endlessly turning the rope, while awaiting, wordless and patient, the briefest of turns. During the hopscotch and marbles seasons she was never able to find a sparring partner unless one of the spottier, plumper girls were temporarily out of favour. Only then did she find a nebulous kind of companionship, so tenuous she was always fearful of its ending, and barely enjoyed what she snatched. But too soon even this simulacrum vanished before the summer rounders with their unpleasant occasion for team selection which drove her unpopularity, her unlovableness home, as at every team choosing she was left wretchedly until last and then added grudgingly – a concession to numerical needs – as if her presence would bring bad luck to her side. "I'll have Vinny," was said, tight smile embarrassed. ("See, you others, I'm saddled with Vinny, but don't you dare think it's because I want her, see.")

Vinny kicked her case viciously, remembering past humiliations still close enough to hurt. She selected a jagged rock from the road edge and hurled it on to the footbridge from where it splashed into the narrow creek that half-circled the town. "Warburton," she said under her breath, and then, frightened of saying it because she had seen her mother beat the daylights out of Royce for using the word and because she had once suffered similarly, she quietly spelt "B-I-T-C-H". After that she felt much better and stayed hanging over the weathered hand-rail until the last circles on the water had melted into the creek margins.

She took the long way round deliberately, left under the railway bridge, then alongside the tracks past the Exchange Hotel, paint-peeling and tawdry. Of a part with it perhaps in its shabbiness, she sighed and hitched her bag into the other hand. Corner neat with chemist and drapery store flamboyant in summer silk led her on past newsagent and milkbar, sick under morning slops-suds-down-swept to gutter, wet patch ending raggedly before the grocer's territory of kerb took her dustily past the next paper-cluttered ramp. A dented utility angled in carelessly across the grass in the side street and backed towards the entrance of the bakery where Sid Ewers, butcher and beefy in stripes of blue and white, lounged in companionship big-muscled across the door, and sucked the last tobacco rags from his cigarette.

"Le boucher est gentil. Il nous donne de la viande," Vinny said sourly under her breath, practising her second-best subject and her hatred together. She patted the side of her bag more to encourage herself as she turned in the school gate, and as every day, so today, first in a new term, she closed her personality into its narrow little room where year after friendless year it learnt to perfect the art of self-containment.

Between the technical block and the school proper was the scuffed grass rectangle where the senior pupils lunched and fooled from twelve-thirty till one-thirty or did last-minute "crams" on the subject for the next period. Cicada-loud with voices, the stridulations of burly boys crashing their cases, it presented to Vinny and to the teetering fringes of giggling girls an equal enticement. But she walked away from the square with an almost cynical world-weariness, up the steps and along the open verandas splashed sun-hot between the spare forms to the girls' cloak room. Peg with name on sticky paper curling back from an area of dried gum marked the place for her hat, but the case had to be humped to the classroom and placed under desk or chair if there were room, or foot-obstructing in the passageway. Vinny dumped it for the moment on the bench that lined the wall below the hat pegs and, going to the bubbler in the corner, splashed water over her hot face and hands. while she was drying herself on a skimpy handkerchief, the bell sounded from the rear veranda, rung jocularly by Mr. Findlay as was his custom on the first day back, expressing cheerful irony for the discipline of the next fifteen weeks. *Tirring-tring-tring, tirring-tring-tring*, repeated with intervals, made into a tiny programme work with the dutiful smilings of the staff as applause, inciting encores of tirrings. Vinny stuffed her handkerchief down the front of her tunic, grabbed her bag, and raced back along the veranda and down the steps to the assembly ground guarded by flag, full mast, pennoned over coleus pots worked by the primary school and senior garden beds with not a thing to show except a few dusty geraniums.

Although she hurried, the lines were nearly assembled and straightening out when, breathless, she panted on to the tail end. Pearl Warburton whispered to her neighbour and moved away from Vinny as she stood beside her. Vinny pretended unawareness. She had pretended it for years; and with a sense of inner comfort she searched among the faces of the staff to discover the one face that was as kindly to her as it was to everybody, that smiled and was angry dispassionately: Mrs.

Striebel, her head bent to conceal her laughter, stood behind Mr. Findlay and to his right, sharing a first-day joke with Mr. Moller.

The headmaster slipped into his diurnal role with the ease of one putting on a dressing-gown. (It fitted him as comfortably, too.) The greetings, the hopes for a pleasant holiday now over, the returning refreshed, the aspirations for a term well spent as the result of stimulating change – all the clichés dear to the educational process were there. Findlay knew, and the staff knew, that though the aphorisms achieved little, they were expected; they capped the moment – these references to God, the empire, duty, the home, children's obligations to parents. What amazed the staff was the enthusiasm that Findlay could bring to the banality, the shining from an inner source that radiated his face as he smiled down on his three hundred charges. Faces fresh or freckled or acne stippled all looked up at him in his transfiguration on the western veranda.

"Like the Sermon on the Mount," Mr. Millington, the woodwork master, whispered.

Peroration ended, the bell was rung again, this time by the senior perfect, and to the vulgar crashing of a march from Miss Jarman, robust at piano and insolent in her treatment of the major keys, the whole school turned right or left according to position and marched raggedly to their rooms. Moller hitched his grey sports trousers up on his thick belly and strolled out to meet the senior class for English.

In their end room they faced him with grinning anticipation, awaiting the customary sapid remark that usually ushered in a lesson. It did not come. Confronted by the twenty polite faces, the wall maps, the "suitable" watercolour prints selected by the school committee, he felt an overpowering boredom. Through the southern windows the scrubby stringybarks crowded down on the Imbil road. Not a house was in view. He gave the order and the class seated itself nosily, crashing back school-case lids in order to burrow through to their poetry texts.

"Silence," Moller said, as he thumbed through his own book.

The September heat was warming the corrugated-iron roof above them in waves, corrugated also, it seemed. He wiped his forehead, his hands, and refolded his handkerchief with the streaked side inward. The class gaped expectantly. What was up? Where was the old Herc ready to have a bit of a joke? Rhonda Welch whispered to Pearl Warburton two desks away and was promptly reprimanded. Vinny watched him with an anticipatory expression only because of her essay. Moller saw the eager look on her face and wondered idly what caused it. He stifled a yawn.

"Open your books at the section on Brennan – 'O desolate eves'. And keep those holiday tasks *closed*! Howard will collect them at the end of the period." He nodded shortly at a slim, handsome boy at the end of the front row. Howard turned and winked hugely at the class behind him, but Moller ignored the gesture and tapped impatiently on the table with his pen. Directly in front of him a gangling lad with untidy black hair was painstakingly turning the pages of his text one by one. Moller watched with exaggerated interest and class became very still as they looked on.

"Peters," he said. "Peters, must you?"

Peters stared back, lovably dense.

"Must I what, sir?"

"Expend such tender care on each page. Turn them, Peters, at least five at a time. The poem is on page sixty-three."

The class laughed, relaxed, and settled back more comfortably. Moller nerved himself for the plunge into lyric poetry with a group of adolescents whose tastes were already fairly well formed by film and comic. He pushed his full lower lip out and then bunched it in over the upper; his hands were trembling slightly when they rested on the edge of the table, and he felt a sharp craving for a cigarette. Another yawn was rising in his throat. He waited until all heads were lowered to the books open before them, but he was not deceived by the external appearance of attention, for he knew quite well that although the eyes might be following the words printed on the paper, not one fraction of inner attention or interest would be being given by any of the pupils in the room except one or two. Distracted by a movement from Pearl Warburton again, he saw that she was scribbling a note on a tiny piece of paper. He smiled. He could not be bothered interfering – she was one of the pupils he liked the least. He could still remember a verbal skirmish they had had a year before when the arrogance of her attitude had prompted him to ask her her age. "Old enough, sir," she had said.

He commenced reading.

His voice had a peculiar resonance not really suited to poetry reading, but what it lacked by conventional standards was atoned for in the emotion he experienced in his reading and which in some miraculous way he managed to transmit, to the few children who really enjoyed his lessons and benefited by them. Intelligent phrasing and emphasis and a personal underlining of the poet's intentions all conjoined to achieve for the listener a wonderful congruity of reason and feeling. But in poems like this – little personal pain-spots – Moller knew that he transferred the writer's reactions to his own being and suffered in the translation. Even as he read to the deaf room, incredibly the longing swept into the quiet rivers of his blood for the old places and the time-lost evenings of twenty years before, sharp with friends' voices. What creatures budded out of this sudden pain laid bare, reason receding until he was only pain and once more forced to explore this unimportant love or that, familiar fray on still-remembered carpets, harsh tongues tasting his foibles. His present was pain with the past. It was all one thing – the wasting of café conversations in the student days and the weekly visits of squeezed-out talk with Lilian now. There was the group waving violently on the church steps – she had insisted on a formal wedding – and here were the empty rooms at night top-heavy with silence.

He paused after reading the last line and looked up at the class.

Warburton must have successfully delivered her note because he could see Betty Klee scribbling what he assumed was a reply. Howard had drawn an over-developed female profile in the margin of his book. Peters, right under his nose, had more juvenile tastes and had inked in every "o" in the poem. He sighed, quite audibly, and the class took this as the signal to drop the pretence of concentration. They rustled with relief.

From farther along the school building the neums of multiplication tables plain-chanted into the morning became part of the heat, the boredom in the room. It is impossible, Moller thought petulantly, utterly impossible to conform happily to the syllabus. And he proceeded moodily to discussion and analysis of the poem, details of technique. Thirty minutes dragged a wounded length round the clock-face. Moller closed his book and asked the class if the poem suggested anything to them about the poet. The twenty faces stared politely but in a hurt fashion at him for half a minute, and then a few tentative hands were raised. Vinny Lalor caught his eye. She had been hoping she would. She was one of the few who listened to and enjoyed her poetry classes. Whenever Mr. Moller read she wanted to cry.

"Well?" he asked, interested in her opinion because of the difficulty of the poem and because he had known her school background for three years.

Vinny stood up with her hands resting on the desk to support her, as her chair was pushed in too far in order to make room for the desk behind. Leaning awkwardly, appearing to topple with her zeal, she shook a piece of hair out of her eyes.

"He was a very unhappy man," she stated definitely. "But he enjoyed being unhappy."

The class laughed. Paradox appeared plain silly. That was all. Moller could not help smiling himself, but because of her cynicism. Kindred spirits, he thought. It takes one sufferer to understand another.

"Perhaps not all the time," he said. "Though it was very clever of you to sense that some people do enjoy their agonies. I think that only people capable of assessing their suffering are capable of writing about it with sensitivity. They stand back from themselves, as it were, and watch their own joy or unhappiness with an interested observer's eye. In a way it is good to be clinical about your personality, for self-analysis should be honest if it is to have any meaning when it is written down."

He did not know whether the girl understood all he said. He felt sure she would understand part of it. Vinny watched him with bright eyes, happy at being the sole receiver of his opinion.

Moller eased his chair back from the table and walked over to the window. Sid Ewer's truck with stinking exhaust crashed across the rectangle and vanished into the receding perspective of the trees. As he watched the red dust settle he told them something of Brennan's life and his unhappy career. There was not much he could tell them, he reflected, for too many of them knew adultery and drunkenness in such a day-to-day fashion in their own homes, its relevance in the life of one of the country's finest poets would be missed.

"Before we finish," he said, glancing thankfully at his watch, "are there any questions?"

He looked round the room without much hope that his invitation would be accepted. Betty Klee was nodding vigorously and giggling at Pearl Warburton. Pearl rose, smiling but with poise, and said, "Please, sir, there's one thing I didn't understand. What does 'niggard bosom' mean?"

A convulsion of mirth shook the room, but Moller preserved his calm. He looked at her sadly and smiled back.

"Howard," he said, "the essays. There's half a minute to go. Is there anyone who has not completed it?"

Three arms waved shyly. He glanced at the owners and noted their names in a pocket diary. "No excuses accepted," he said. "Remain after school."

The class shuffled as the period bell rang. Some of them stood in an attitude of respect when he left the room, but most of them sat giggling with their neighbours. They watched him go, solid under his cheap tweed jacket, fingers already fumbling for the makings of a quick puff between classes, groping in the pocket where the tobacco crumbs fell from the loose pouch.

Vinny looked after him with something near to love as she handed in her essay to Howard, recalling what he had said about pain and sensitive people and writing about it. How did it go? "Only people able to something their suffering could write about it sensitively." One day she'd show them, Warburton and fat old Klee and the rest. Fame and fame and fame . . .

"Open it up, Lalor," Howard snapped. At sixteen he already hated plain girls.

"I don't know how the population increases," Helen Striebel said gloomily as she watched the barbaric young killing time mercilessly, slaughtering the lunch-hour. "That is, I understand the fundamental principle, but I cannot understand its repetition." She turned away from the window, teacup in hand, to her lunch spread out between the exercise stacks on her desk.

The men roared with laughter.

"What's this? What's this?" Moller said, coming in rubbing his hands. "Sex rearing its lovely head?"

He went to the battered teapot near the wash-basin and filled a cup.

"Weak brew. Who's guilty? Helen, what was that remark I surprised you in?"

She laughed with the others. "These *children*. I explain a perfectly simple trigonometrical problem, I set a similar one, and not a soul gets it right. Peters said he thought it was a quadratic equation. . . . Still, I was pleased he even knew the term. His idiocy is rather endearing."

"No shop first day back," Sweeney roared heartily. His coarse good-looking face stuck out arrogantly above a footballer's frame. He tapped another memo for Findlay, using his typewriter in somewhat the way emotional pianists use their instruments, crouching low and leaning back and making rather unnecessary arm movements. "How's your wife, captain?" he asked Moller, when he had come to the end of the memo. Moller, watching him, felt like bursting into loud applause. ("Brilliant, my dear fellow! Positively brilliant!") Hesitation patterned his plum face and he lit a cigarette before he answered. He could sense the others waiting for his reply also.

"Much the same. Worse if anything, I suppose. Her right hip is affected now."

"Sorry, old boy." Sweeney gulped back lukewarm tea and felt safe; safe in his job, safe in his health, and safe in the campaign he was conducting towards achieving a profitable marriage. He eyed Rose Jarman sideways where she sat, not quite plain, and not quite good-looking in her expensive one of many linen suits. Her father owned a large dairy farm in the Mary Valley, a seaside cottage at Inskip Point, and a big, fast black car. Sweeney coveted all these things, and his covetousness was understandable, for Rose was an only child whom her father loved in a completely foolish way, lavishing on her practically anything she wanted. At times Sweeney felt too young for marriage at twenty-four, but, realizing an opportunity such as this might not come his way again, he was prepared to make the ultimate sacrifice of the male. Although he was not interested in easy seduction, it was on no moral ground. Rose was not sufficiently attractive for him to labour through the preliminary details of an *affaire*, and he was, if nothing else, a man who demanded value in kind for his money.

Mrs. Striebel marked another book, unnecessarily conscientious on this first day back. Elderly Miss Rowan, disappointed in love, in life in the broader sense, and in occupation, grizzled into the room from the infants' department.

"Sixty-three! Would you believe it! Sixty-three in that tiny room. I'm resigning at the end of the year, I tell you."

"Go on with you!" Moller said. "You've been saying that for years, Rowie. I bet you'll be teaching their grandsons. Have a cup of this appalling tea. I don't think the dregs were emptied last term!"

Miss Rowan shifted her glasses higher and flopped into a chair.

"Dear, it's awful," she said. "Why do we do it? Why on earth do we do it?"

"Because we love little children. We see their essential innocence, their kindness to each other, their respect for old age. It's all so rewarding." Moller sipped tea and sucked at his cigarette alternately. Sweeney shoved a paper of sandwiches across the table and Moller took one absent-mindedly. Chalk dust still in corners, rolls stacked on corner press, programme registers along tables, tea-cup rings – all the impedimenta of teaching. The eight members of the staff squatted uncomfortably with them, acting no longer with each other, now that familiarity's offspring banished politeness and allowed the idiosyncrasies – shortness of temper, oddly enough, and the uncalculating kindnesses – full play. This laying bare of the personality made in a general way for more harmonious living together. There was no necessity for pretence. Although the end of each school year found nerves frayed from irritations that were part of the job, the staff returned each February, prepared to live out again a union more intimate in some respects than marriage.

For the past three years there had been no transfer of staff, and daily interchange of ideas and school gossip had given these eight people a relationship intangibly binding one upon the other. That this was a dangerous thing did not make itself immediately apparent; yet month after month of limited companionship, limited conversational gambits, threw the staff in upon themselves in a desperate circle of self-concentration. The school and its problems became over-important; the behaviour of one member of staff to another, the fortune or otherwise of any of them, was balloon-swollen and treated as if it were the concern of all. Partisanship reared up in sudden ugly growth about trivia, and though it withered away in the calmer moods of the men and women, memory had still many limbs to spread tendrils of discomfort and dislike.

I will remember this room, Moller thought, though the years deny all cognizance of time and place and mood. I will remember it by the positioning of chairs, the ink stain on the corridor wall, the windows looking out on the school field and the courts and the mountain sky-threatening behind the township. Glancing round, he reflected with amusement that the seating habits of the staff had remained unchanged since he had been there – and that was three years. Helen, calm, straight-backed near the end window; Sweeney sprawled huge and boorish over typewriter at the centre table, and Rose Jarman beside him with Miss Rowan, slicing the townspeople into tiny pieces and serving them up with their sandwiches and cake; Millington, blond and good humoured, near the door beside Corcoran, late-comer to lunch, over-bellied, tonsured at forty, bullying the seventh grade into examination passes at the end of each year. Only one person was missing – Mrs. Ballard, efficient as an egg-whisk in the home science section, all gleaming like a hard baked stove, ate, often as not, in her separate teaching wing the left-over fricassee and pastry prepared at her classes. Eight of them, nine with

Findlay, all marooned on this educational islet, aching from each other and from the town, ingrown like nails, throbbing with self and other self.

Below the end windows a surging and unexpected clamour of singing broke on them.

"Oooooooooh – the tunnel of LOVE, the tunnel of LOVE!" It was chorused with the heartiness of bush-hikers and a salacity of emphasis remarkable considering the age of the performers.

"Vulgar little bastards," Moller said. He leant out the window and glared down on four boys from the senior school. They were squatting with arms linked, and swaying to their singing.

"First day of term is hardly one for rejoicing," he said. "Get out of there. Right out, you fellows. You know this section is forbidden. Get down near the technical block."

Four pleased faces, upturned to his, smirked their satisfaction, happy with the result they had achieved.

"Sorry, sir," Howard said, all melting politeness sauced over a crustacean shell of insolence. "We forgot. We didn't mean to be happy."

"Go on!" Moller roared. "Out!"

They sauntered off, slowly, provokingly, while Moller watched them until the corner of the building cut them from view.

"There you are," he said to Miss Rowan. "There's your answer. We do it for absolutely nothing. We do it so that any manners or good taste we attempt to give them may be thrown back in our teeth. We correct so that parents may criticize our harshness, and we neglect through sheer weariness and hopelessness so that parents may criticize our indifference. But all the time, *all* the time, mark you, we must be cautious of ourselves; we must live righteously within the law and the sub-sections of the Education Act. Circumspection is our ruling word."

Sweeney clapped ironically. "Well said, captain. Have another ham and pickle. They're doing you good."

Helen Striebel rolled the last of her crumbs into a

brown paper bag that she screwed up and hurled into the wastepaper basket.

"Everything you say is right," she agreed. "And add to it the necessity for near-perfect technique in our subjects. I remember when I was teaching in Sydney, before Tom died, the headmistress of the school I was at being displeased with the writing of the English staff. So one afternoon – and though this is incredible, it's perfectly true – she took the five of them, all graduates mind you, and some of them middle-aged, and gave them a writing lesson in cursive alphabet formation for forty minutes. She made them practise each letter as if they were children."

"My dear, I can still help you," Miss Rowan said bitterly. "Crushing a sixty-fourth into the prep room will be a matter of no importance."

Corcoran knocked his pipe out against the table edge and brushed the ash carelessly from his grey flannel trousers. His entire life was governed by routine and examination cramming; it was not a pose and it was not that he wanted particularly to get on in the department – he just preferred it that way.

"Playground duty," he said. "Who's for it with me?" He knew – he always checked with the roster – but a pretended joviality over tasks was his one concession to flippancy about the job.

"Mercy on this first day," Sweeney pleaded. But he got up, nevertheless, nudging Rose on the thigh as he went past.

When they had gone silence fell heavily and accustomedly. Miss Rowan rose after a while and stamped off to her room to prepare the afternoon's blackboard of objects so carefully drawn they appeared unnatural – apples, oranges, books, dogs and cats whose outlines were executed in vigorous lines and scarlets and purples to gain the interest of her class. Rose Jarman washed the cups in a small enamel dish, dried them quickly, and then called a child to empty the slops. Moller sighed and opened the first of the essays piled on his table and began reading unenthusiastically. Most of them were two pages in length, eked out with wide margins, large writing, and generous paragraphing. This is where I cry for my dividends, he thought, where I long for some seed of original thought to display even the minutest germination. He knew that in attempting a lesson on Brennan he had been ambitious, but after all the poem was in their set text and he always subscribed to the argument that if only one child responded to the challenge of something both beautiful and difficult, then the waste upon the others was worth it.

So now, ploughing through this weed-rank jungle of holiday tasks that all seemed to be a dull résumé of unreal picnics, fishing trips, and bush rambles, or else adventure stories so garishly coloured they were childish, it was with a feeling of wonder that he paused finally before placing his red-pencilled approval at the end of Vinny Lalor's precise writing. He looked up. The room had emptied while he was working save for Helen, who shared the next period off after lunch with him, a period of relief while Findlay, godlike above the test tubes and the bunsen burners, took the combined school for chemistry.

Moller looked across at Helen through the thin planes of silence in the room. Outside the bell shrilled suddenly and the inner silence was united with the outer that spread like mist all over the grounds and found the very last whisperings and the very last scuffle melt away. He could hear the lines forming as Corcoran gave the orders, and then the tapping of Rose Jarman's expensive tittuping heels when she went along the veranda to the music room to wrest cold technical sense from the untuned keys. The boredom that he had endured all morning dissipated as he saw his teaching partner calmly turning pages of books and impressing her ideas on them in a thick blue comment. She sensed his eyes upon her and smiled without looking up.

"Just a moment, Robert. I'm on my last one, and then I'll join you in a cigarette."

Moller watched her smooth face and drank in the quietude of her lowered eyelids and sad mouth. She had joined the staff a year after him, widowed and withdrawn for at least six months, until he, about to lose his wife in a permanent illness, found his being's purpose running parallel with hers so that it would have been a wild and incredible thing had not each found the other a solace, at least in the daytime hours. Her practicality, which he lacked, and her humour, which kind he possessed but enriched male-fashion, drew him, the impractical and the dreamer, into a companionship that tempered their teaching relation. Affection existed between them. They were both aware of it. But they were circumspect, careful of staff and town that lay idle under the hot sun waiting to devour reputations. Sometimes, but never often, they would stroll down from the school together in the late afternoon, watching Bundarra fling its hammer shadow across the little streets and shops and houses, and when they reached the hotel where she boarded he would turn away after the briefest of leave-takings along the road beside the railway line to his empty house.

He kept it going. There was not much point in selling it until he knew exactly what to do about Lilian, whose paraplegia was now so advanced. They were separated physically by her illness and absence and spiritually by the despondency that had enveloped her to such an extent that even his weekly calvaries of pity to visit her meant nothing really to them, who were childless of the body and no longer shared offspring of the mind. He kept the house going largely as a place for his books, somewhere to play a record and cook a quiet meal; or just to lie around in the months of June and November, unhappy in the debris of unmarked examination questions.

At those times when the summer evenings drifted in

from the sea in a green translucence that lay over the hills and paddocks like clear water and the after-tea hours lay ahead as empty as the sky limits, he would have liked Helen with him to share the silence or the idly dropped word. But his neighbours watched with unkindly interest the most trivial actions of a man who did not belong to any of the local clubs, refrained from attending any church, and found horses and bridge boring beyond endurance. Occasionally he played an uninterested game of badminton at the doctor's home, but that was not sufficient to excuse his lack of interest in sport. His love of books and music made him immediately suspect, and his preference for drinking at the hotel bars with the working class, instead of the private polite parties, marked him down as rather common. He did not know, and he certainly would not have cared if he had.

In much the same fashion Helen Striebel was criticized by the women of the town, who resented the way she was able to keep to herself, disliking her because of a self-sufficiency that precluded the need to swap knitting patterns and sponge recipes and allowed her to retire blamelessly to her room at seven. This sort of behaviour was accepted as a personal affront by the active women's organizations, who regarded it angrily as voiceless criticism of their behaviour. In a way perhaps it was, though it was unintentional.

"In a place like this," Moller used to say to her, "you may detract and calumniate with impunity, but sneering at *mores* and traditions is unforgivable."

By now Helen had put down her pencil and pushed the bundle of closed books to one side. She fumbled in the bag that she kept slung over the shoulder of her chair and drew out her cigarette case. Through the thinly fanning smoke they looked amusedly at each other, he finding her devotion to the tedium of correcting exercises as much a part of her personality drive as she found his amusement at its part of his. Their ability to predict each other's reactions pleased them both. Finally Moller spoke.

"It's good to see you again, Helen. The holidays were no holiday for me."

"It's good to see you, too." She paused. Her eyes looked away into her own shyness. "Robert, I heard you tell Greg Sweeney that Lilian was worse. I'm so sorry. Won't she get any better? Not any better?"

"Not a scrap." Moller remembered the tossed bed, the crumpled pile of women's magazine, the sweet smell of ether and the oranges, unwanted, piled beside the flowers. Remembered, and felt a frightening weariness at the thought of it again next week and the next and the next with the tossed bed, the magazines, the sweet smells of ether and the oranges and the flowers.

"Not only will she not get any better," he said, "but she is slowly, very slowly, becoming worse. And indefinitely, it seems. Only one thing is definite, Helen, and that is she has completely lost the use of both legs." He tapped the ash off his cigarette. It fell into the light layer of chalk dust below the table. "She's too miserable to be interested in much. Each week-end I see her she plucks nervously at the covers most of the time and hardly has a thing to say." He stood up agitatedly and walked over to the window. But his agitation was not really with Lilian.

Helen sensed that he wished to say no more about it so she said abruptly, "My holidays weren't the best, either. Margaret was down with 'flu. The city was jammed with Show visitors and I lost a tenner first day there. I'm glad we don't have to write a holiday task about them."

"Talking of holiday tasks," Moller said, swinging round from the window, from the pain in his mind, and hurrying back to the pile of books on his table. "I've got something here that might interest you, Helen. A child with an idea at last."

"Who is it?"

"Vinny Lalor. Yes, Vinny." Moller laughed as he saw

the disbelief on the other's face. "Not brilliant, but original. It gives quite an interesting sidelight on that unhappy kid's existence."

He sorted through the books until he found the grease-spotted cover that badged most of her exercises, and opening up the book he read, " 'A Family Day'." He stopped "Get that, Helen. Even the title has escaped." He glanced down at the book again and flicked the page over. "Would you mind if I read it?"

"No," Helen said. "Go ahead. The staff is as one when it's a question of discovering a little intelligence."

Moller hooked a chair out with one foot and having sprawled easily in it he continued to read in his soft voice:

" 'All yesterday I wondered if families were like ours. At first I thought there could be no answer to this and then quite strangely I found that there was. Very early I began to walk from our home which is at the top of Duncan Hill and passed most of the houses on this side of the town well before ten. At one place after another the same scene repeated itself, a crying child, a woman shaking a mop over the stair rail and a man lounging back in his chair and shouting an order.' I like that bit," Moller said. "This part was different because my father shouted his last order three years ago and then left. I think this is a pity for though it is bad to be shouted at, it is worse to have no one to shout at you. I feel if he were here with us, shouting or not, we would be more like other families.

" 'In the evening I went past the same houses and from each the lights shone boldly in the darkness. In one house there was a piano with someone making a mistake over and over and in another I could see people laughing over their tea. It was like looking into another world. But from nearly every home in the street blared the radio tuned to a talent show. The announcer was so kindly he was false and the performers were so sincere they were sad. And when I crept home, there was mum listening quietly to some classical music because she has always wanted us to be more refined. So when she became busy with the ironing, I went softly to the radio and tuned in to the talent show too. Listening to the bad singing and the hill-billy guitars I felt happier than I'd ever felt before. Our house was the same now as all the other houses in the street, and I was part of the sameness.' "

Moller looked up at Helen's disturbed face.

"Not exactly the usual style of holiday task, is it? Poor little beggar!"

They both thought of the child and her isolation. Helen saw the playing-fields curving back to the pepper-trees and the tennis courts, and the senior pupils in groups forming permutations of gossips over their lunch hour activities; and apart from them, outside all the groups every day, the hair-bright, plain-faced child trying desperately to look as if she were walking purposefully, as if there were a goal somewhere – and not succeeding. Sometimes when Helen was on playground supervision she would come up to her and ask a trivial question about the afternoon's mathematics class. Her requests were such thin ruses to give her approach some point that Helen, filled with pity for the child's friendlessness, would walk across the grounds with her, talking about school work and the girl's interests as long as the lunch duty lasted. This was bad in a way, for it not only set Vinny Lalor apart but it made her the butt of unpleasantness, charges of currying favour. Yet neither the child nor her teacher felt capable of acting otherwise. Moller spoke to her, too, in the yard, but less frequently; and then after a while, when it was discovered how she loved reading, both of them lent her books of a better quality than the meagre contents of the school library could provide. Despite this particular attention, however, her essays had never before revealed, apart from an occasional felicity, any mark of the sensitivity behind her observations.

"It's quite incredible," Helen said. "By the way, how do you think Vinny would know what was bad singing and what wasn't?"

"I suppose she heard her mother criticize the talent shows."

"That's so. Incidentally, I had no idea the father had left home. I was under the impression he was dead."

"It happened just before I came here," Moller said, "but it's such an old story no one ever discusses it. Mrs. Lalor seems to manage somehow. Better off, probably. Two of the kids still home are working, and they help out. You've noticed Vinny's clothes are never quite up to scratch. That seems to be the one thing some of the nasty little beasts in her class can't forgive."

"God, they're cruel," Helen said. "And there seems to be nothing one can do about it." She paused. "I feel," she said deliberately, and thereby setting up the first piece in a dangerous montage, "that I would like to do something special for that child. Give her a treat that she'd remember with pleasure for a very long time. How about running her down to Brisbane with us next month and taking her to a ballet or a play or something like that?"

Moller jerked his head back in surprise. "Are you serious?" he asked.

"Perfectly. I've always had a weak spot for that girl."

"But think of the complications. There's the mother to ask. Findlay probably will think it odd and the rest of the kids will give her hell."

"There's no need for Findlay to be told and Vinny won't mention it to the others. I'll see to that. As for Mrs. Lalor, I'm sure she would be pleased. I know her."

And did know her: the seedy dresses, the hair worried through its curling pins, tortured by steel waving grips, the grammar struggling desperately to surface the swamp of local carelessness, the seedier finance behind the upbringing of six children, Vinny last and least lovely; knew her in her gaping timber house behind casuarina and lantana hot-prickled-red-yellow-freckled maze of overgrown hedge, up garden path between the asters and chrysanthemums tangled in fertility to the wistaria'd veranda; as a pale face through leaves and worries.

"She would be pleased," Helen repeated. "Vinny could stay at Margaret's with me and be perfectly safe. Robert, I'll enjoy the variation in my routine, so be a little more enthusiastic."

"When will you ask?"

"I think I'll stroll up to Lalor's this evening while the impulse is still fresh."

"If you're determined . . . it might be a good thing at that," Moller said. The tiredness was sweeping over him again in the rising afternoon temperatures. He stretched his knotty hands painfully-pleasurably, above his head and grunted. The period bell would ring in five more minutes. Placing a hand on Helen's arm, he patted her lightly. A fly drummed backwards and forwards across the ceiling, and Corcoran's voice raised in sudden anger throbbed along the veranda. All the newness of term opening was gone in the establishment of routine. Everything was as usual. Findlay came into the room through webs of heat, ovoid and perspiring and genial, but relentless in his pursuit of minutiae, to post another notice on the staff-room board.

TWO

The repetition of the cottage pie drove Helen from the green cave of a dining-room earlier than usual. Where calendulas spiked multiple suns above the five dining tables and cloths gravy- or porridge-spotted from earlier meals, the six permanent boarders had sat tense in their dislikes of each other's eating habits, seeking conversational refuge with the commercial travellers or the dairy inspectors or the forestry officers on their way to the Brooloo station. The sucking action of one mouth dreaded and fought back the clicking dentures of another. One pair of hands chopped all the food into prissy segments, another forked in clumsy gobbets, angry plugs. Conversation was sterile from two meals a day, seven days a week, four weeks a month, curving its full cycle through weather and politics and local scandals back through weather and scandals and local politics. Mouths minced or pursed or dogmatized or vanished altogether in refined outrage and jaws became prognathous over unimportant points of view.

Sharing the salads and the roasts with Helen Striebel were Alec and Jess Talbot. The husband, young, graduate in science with the views of a respectable lady church-worker – and the face – was bacteriologist for the butter factory for a year. His wife, all amazon-thighed, huge-busted, and gone to seed at thirty from over-zealous hockey and basket-ball playing, plunged with desperate seriousness and ellipsoidal vowels into every new piece of gossip as if it were a pool, and surfaced refreshed and whale-like with a struggling little fish – the privacy of some local wrongdoer. Under the guise of interest in their fellows and the pretence of purely disinterested analysis, they tossed the wretched thing back and forth between their careful grammar, their nominative pronouns after the verb "to be". What wallows of refined moralizing! She had failed to graduate but constantly referred to the fact, so that, first having driven home the point that she was university-trained, she made the listener wonder how such a leaping, pouncing mind could possibly have flunked the course. Helen always longed to shout "Goal!" as another reputation bounced its full career and succumbed to a final, hearty schoolgirlish blow.

Alec Talbot loved music. In their bedroom he kept a tiny radio that he played softly at night, a gentle background to the raucous vulgarity of the quiz and give-away shows that pounded from the other rooms. As he went about the hotel on mundane errands, he would whistle with infinite detail and piercing clarity whole subjects from symphonies, sometimes whole movements of the more esoteric chamber music. However, as Helen was the only person in the hotel who recognized the works, no one else knew how cultured he was. So all this effort with Brahms and Mozart was rather a waste, for Helen had ceased to discuss music with the Talbots when she discovered that they used it merely as a dividing line between themselves and the hicks.

"And what is it like being back, Mrs. Striebel?" Jess Talbot had asked.

Helen only smiled – she had become expert at facial answers – and continued eating.

"I suppose," Jess Talbot pursued, smacking the ball straight between the goal-posts, "that you saw Mr. Moller when you were in Brisbane. He told me he was going down for the fortnight."

Helen looked up coldly.

"Brisbane has a population of nearly a million. There must have been several thousands of Show visitors as well. Would you be surprised if I said we didn't meet?"

The other woman laughed carefully. "My dear, how silly of me. Of course. I just thought you were such friends, you know. Always deep in conversation when I see you coming home. Alec, pass Mrs. Striebel the bread. No. I don't think I missed seeing the Show this year. After all, Alec's work means so much to him, and the factory was very busy, if only because of the Show. Isn't that so, Alec?"

His face, sallow with idealism, gazed seriously across the table.

"To cap it all" – he looked away and his chin shook earnestly – "the cooling system collapsed on the Wednesday and we were working non-stop for eighteen hours putting it right."

Helen fidgeted with her soup spoon. Along the wall sombre horses glared moronically at her from the sporting prints. Opposite, the Talbots stared critically. She regretted not bringing a book to the table; she would have enjoyed the Talbots' reactions to her breach of manners. Between the green hands of a monstera deliciosa she could glimpse the Farrellys sipping fastidiously, bowed down by their profits, starved by their economies, and respectable, respectable, respectable. The tweed that formed around him a loose circular lovableness repeated itself on her in spinsterish outlines of propriety. They inclined genteelly towards her as she watched them, and Jess Talbot, diverted from a particularly savage anecdote, wreathed her face in godliness and dabbed essence of Christianity behind each honest-to-God, straight-forward, head-girl smile.

"They're pets, aren't they?" she said, turning to nod. "So open to deal with. And regular church-goers, too. Though of course I don't hold with popery, but it does seem to go hand in hand with hotel-keeping. However, one thing I will commend them for, won't you, Alec? I will commend them for their kindness to young Allie when she had that trouble."

"What trouble?" Helen asked bluntly, knowing, and resenting discussion of it.

"My dear, you know. You did know, didn't you? You must. It's the most fascinating tale. It appears that last February one of the bank clerks who –"

"Jess, please," Alec interrupted. He took the last portion of the butter in his abstraction. His chin shook. Helen consulted the menu and ignored Jess Talbot's confiding eye that promised "later". Behind her at the next table she could hear the railway clerk in heated argument with the bank teller, each riding a horse to win and backing it with anger.

All blossomed in pink, early for the pictures (a love story and a Western), and ready to race away after the last plate was cleared, the second maid took their orders with indifference, dreaming of the brilliantined, tight-panted hero who would later compromise her in return for three shillings' worth of tears and giggles. She could hardly wait. She returned with the pie all pranked in weedy greens and ice-cream mounds of potato, so uninviting in appearance that Helen felt she could not eat it. She cut neat bays and inlets into its outer edge while the Talbots whacked into their heated-up roast. Ron Coombes, chief boiler hand at the factory, coarse and good-natured, bachelor and pleased to be, bounced in late to join the teller and the railway officer. The Talbots nodded coolly. They were very conscious of the social gap between Coombes and themselves, and they were always fearful of some dreadful familiarity following upon a lowering of the barrier.

"It makes them uncomfortable when we're friendly,"

Jess would say, wrapping her self-justification round her like a chenille gown. Helen sighed relievedly, seeing him approach, and gave him a wide and grateful smile. She decided suddenly against finishing her meal.

"Hullo, Ron," she said, and rose. "Excuse me" – briefly to the Talbots. "Ron, I must see you later about some lighting I wanted rigged up for the school dance next month. Mr. Findlay said you were the one who did it last year and wondered if you'd be kind enough to help out again."

"Glad to, Helen," he said.

The Talbots shuddered at the exchange of first names and Jess was later to say to her husband that she thought perhaps Mrs. Striebel was just a wee bit common . . . well, not . . . you know . . . and the Beethoven Seventh thundered on behind her, for she always talked through the very best music.

Helen went upstairs to her room that was really nothing more than a cavity veranda'd and corridored at each opening, with a monstrous wardrobe against one wall, a leprously stained mirror, and a bed. To these basic forms she had tried to introduce the intelligence of personality with prints tacked on the wall, a mantel radio, a clock, books and magazines. But when at night the clean-cut angles of light sharpened themselves against the furniture edges and behind the milky looking-glass she saw her thirty-two years staring back at her with placidity and resignation, she knew what mockery four walls made of the prints and the books, the mantel radio and the clock.

She took a jacket from the wardrobe and then sat on the edge of the bed to change her shoes. The sagging wire moaned and shuddered, the fluff from the mattress sifted imperceptibly. Oh, the infinities of daily boredoms, she thought, the sun driving her each morning to the grind of work that was mainly thankless, and in the evening driving her back again to the hotel with its patterns of boarders and meals. Tonight the longing for escape was intolerable. there seemed to be no fellowship in the new books she had brought back with her from the city. With both anger and pleasure in her mind she shut her door firmly and locked it. Below in the street the evening lay in grey points and streaks tattered by late dog-barkings and flapping newspaper sheets. Smiling, she entered its anonymity.

Once out on the road with the gums crowding in rapidly upon her, the bracken-scented wind curling round her, she felt immediately better. Two people passed her in the darkness and called out good-night. She was pleased to answer them and walked contentedly up the long hill that led to Lalor's. A peculiar feeling that the evening divergence from habit – the seven o'clock bathing, the eight o'clock reading, and the ten o'clock sleeping after the Gympie mail had passed through pratically under the hotel verandas – was in some way a focalizing of the whole of the day's trivia into one important central point filled her with elation. She walked even faster.

By the time Lalor's fence came into view it was nearly seven-thirty. The front of the house was in darkness, but a square of light shone from a back window. Helen pushed open the gate and the shadows of the miniature jungle swallowed her, the splintered veranda steps offered her silence, and in the constantly moving night of the veranda itself with the thin moonlight probing the wistaria, she hesitated just a few seconds before ringing the bell.

It excursioned into the bungalow recesses with an alarum like beaten gongs. The drone of voices that had reached her ears faintly ceased at the signal, and a light switched on in the hall shone through the stained-glass panels of the door with a religious significance. Bathed in a liturgical glow, she blinked and smiled as the door open widely on Mrs. Lalor searching short-sightedly for her own surprise as the worry on her face changed to the anxiety of recognition.

"Mrs. Striebel!" She rubbed her hands nervously down the front of her apron. "What a surprise! Come on in."

She stood aside and Helen went in and down the long hall. It had a nightmare quality in its narrowness and length, but the shock of light in the sitting-room ahead was the essence of comfort. Two of the other children were sitting there and they grinned at Helen as she came into the room. Helen recognized Vinny's brother Royce and the eldest girl, Rene, who was twenty and working in the local dentist's rooms.

"Done real well for herself," Mrs. Lalor would boast proudly to her neighbours. "I always knew I could make something out of Rene. Types and does shorthand and all that sort of thing as well as helping in the surgery. Mr. Lunbeck says he doesn't know what he'd do without her." (Nor would he, some of her neighbours thought viciously, knowing Mr. Lunbeck's little fancies and Rene's high self-evaluation.)

The two women sat down in the cane basket chairs where cushions and arm-rests had been reduced by the violence of the children to a secure drabness from which nothing could redeem them. Now and again Mrs. Lalor, teased by magazines into an effectual activity, had licked them over with a glossy enamel in a fashionable shade or prodded the cushions to brief life and packed them into new linen covers. It was hopeless. Royce spilt ink or put his muddied shoes on them, and Vinny read and munched fruit in them, and it all came to the same thing in the end.

"Well," Mrs. Lalor said, "I hope you haven't come about Vinny. Getting into trouble or anything like that, I mean."

Helen picked at a loose end of cane but stopped when she noticed Mrs. Lalor's anxious eyes on her.

"It is about Vinny that I've come," she said, "but I assure you she's in no trouble. Certainly not with me, anyway."

"Is she working hard, Mrs. Striebel?"

"She tries very hard indeed, Mrs. Lalor. You've no worry at all on that score."

"That's a relief. Always worried about that one. She never says much." Mrs. Lalor breathed deeply and settled back in her chair.

Helen paused. The two women gazed awkwardly at each other. The business was harder than she had thought it would be. "Look," she said, "I'll come straight to the point. Today Mr. Moller, her English teacher, showed me the essay she had done for her holiday task. Where is she, by the way?"

"Her turn," interrupted Royce who was now crouching by the radio. "She gotta wash *and* dry up tonight."

"You shut up, Royce," his mother said, "and lower that serial. Rubbishing stuff. Vinny's in the kitchen. They all get their turn, Mrs. Striebel."

"Good idea," Helen agreed. "I like the closed door, too. Keeps them working without distraction and stops their unhappiness spoiling what you're doing."

Royce grinned. He had just left school and was working as a grease boy at the factory. He had lost a front tooth.

"You were real tough on us, Mrs. Striebal," he said. "But it was good."

"Thank you, Royce," Helen said gravely. "You always responded well to my treatment."

Royce's big face, freckled and pimpled, grew red with pleasure. Embarrassedly he rubbed his large nose.

"Now go on, Royce," his mother pleaded. "Listen to your old serial please, and leave me to talk with Mrs. Striebel a minute."

"Well," Helen said, and stopped, perplexed. "Look, I really don't know how to put this without sounding as if I'm exaggerating and that's the last thing I want you to feel I'm doing. But after I read Vinny's essay today, I must confess, Mrs. Lalor, that I think your little girl has quite a deal of talent."

"She was always one for books, you know."

"Yes. I know that, and it's a most important thing."

"Vin showed me some of the ones you loaned her."

"Did she?" Helen smiled. "I hope you approved."

"I read them meself," Mrs. Lalor said. "Vin and me fought over who had them next."

Helen felt more relaxed. "Good," she said. "Now I do hope you won't mind what I'm going to suggest. I would like – with your permission of course, Mrs. Lalor – to give Vinny some little treat – an outing in Brisbane, a play or a concert. Something like that. I feel sure she'd appreciate it and get a lot from it. And between you and me, that's a lot more than I can of most pupils I've ever had."

Mrs. Lalor's thin body sat up eagerly straight. "Why, that's real nice of you, Mrs. Striebel, but we don't know anyone in Brisbane she could stay with."

"That's easily fixed. My idea was for her to drive down with me and Mr. Moller next time I go to Brisbane. I always stay with my sister at Hamilton, and Vinny could fit in nicely with us. My sister's single, the house is far too big for her, so there'd be plenty of room. All terribly respectable, of course." She laughed, not nervously, but dubiously.

Mrs. Lalor's lumpy, overworked fingers embraced tightly. In a way she was puzzled as well as pleased by this sudden offer. It was the first time anyone at the school had taken a real interest in any of her children and she found it odd. In addition, she had no knowledge of Vinny's unhappiness at the school or her friendlessness. Royce, the closest to Vinny in age, had never noticed, being busy with the male gangs of the upper school, and his sister kept her own unpopularity to herself. Vinny was sensitive at being a pariah even in her earliest years.

"It sounds wonderful for her. I bet she'd be real happy to go, Mrs. Striebel," she said doubtfully.

Helen smiled with relief and at the sight of the smile all Mrs. Lalor's doubtings vanished.

"You're real kind," she said and laughed in her enthusiasm. "Real kind. Have you said anything to Vin?"

"Not yet."

"Then let me call her. Vin! Vinny!" Mrs. Lalor heaved herself out of the chair and opened the kitchen door. The clattering ceased and Vinny, arms sud-dripping to the elbows, her old jumper white-flecked, ran in from the great pile of washed and unwashed dishes. When she saw Helen sitting calmly in the basket chair, at home in her house, the sudden upsurge of joy almost made her choke. She could say nothing. How much more satisfying it is to worship than to be worshipped! Her love for this woman shaped her entire day, caused her to count through classes to hers, to plan her lunch-hour round an opportunity of talking to her. Although she had little ability at mathematics, she slaved at the subject merely to win Mrs. Striebel's commendation. For her the whole relationship's huge flower spread its corolla in petals of kindliness, and tented her in with a form of affection and security, excluding the daily indifference offered by the others. And in the evening, after all, there was her home where other people spoke and moved and, to a certain extent, needed things from her. She knew already that to be needed placed one within a scheme – that therein lay the crux of her problem. At school among her contemporaries she was never needed. If she were absent the class surface showed no ripple of awareness or concern.

Her eyes met her teacher's. Their luminosity drew her like a moth. Uncomfortably her arms dripped water on the floor. Then Helen said, "Vinny, my dear," with deliberation. The girl, appearing even thinner in her sloppy cardigan, stood very still glancing from Mrs. Striebel to her mother and back again. The room was caught by the moment. Here were flowers curving in sleep upon the table, there the framed wedding picture had became a lake of light. The floor slid away beneath its seagrass matting, and the walls moved in with their unpainted cypress planks. She was being squeezed forward down an interminable corridor to where the day's purpose smiled and said, "Vinny, my dear."

In an attempt to dry her arms she rubbed them on the side of her skirt. Royce huddled closer to the radio in love with mediocrity and outer space. Mrs. Lalor took up her knitting, and her hands moved independently of her mind. And Helen kept smiling with incredible kindness into the child's vulnerable eyes. Now I know, she thought, with surprising insight and unexpected poetry, on what frontiers she stands and for whom she knows the violent chasm of each day ahead, poised brinkwise.

Gingerly her mind moved forward to crumble words as one would bread for swans, and she said, "I've come to obtain your mother's permission to give you a little treat."

"Oh, Mrs. Striebel!" the girl breathed. She accepted this material manifestation of reciprocal love as natural and miraculous at the same time. Children alone can preserve aplomb confronted with the most abnormal situations, and are able, having translated them to their own special purpose, to see in them – with reason or without being no matter – the genius of their own fantasy.

"We were wondering, your mother and I," Mrs. Striebel continued, cunningly adopting the older woman into the freeemasonry of her plan, "if you would like to come to Brisbane with me one week-end and perhaps see a play or go to a concert."

She did not volunteer a reason for the gesture because she realized that the sheer pleasure of surprise drowned all sense of inquiry. Perhaps at some later time she might mention the essay that had so impressed her and prompted her action. Certainly the child's mother would and then Vinny could draw what conclusions she liked.

"Would I!" Vinny said. "Oh, Mrs. Striebel! Oh, Mum, may I? May I please? Mrs. Striebel, I've only been there once that I can remember, and it was so big after

Gungee, and exciting, but it's so long ago I can't really see it much except as hot and big and dusty."

They laughed, in the contagion of her excitement, infected. Outside the loquat tree tapped and talked to the water-tank and shifted its black paper double across the glass. A goods train cutting a furrow through the valley screamed twice as it took the southern bend, and in the loud silence coming after, so filled with tiny sounds – the gaspings of burning wood in the stove, the soft signature tune on the radio, the grunting of the kelpie under the kitchen table – the three faces repeated the pattern of pleasure with ever such a slight variation. Vinny's joy transfigured by worship was duplicated with anxiety on her mother's face and behind that, further still, a shadow of jealousy of the woman whose face bore happiness and also the arrogance and the humility of the giver.

"I've told Mrs. Striebel it's all right, Vin. We've only got to pick a week-end."

"How about the Friday after next?" Helen asked. "Or have you something arranged?"

Mrs. Lalor laughed, and even Royce glanced across, hearing the bitterness in her voice.

"We don't have nothing important happening here. All week-ends are the same to us, unless maybe we waste our money on the pictures. I reckon they'll go on being the same, too, until they carry me out of this old place."

"Oh, Mum!" Vinny protested. This bright coin of pleasure seemed to have been come by guiltily. Helen edged uneasily along the striped canvas cushions and formulated a trite leave-taking. There were offers of tea, but she refused, wanting now her errand had been achieved to be out in the clear starlight. Mrs. Lalor kept saying how kind it was of her, and when Helen protested that the action was giving her the greater happiness, she felt gently on her elbow a hand placed lightly as a leaf. Vinny was standing behind her, testing the reality of her presence and purpose with touch. She gave the searching fingers a quick squeeze.

"We'll decide on details during the week, There's plenty of time."

"Plenty," echoed the girl, vague in the corridor dimness. The three of them moved to the veranda where the moths blew whitely across the darkness from garden to hall. They brushed the softness of them from their hair and necks.

"Great place for the brutes," Mrs. Lalor complained. She knocked down one large moth that was circling insanely about her face. "Mind the step, Mrs. Striebel. Vin, you never said thank you."

"There's no need, I assure you," Helen said. "Your trust that I will look after her is quite a compliment. Good night, Mrs. Lalor. I'll see you again before the twelfth and we'll settle everything."

The two figures who had been watching from the veranda and the one figure moving into the darkness were still linked emotionally even long after the gate had clacked behind the one and the door had shut in the others. Two paddocks away a late fire burning flung an orange wind-blown rag against a sky that was curdled with cloud and moist with stars. To the west the road ran back under the fig trees to the township, and to the east it described a glimmering arc among the striated ranks of gums and came in again on the northern end of the railway-line, touching with its familiar finger the would-be suburban gardens clustered behind chain-wire and timber pickets.

Reluctant to turn back yet to the hotel, merciless in its boredom, Helen thrust her hands into her coat pockets and strode off to the east, following the curve of the hills above the town and seeing them melt into quiet debate with hill on hill towards the sea. When at last the swing of the road took her in by the first houses, she thought of Moller, wondering if he would be in his shrub-thick garden hosing the browned couch-grass. With a sense of recklessness compelling what she knew to be a foolish action, she decided that if he were not in his garden she would still call on him. Light behind his windows banished hesitation and she opened the gate unhesitatingly and went towards the house between scent-drunken native daphne to the unfamiliar porch and door. Through the open windows poured a stormy music of cadenza'd brilliance illuminating a backdrop of mountainous brass that made the virtuosity of the pianist appear an effortless facility. It is brilliance only, Helen mused, pausing for the record to run its course before knocking. She went back into the garden and broke off a sprig of daphne. Islands of crazy paving floated away across the lawn to the side of the house swimming on the dark wet grass. Everything was so magical, she laughed, but, protesting against raptures, refusing to accept the imagery of music or garden, she even repeated the words, "It is brilliance only." As the first movement of the work drew to a close with a long-drawn warning on the horn, she climbed the steps again and knocked loudly on the door. Moller could not have heard, for she recognized the pause between bands on the record and then she heard the strings take up with moving tenderness the first chords of the adagio. She knocked more loudly, and after a little while she could hear his feet, lazy across the floor. The music stopped.

"Such unconventionality," Moller said, after he had opened the door and had seen Helen's pale face smiling – laughing nearly, she was so happy.

"I know. I know." She pressed the daphne to her nostrils. "It was sheer impulse. I've just been to Lalor's and on the way back I thought I'd like to do something different."

"The boredom of the first day back is worse than any other time."

"Correct." Helen laughed. "I couldn't even finish dinner tonight. There was something about the pub that drove me out. Anyway, I thought I'd let you know everything has been arranged satisfactorily – for Vinny and me, that is. I feel mother was a bit dubious about it.

Still, there it is. And then I wanted to tell you, and hatred of all the little gossping tongues urged me. Sheer bravado!"

" 'One braver thing than all the Worthies did,' " Moller quoted, " 'and yet a braver thence doth spring, which is to keepe that hide.' So come in quickly, my dear, before you outrage the sensitivities of the Lunbecks."

He held the door more widely for her and she stepped into a foreign country that was foreign only in its primary aspect, for his presence familiarized what was new. "They love to think of me lonely and celibate, brave in my misfortune, living from day to day all the momentous clichés of the women's magazines."

"So in effect you're glad I've come? Even if it is only for a little while?"

"Of course. How often I've longed to ask you over for some records! But I was always afraid you'd be frightened of neighbours' opinion. So I'm glad it was you who came to me. I hate being refused."

"Thank you," she said. Words are nothing. Are everything within their moment.

"Still," Moller continued, piloting her into the side closed-in veranda that he kept for his own, "now you have dared for me, you must stay at least to hear the Fifth out, and have a coffee."

He turned away, large and dark, slightly flabby with his gaberdine trousers slipping untidily below his relaxed stomach muscles. His fingers were spatulate and long, gingered from nicotine; his eyes were troubled with irony and kindness, and his mouth had the mobility of self-humour. He went across to his record-player and Helen sat in a chair by the windows. Carefully he replaced the needle on the second band and they sat exposed under the glare of the unshaded light bulb to the second and third movements of the Beethoven. They smoked, and they smiled occasionally at each other through the cantabiles and the diminuendos, cloistered in simplicity until the bassoons and horns eased in on the piano's muttered chords spelling out the dramatic final theme. The tiny silence held to just that point where it became unendurable. *Attacca.* They were away on the allegro and its dogmatic statements of melody, and Miller and Helen lay back in their chairs and under cover of gigantic fortissimos, shifted into more comfortable positions and lit new cigarettes.

"How was that?" Moller murmured when it was all over. "That your pals the Talbots could see us now wrapped in compromise and culture! It would support their conversational sorties through a month of badminton. Is there anything else you'd like to hear, Helen, or will we get busy on some coffee?"

"The coffee, I think. And after a while some soothing trio or quartet if you have it. I heard Alec Talbot whistling something last term I meant to ask you about. I think it was Schubert, but I wouldn't be sure."

"When you're strengthened by coffee," Moller said, "you can sing it for me."

"I'll have to be really strengthened, Robert. I think I'd just as soon look through your record pile and work it out by trial and error."

"So be it. Come and help me brew this stuff, Helen. I'm still trying to achieve the perfect elixir."

Helen rummaged in the cupboards, found bread and sliced it, and began making toast. Moller put the coffee on to simmer in a saucepan and leant back against the sink watching her as she worked. He found it unbelievably pleasant to have her there with him and was smiling happily when she looked up and saw him.

"After a year," he said.

"What? What after a year?"

"This. Just this. You working away in the kitchen, coffee on the hob, a record digested. Here, you'll need some cheese for that toast."

Bending down to forage in the cupboard behind him, he kept his broad back turned to her so she could not sense his emotion. Among the dim edges and corners, the uneven planes of grocery packets, lonely as a late night city, he became suddenly still as he peered down the lanes between the prisms and cubes of food. The vision of his aloneness and the aimlessness of his progress blew like a gale-blast along the thoroughfares of this toy-town, and he touched the sharpest of points that indicated barren evenings and days, became lost in his mental projections among the alley-ways between the biscuits boxes and the flour, and shuddered at the solitude of this new landscape. With an effort that was painful he straightened and turned heavily and smiled and then not-smiled into Helen's face. During the cessation of speech the very climate of the room had changed, though there were still the red cotton curtains and the cheap imitation tile work above the sink and the bread bin solid as a Bible behind the door.

"There's one thing I must make clear, Helen," he said, and did not touch her in spite of his wishes, but she felt as if she had been touched all the same, "that after tonight I'm afraid I can't reject the situation between us any longer. I have decided that I shall have to reject Lilian – not in so far as there are oranges and magazines and the exchange of platitudes, but in so far as you are concerned with me. Quite suddenly, Helen, I seemed to have lost the wish to control my impulses towards you."

He touched her arm with his large gentle hand and rubbed the sleeve of his other arm across his forehead where moisture lay in the furrows like dew. Helen looked down and seized mentally on the three objects within her grasp – the bread, the knife, the butter. She learnt them by heart and shut her eyes and memorized them and opened her eyes and found them still present like a talisman. Having reached this stage of the journey together and having desired it sub-consciously so long, yet still she was doubtful of how to reply. The disturbance in the blood made speech impossible for the moment, but finally she looked at Moller's sad face and was shocked into the beginning of a smile.

He essayed one, pitifully, and said, "Helen, please. I wish to court you to the ultimate old-fashioned scandalous end. My intentions are dishonourable. Please accept this as the warmest compliment I can pay you."

She laughed and the tenderness between them merged more comfortably with the bolder stream of their old comradeship.

"That is the way I accept it, Robert?"

"Do you, then?"

"I think perhaps I do."

"Helen," he said, "Helen, let's hurt no one else in doing this. Especially Lilian. We must be sure that this snivelling bloody-minded town is unaware of us. How it would salivate over this conversation!"

He let her arm fall to her side and turned to the coffee that was bubbling. He took a strainer from a drawer, poured coffee into cups, and snapped the switch down on the stove. Helen buttered toast and set it out on plates, finding in the simple domestic actions a kindling delight. And as they sat over their supper they investigated the possibilities of silence together and on its quiet plains they mustered the flocks of their gentleness. They sat a long while, hardly saying a thing but utterly content. Moller watched her fair head, her intelligent eyes and the curve of her mouth with a dreadful hunger, but still did not touch her. She was, he reflected, all the day and all the night he could wish to know, the goal of his heart and thought. He tried, in this room that was so full of Lilian, not to think of his wife, and the struggle between pleasure and pain must have shown on his face.

Helen asked, "What are you thinking?"

"Of you – and Lilian."

She was surprised to see tears spring to his eyes and he turned his head quickly away from her.

"It was Ulysses' private woe – the endless pattern and perplexity of never-ending oceans."

He laid his head on his arms in a defeated way, and

Helen moved so quickly round the table to him it was as if she had not moved at all, but had always been there with his head cradled against her. Their bodies moved as naturally to each other as flowers to light and they comforted each other so until their time for parting came under the clock's warning.

The daphne was still clouding the garden with scent under the china-white moon. Shadow made their faces featureless, but not their voices when they parted by the gate, and Mr. Lunbeck, smoking quietly beneath his guava tree, was overjoyed to find he was not alone in his pursuit of Eros.

The pattern on her pyjamas was washed into an anonymity of design, yet Vinny still found upon the yellowed surface of the flannelette the ghosts of scrubbed daisies and leaves. She stood skinny in her singlet before the wardrobe mirror, and thrust her arms absentmindedly into the coat sleeves. The elastic at the top of the trousers was loose now from boilings. Every so often she had dragged it out through a little opening and made knots to tighten it, so that it was beaded like a girdle of discipline, but incapable of combining further elasticity with the shortening process. She held her pants up with one hand and switched off the light while she shouted good night down the hall to the family. In the darkness she heard their mingled replies, and then she edged between the layers of chill that soon would become layers of warmth, curling in a ball with her head turned to the sash window opened a few inches at the bottom. The sky was filled with pastings of cloud. She watched them and said little phrases to herself and whispered, "O desolate eves along the way", and could get no further, her memory tricking her. Over and over the words emerged, passing like smoke between the old washstand and basin and the wardrobe, curling mistily in the darkness-becoming-lighter of the room with less and less meaning in the words as scenes from the evening repeated themselves in profiles of invitation from Mrs. Striebel's clever face, or her hand touching Vinny's shoulder, or her words "my dear".

"My dear." Vinny said them aloud and turned to hug the pillow in a paroxysm of ardour. She smiled foolishly and ached with love and joy and a desire for martyrdom for her idol's sake, and then went into a raptuous fantasy of herself and Mrs. Striebel in dangerous climates, with herself heroic at dying moments, nobly trying to stanch the flow of her friend's tears.

A wind rising all seagrass-scented and smoky from paddock burnings threw violence across the screen of her window with the clumped foliage of the bloodwoods flung like crazed mops across the star-white sky. Through their turbulence she sensed the outlines of her classmates' hostility, their indifference; and although she tried to fight the image and recapture the tenderness of a few minutes before, she found herself whimpering with part-pain, part-annoyance in the darkness and burrowing her face into the pillow to cut out the vision of the sharpest shame of all. "No," she said, "no", and ground her knuckles so hard into her eyes that the night exploded in flashes of colour that washed and waved together and changed shape like watermarks on paper and then became a steady golden oval with a diminishing black centre. It was ringed in orange light that was metamorphosed from diamond shape to cruciform and then it sputtered out into the soft blackness of her relaxed eyelids. The pattern was always the same.

It had happened last summer term, her birthday term.

Her mother had suggested asking them, but Vinny protested because she knew it wouldn't be any good, anyway; yet in the end her mother won. So she had invited, with almost Christ-like humility of purpose, the very girls who disliked her most, hoping at the back of her mind that some miraculous *volte face* might occur, that after this birthday treat she would be accepted.

The five of them came. They all lived on her side of

the town. They came in their best frocks – which were not so expensive, perhaps, but made Vinny's shrunken voile a sad matter. And they bore token gifts of the cheapest kind – a small bottle of perfume, a pocket diary, a plastic brush-and-comb set.

"It's your first teen year," her mother had sentimentalized. "You must have a party, love. Oh, I can still remember mine! What a time! Dad, stingy though he was, God rest the old basket, asked every kid in the street. And they just loaded me with things. Hankies and books and stockings and undies."

Remembered Vinny bitterly, as the tiny packets lay insultingly on the blue quilt of her bed. The guests had jostled one another, giggling and gazing curiously at the poor room. They primped before the wardrobe mirror and plumped out fat fringes above their freckled or browned country faces. She saw Elizabeth Turton notice the hole in the mat beside the bed and with loathing watched her nudge Pearl Warburton into a shoulder-shaken spasm of suppressed giggles. Betty Klee's great moon face swung round the room like an arc light. Her fat calves bulged over the tops of bobbystocks, and her feet bunched out the shiny leather court shoes she was wearing.

"Well," Vinny said awkwardly. "C'mon outside under the trees."

She led them down the dusky hall to the sitting-room with its cheap home-made cupboards and its drab easy chairs exposed in the afternoon sunlight that slanted through the windows. I hate it, she thought sulkily, but I won't let them see it.

All her visitors looked about them in an appraising fashion.

Making adult conversation, Pearl Warburton said, "We just bought a new lounge suite in Gympie. Genoa velvet in autumn tonings. Very fashionable, I think."

"Ooh, it's lovely!" her satellites chorused Greek fashion. "Ooh, so soft when you sit down you nearly vanish and your legs just come right up off the floor you go back that far."

"That must be fun," Vinny said sourly, with the obscene image of Betty Klee's monstrous baby rolls of white fat in lavish display.

Her mother was busy in the kitchen, red and perspiring over the fuel stove, making sausage rolls for the afternoon tea. She whispered to Vinny as she stood near the door, "Go on, lovey. Take the girls out to play in the yard. It's too hot in here."

"Why couldn't you have made them this morning like I said?" Vinny whispered back resentfully. "I wanted to help."

"Now that's enough. You know I had to finish Rene's dress so she could wear it this arv."

Vinny grumbled an unintelligible reply. Rhonda and Janet Welch heard and sniggered uneasily. Their broad stupid faces did not register the year between them.

"Cost sixty pounds," Pearl continued, unwilling to release this social weapon. "Cash. More if we got it on terms. Mother says terms are just helping the Jews. Don't you think so, Mrs. Lalor?"

Mrs. Lalor looked up startled by the phenomenon of adolescence new since her day. "I suppose you're right," she said. She felt a strange discomfort in the presence of this over-developed girl with the cold eyes and the full, wet-mouthed smile. "Still, we got all our stuff on terms and glad to, things being so dear and us not being able to rake up the money. Wouldn't have had a chair to sit on otherwise."

Mother, mother! pleaded Vinny's mind. She saw the others smirking and staring critically at the cane settee and the cut-out calendar pictures spotted with fly dirt and the hideous carved clock that never went.

She managed to lead them outside down the five back steps, counting them silently to herself and clinging to their numerical fact as a thing of strength amidst all this half-suppressed criticism and mirth. The mango trees were green cumulus of shade and coolness along the back fence with the pattern of their foliage overlaying the trunks with black. For a few dreadful moments they all stood in complete silence. Vinny was uncertain how to entertain these girls with whom she shared no common denominator save that of age, for she was an immature thirteen and under-developed physically alongside their boy- and bust-conscious selves. They were playing the part of young ladies visiting – below their social inclinations and in adult guise. So that when after many false starts and awkwardnesses the group degenerated into hoydenish hide-and-seek and tag, the spectacle of large, ungainly girls throwing themselves among the privacies of tree and shrub, shrieking at contact or an avoided one, was entirely grotesque. Vinny felt peculiarly apart from the boisterous group. She would have enjoyed the games far more than any of the others had they been played with any genuineness; but she was conscious all the time of a condescension and an innate burlesque of what was happening. So after a while she excused herself and went to the lavatory at the end of the yard.

The four narrow walls enclosed her in a prism of stifling heat. She sat looking at the sawdust and the neatly cut squares of newspaper hung on string and the sunlight coming in yellow planks past the door jamb and the cracks between the timbers. There were spiderwebs thickly in the corners and along the roof beams and between the floorboards rows of paspalum spears. She felt safe sitting there and listening to the squeals of her visitors with a sullen but contemptuous distaste. Three minutes passed. The sunlight slid quietly across the floor. Outside the squeals suddenly gave way to silence, followed by sly giggles and a murmur of voices. The visitors must have come closer to the acalyphas crowding the lavatory walls and sheltering it from the lawn, for she could hear but not distinguish Pearl Warburton's glib tongue licking a piece of gossip into shape to start it rolling from one to another of her listeners in a variety of exclamatory noises.

Vinny rose softly, prickling with curiosity, and opened the door on sun and dark-red acalyphas chinked with the white and blue dress of the guests. She stood very still and caught her breath and then moved in closer to the shrubbery.

"Silly old bag," Betty Klee was saying. "Bet she burns those rolls. And there won't be enough, anyway."

"Not if you're around."

They did not spare each other. "You trying to build yourself up?"

"No wonder Vinny's queer," Rhonda whispered. "It's that poky old house and that awful looking furniture. It'd be better if she burnt the house, not the rolls."

There were shrieks of laughter at this and then Pearl Warburton's voice unctuous with insincerity.

"Ooh, you are awful, Rhonda, saying that. Why –" She hesitated with artificial coquetry. "Why, Royce is rather nice, don't you think?"

The silence following held its expectancy flower-tilted to the girl behind the shrubbery and the germinating lasciviousness of the girls hidden from her.

"I sat next to him at the pictures the other night. Mmm . . . *mmm*!"

Vinny trembled with rage. She could visualize Pearl's eye-rolling salacity in the telling, the implication of omission. Royce, whom she loved best of all the family, could not thus be kind to her enemy. She bent white and sick against the branches.

"And then after the pictures were over we . . ." Here the insinuating voice became so soft Vinny could not hear anything but the flow of its murmuring and the listeners' giggles which punctured it like reefs.

She heard Betty Klee exclaim admiringly, "But what did you tell your mother when you got in so late?"

"I told her the pictures were slow getting out, and anyway I put the clock back half an hour before I left."

"Ooh, Pearl!" Choruses of acclaim and admiration. "Ooh, you are awful!"

Royce, thought Vinny. He likes this girl who hates me and who has made me unhappy for years. Tears scalded her pale lids and hung upon her colourless lashes. She backed away softly from the shrubbery and came up to them from the orchard end of the yard, trying to appear casual and indifferent to the tight-knotted tortoise of their gossiping heads. The brown, the black, the blonde jerked apart, the white and the blue emerged individually from the pastiche in five variants of nastiness and arrogance. When she hailed them they turned to her with foolish and knowing smiles and queries as to where she had vanished. The sun was shining splendidly on the green and the red making rich splashes of shadow. The grass washed backwards and forwards in a breeze. The figures had that sudden clear arrested appearance of a photographic "still" and when their lips moved the sound came as if from a dubbing. At the back door her mother appeared and called to them; yet even though they all heard there was some intangible relation binding the six of them in cool enmity on the lawn. They stared at each other, and the Welch girls squeaked with nervous laughter, until the moment when Mrs. Lalor's voice sliced again into the silence. Wordless, they walked to the house and the back sitting-room where the long homework table bore the best table cloth and the best crockery.

It was not an exciting display, but the food was well cooked and there was sufficient. Memories of magazine spreads with the tables' momentous works of gelatines and ices, in sandwiches and open glazed tarts, came to Vinny as she looked at the plain sponges, the neat fish-paste sandwiches and the rolls. There was difficulty in seating the guests, too, for Vinny was quite determined that Pearl Warburton would not be placed either on her right or on her left. Finally, safe more or less, between the Welches, she poured syrup into tumblers – making sure to keep the chipped one for herself – and handed them round in silence.

"I'd prefer tea, thank you, Mrs. Lalor," Pearl said. She smirked swiftly at her friends. "That's if it's no trouble."

Started by the self-assurance, the older woman said, "Why, no, it's no trouble. I did intend making some later. It won't be a minute."

The rolls and the sandwiches made an unenthusiastic round, during which the guests discussed a gigantic meal they had once had at the Turtons'. Mrs. Lalor brought in the tea in the dented silver pot and Vinny realized her mother was making an effort to impress. She could have wept with love and shame – but mainly shame.

"With lemon," Pearl said, graciously declining the milk. "And two lumps."

All the incidents of the afternoon became huge intolerable rocks in the avalanche of Vinny's anger – the presents, the sneers at the furniture, the talk about her brother, the prissy dissatisfaction with food of which she too was ashamed – the whole thing roared its tumult through her mind and hurtled from her lips.

"We only have this sort of sugar!" she shouted. "We don't have lump sugar. Only this, Pearl, only this awful old ordinary sugar."

She kept saying the words, "this awful old ordinary sugar" over and over, and, as if unable to stop and unaware of her action, had risen to her feet and was leaning forward, her arms jerking with rage. She shook the sugar bowl in the other girl's face and Mrs. Lalor gasped a protest.

"Vinny, what's up with you? What's got into you?"

"It's her!" she yelled, now beside herself and enjoying the scene. "Nothing's right. All she does is sneer and criticize us." She swung sharply round on Pearl. "Why do you stay?" Pearl listened appreciatively, her full red lips moist and ever so slightly curved into the crescent of a smile. "Why don't you go home instead of crumbling our cake into little bits to shove to one side. Go home and whisper about Royce. Go on!" She summoned all her courage for the final insult. "You bitch!" she said.

The room became for a second very still. Then Mrs. Lalor, moving swiftly to a misapplied vengeance, was also unaware of her action until it was completed. The shock of her hard palm rang against Vinny's thin face with dreadful concussion.

"I won't have those kinds of words," her mother said. Trying to explain this uncontrolled situation to herself. "You got to apologize, Vinny, because I won't have it, see."

The girl stared at her mother, the bright red of the hand print on one cheek and the other cheek paper-white. Then without a word she pushed her chair roughly aside and raced from the table down the hall to her bedroom. In its dimness she shoved the dressing-table quickly against the door and then flung herself, fingers pressed to her ears, upon the quilt among the paper wrappings and the gifts. Faintly she could hear her mother ordering and then pleading with her to come out, but she would neither move nor answer, and after a while the visitors left, all sounds died away, and the tears came at last to comfort her spasmodically until long after darkness drifted into the room.

Lying in the darkness now, Vinny saw the whole afternoon telescoped into a brief minute of shameful memory. Her mother had questioned her later about her behaviour, but she had not explained why she had become so angry and she did not talk about what she had so nearly heard in the acalyphas. But ever afterwards she felt cut off from Royce almost entirely, and certainly from her mother. She blamed her for the failure of the entire affair. With the sweeping generalizing of the adolescent she turned all her affection upon Mrs. Striebel, and cultivated what might have been a mere "crush" into a disproportionately deep attachment. As the end of the year drew near, she made in the back of her work pad a calendar of schooldays with the periods to be taken by Mrs. Striebel numbered off. She dreaded their ending, for nothing awaited her after the public examinations were over but a job in a Gympie office – if she were lucky – shifting figures from one column and one ledger to another, sifting the relationship of money and goods.

Down the hall came the distant crash of the back door and her mother's voice raised in protest as Royce clumped noisily to his tiny den off the side veranda. Vinny frowned and twisted under the worn sheets. She shut her eyes and Mrs. Striebel, dark and adorable, loomed up between the bloodwoods and filled the sky with sleep.

Three

Robert Moller yawned stalely into the spring. He started up the decrepit Buick and then backed it down the drive and out on the roadway. Ruth Lunbeck waved over armfuls of flowers and gardening shears, poised with just that right amount of poetry above nature. Her hard, pale face foolished a smile under expensive leg-horn and brand new linen and tweed. He smiled back perfunctorily and then groaned softly to himself and twisted the side of his mouth away from her downwards into an expression of contempt. With a roar the car vibrated into life and wrapped watcher and watched in an orange screen of dust – a fact that he endured with pleasure as he thought of the new clothes and the agitation behind him.

When he pulled in by the hotel Helen and Vinny were there waiting, Helen with a large overnight bag and Vinny with a hat box. Behind them, through the half doors of the pub, the noise of the drinkers – the morning shift from the factory – rolled out in a blurred wordy wordlessness. Behind the press of workmen Moller could glimpse Farrelly, trim as a bottle and an impersonal dispenser, playing the cash register like a miniature organ, venturing into passacaglias based on short-measure and short-change and tips. Helen followed the direction of Moller's sardonic smile.

"The moment of truth," she murmured to Moller, nodding towards the bar.

"How right. In with you both." He jerked open the front door for Helen and then leant back and opened the rear door for the child. "You'll have to put up with my ungentlemanliness," he said to them as he took Helen's bag and slung it on the rear seat. "We're running a bit late. The damned engine played up again." He let in the clutch and the car moved forwards. "Yes. Friend Farrelly simply thrives in the odour of sanctity."

Vinny sat forward close to the window, grinning nervously with excitement. Her hair had been combed back hard with water and shone pleasantly above her best jacket and skirt. On her lap she held a bottle-green coat that, Helen knew, long before it proved the fact, would be several sizes too large. Helen laid her hand for a minute on Moller's plump knee bulging beneath his shiny sports trousers and he patted it in a businesslike way.

For each of the three the journey held the magic of giving or receiving or of helping to give or to receive. Caught in a present temporal elation, bounced into unison on worn leather and ageing springs, they received impressions of slope and hill distance in melting spaces between the telegraph poles and the blurred oneness of the fence-posts. The road twisted south and east from the township, and then south again, once the hill cupping the town had been crested, and moved ahead of them in the mild September afternoon amongst flat grey shadows.

A mile or so out of Gungee, near the beach turn-off, Rose Jarman's car passed them with her future husband (though she did not know it) lovingly fondling the wheel. A stuttering shriek of the horn and the big black car skimmed them so closely they could still read the obscenity some school wit had fingered on the dusty duco of the boot. Moller grunted with annoyance as he pulled the car in closer to the road edge.

"There goes one of the seven wise virgins," he said. "And I don't mean Rose."

Helen laughed. "Shush!"she said softly. "We have a passenger, remember?"

Moller grinned and nodded good naturedly. "I'm suffering from a severe attack of week-end. I'll be careful, I promise."

Now that he had arrived at his decision, had achieved a certain exposition of his feelings, he was conscious of an astounding relief. Whether or not his decision would prove wise for himself or for Helen or even Lilian, who still made claims on his conscience, he did not know, though he was, naturally enough, much given in his frequent analyses of the situation to a specious form of rationalizing that applauded his purpose. He sought the self's bright centre, urged by tempest in his own blood, and now was happy that he might in future let slip aside each day's disguise and loosen the sophisticate masks that plied chalks and words of reprimand and menial actions into an impression of surface acceptability.

They raced over Eumundi's green hills in the limelight of five o'clock, down through deepening tones in paddocks and trees under a threatening spread of nimbus moving in from the sea-line.

"God! Not this week-end," Moller pleaded, glancing up at the sky. And then, "*Wie bist du meine Königin,*" he sang in a sudden exhilaration, on key and fulsomely exaggerating. He da-dahed the piano accompaniment that followed and Vinny blushed frantically at the sight of her lords relaxing. "Happy, Helen? Happy, Vinny?"

"Yes, sir," she replied shyly, and turned to look at the racing scrub under the racing sky.

"Well, baby, I'm happy. Happy to be out of school and out of town. You'll have to excuse us, Vinny, and be very tactful if you see Mrs. Striebel and myself acting like escaped prisoners. We are. So relax, my child. We are normal under the job exterior."

Vinny pulled her coat over her thin knees and pressed them hard against each other. She swelled with happiness and looked at the backs of the two adult heads in front of her with uncritical pleasure, denying their physical faults and seeing in them a near-Olympian beauty.

"Back to your Brahms," Helen suggested softly as they passed over the shallow reaches of the Maroochy River with its mud flat stampings of greyish white below the bridge. So he resumed singing and passed through the matching inflections of Daumer's words and Brahms' music until he reached the end of the first stanza:

"Wie bist du meine Königin,
durch sanfte Güte wonnevoll:
Du lächle nur,
Lenzdüfte weh'n durch mein
Gemüthe wonnevoll, wonnevoll."

Both Helen and Moller were aware of the emotion behind this half-clowned performance of one of the loveliest songs either knew; and Vinny, sitting quietly and embarrassedly in the back seat, became apprehensive of an adult emotion in the air that she could not fathom. She felt, too, a curious stirring jealousy as she, the acolyte, watched them, the priests, performing a wordless, actionless rite in front of her.

The sky was nearly dark now, only hachured by drizzle that had whispered across them since passing the Buderim plateau. The ginger and pineapple farms lay mistily under the quiet rain through which they could still see the big sawdust mulch heaps lying damply along roadside and paddock fences. Moller set the windscreen wiper going and they drove for a long while in silence under the steadily increasing rain that barricaded, with points of quiet on the canvas roof, the car and its three occupants. Rain stipple and trees and the sudden chromatic gurglings of a creek freshet. Ngungun loomed up in the rain, its huge hump of trachyte theatening the sky, and then Tibrogargan and Beerburrum crowded in upon them, black and ugly and well loved by Moller, who passed them every week-end with a sense of journeying half done.

Today each familiar section of road, each familiar action with the car whose foibles were old friends, had become endued with a newer connotation. The lights of Caboolture, blurred and wet, sucked them into the main street, and by a corner store the car shuddered and pulled up in the racing gutter. Moller dived out his side and splashed into a bright doorway, reappearing in a short time with pies and chips. Helen wiped his shoulders and hair with a scarf she had tucked in her coat pocket, and then they ate noisily and happily in the half-light, with the roar of the storm-water drains right below them.

"A pity," Helen said as the rain thudded and thumped on the roof of the car and splashed in under the mica window screens. "But we shan't let it spoil our two days, Vinny. Never fear."

"I like it," Vinny said. She bit off half a chip. The hot potato burnt her tongue and she let it fall back into the paper. "I feel cosy like this. I wish this journey could go on for hours."

"It will if this rain keeps up." Moller glanced at his watch. "We're twenty minutes behind on my normal schedule. I shall have to put my foot down and keep it there if we're going to reach the city by seven-thirty."

"Must we?" Helen was surprised that anyone so normally uninterested in routine or the appearances of it should have this particular compulsion.

"Helen. It's my old bomb's reputation that's at stake. And besides, I forgot to ring my people and let them know I was coming. It's unlikely, but they may be out after eight and I'll be left homeless in this filthy weather until they return. Unless you like to take me in."

He crumpled the newspaper from round his chips and tossed it out of the window where the rainwaters snatched it away in a flash.

"There she goes," he said, peering out after it in the darkness, "running a banker." He watched the sadness of the runnels under the lamplight awash with twig and paper and leaf, the exhausted cartons of week-old theatre crowds damming the gratings in grimy piles. He rolled himself a cigarette, lit it, and turned to Helen and then to Vinny. "Well, you girls? Are you ready?"

Helen nodded with her mouth full and Vinny said, "Yes", as she scooped up a lump of pie gravy from her skirt and popped it into her mouth. She had never been so happy. Absent-mindedly she rubbed at the stain with a corner of her coat and then abandoned the idea as the car spluttered and started. Taken hold of by a common feeling of irresponsibility they sang current popular songs loudly for most of the way.

"I don't wanner set the world – on – fiyuh,' " Moller roared through the beating rain. " 'I jus' wanner start – a littul flame in your heart!' " He accelerated sharply with each strong beat. Vinny giggled delightedly and timorously joined in.

Helen sank down more deeply into the seat and huddled under the warmth of her coat, her head dizzy from the small enclosed space that was stuffy with the smell of damp upholstery and petrol. Soon she was merely a voice augmenting from time to time the undiminishingly cheerful singing of the other two; her eyes, dazzled from watching the headlamps flinging the crouching country back in elongated stripes of yellow, gradually closed. She was reminded of a similar pattern – the truck drives in each week-end with the workmen, bucketing between the school where she was a five-day boarder to her home near the town filter beds. Along the old Moggill Road at night under glacial stars above and cigarette ends burning stars around her in the darkness, with the smells of sweat and earth and cold wet grass and gums, and then the river opening up beyond the trees a sheet of argentine light. Huddled with knees knocking and "sorry miss" and trying to doze against the back of the driver's cabin on the cold winters evenings flaming with frost. It all seemed to be part of the present, until Moller would pat her kindly in the dark, bringing her back to the actual now; or until she could hear him snarling at another car, "Dip them, you bloody fool! Dip them!"

It was pleasant, she thought, remembering Vinny's thin face eager-bright under the wavering street light at Caboolture, to be performing a charity; pleasant to balance in part the guilt sense that coloured her mind when she thought of Moller. She wished Lilian were cruel or domineering or repulsive physically, but in fact she was none of these things. Confronted with an overwhelming illness, she had, Robert said, become, naturally enough, more and more intolerant of daily ministering to her person on the part of nurses or friends. She had grown farther and farther away from all the interests she had once indulged. With the withering of her limbs her mental life seemed to be dying away, too. Helen wished there were some alternative solution to her present situation other than physical fulfilment. She could, she knew, deny that it existed. But that would be false also. And in the darkness she sighed and leant her head against the hard edge of the window, suffering the discomfort with determined self-punishment. Rhomboids of windscreen glow lit her wide pale face, her hands, locked for warmth, not in humility or supplication, upon the heavy stuff of her coat. She picked away the torn crescent of a finger-nail and abandoned her problem to the scattered lights of the outer suburbs.

The suburbs scrabbled into the greenness and at night their lights pricked into darkness with edges furred now from rain. The lights came with increasing frequency until at last they crowded together along the treeless streets with their meagre gardens. The street lights splashed every twenty yards a puddle of yellow on slippery bitumen or white bus stop or shelter shed. The first brightly lit tram scuttling away with its explosions of green light on the overhead wires was for the three of them a quick urban excitement, a severing from Gungee that lay behind them at this moment with its facets of work and friendship and friendlessness as unreal.

"There, kid," Moller said over his shoulder to Vinny. "There's the big, exciting city." He laughed at the loneliness of tramline and at himself. "Packed with people and movement and pulsating life." He stared along the wet empty road. "Not even a damn' dog. Oh, bloody weather!"

"What do you want?" Helen asked. "A ten-gun salute?"

"There'd be some point in that for all of us," he said softly.

He waved a fast car past him and the Buick pulsed along evenly by the cluster of shops and the waterproofed film lovers huddled early in vestibules with that look of stupid anticipation in eyes that were shortly to become like celluloid. Fortitude Valley was bedraggled, a woman with her hair in pins, feet thrust into slippers. Frowziness loitered round shop corners with the tight-panted sailors just fed at the Chinese cafés, dawdled at the railway entrance in boxy jackets and black shirts, behind tills in the empty milk bars and coffee shops.

Vinny regarded all this close-packed squalor with no sense of depression at all, but as part of a city's magic. Now, she thought, now I am really out of Gungee and in town, and everything I see I want to store away. With what avidity her eyes ate up shop windows, people, trams and neon signs, and when at last they swung out along the river road by Hamilton Reach the breadth of water and the shadowy hulls of ships with their lights glowing flatly in the darkness all caused her to catch her breath with wonder. The reflections of the lights shuttered in red and green and lemon over the river for hundreds of feet.

Moller stopped the car outside the large bungalow where Helen's sister Margaret lived. The house sprawled white and untidy across most of a large block of land, gardened haphazardly into a jungle of scent and exotic tropical mussaendas, hibiscus, and today-and-tomorrow bushes. He switched off the ignition, glanced at his watch and scowled.

"Fifteen minutes late."

Helen, combing her hair, looked solemnly at the polished street. The street-light in front of the house burnished the camphor-laurels on the footpath with an electric green.

"The main thing," she said, "the most important thing is that we're here. An epochal week-end. Thanks, Robert, for bringing us down."

"Shall I see you at all?" Throwing caution to the darkness and the rain. The canvas roof pattered no replies. Helen felt excitement edge quickly in the back of her mind. She leant forward and struggled into her coat, her fair head touching the dash-board. Vinny prickled with unexpected jealousy and then repressed it in the knowledge that she was no longer on the fringe of things. She was becoming part of a private circle of knowledge that would support her in the friendless weather at the school. Amongst gossiping speculators she would be privy to truth. She pretended to be busy with her coat.

"Well?"

"Perhaps – perhaps tomorrow night. Tomorrow afternoon is Vinny's, you understand, and Sunday as well. Margaret has booked our seats for a matinée tomorrow, and Sunday – well, I thought a quick visit to the Art Gallery or Museum if there's time, and getting Margaret to run us out to the tram terminus to pick you up."

"All very educational, Helen. A little profanity, you know. . . . Still, never mind. I'll ring you round six or seven tomorrow evening to see if you feel up to a late coffee. A late anything," he added, half to himself.

Helen seized his left hand and pressed it with a swift tenderness that made speech unnecessary; then quickly she opened the door and jumped out over the running gutter. Perched on the kerb, she grasped the handle of the rear door, and for a moment she and the child struggled against each other; then the door jerked open unexpectedly and Vinny tumbled forward off-balance on to the roadway. By a miracle she kept her feet and Helen's firm hand intercepted her elbow and supported her during this moment of ludicrous spasticity. Together they yelled goodbye to Moller from under the front gate's dripping arbour, and when he had turned the car and they saw the red tail-light vanish the way they had come, they raced up the cement path to the lighted veranda where Helen's sister was waiting.

For a moment it was all confusion and greetings and well-wishings with the hands and the arms forming the proven theorems of personal relationships; and then it became bright rooms and shadowy, good furniture and old, a bathroom tiled and chromium plated and reflecting from a dozen surfaces the awed, the excited face; and then it was chairs to sink, to vanish in; and kindly questions pursued the comfort, and ease of mind followed with cocoa in splendid red cups and intricate open sandwiches like problems in stained glass. It must have been quite some time before either of the women noticed the tears running unchecked down Vinny's smiling face. Their anxiety was afraid to question but did nevertheless, and she assured them both that her tears were of pleasure.

"I can't help it," she said. "It's just I never had such a nice time before."

And they were sensitive and sensible enough not to pursue the matter, though the wet-streaked cheeks were provocative and the ill-kempt hair and clothes.

Helen saw Vinny tumble into bed in the spare room, cheerful with suburban cretonne and hooked rugs – a deliberate affectation on her sister's part, running counter to her natural taste. But it was unglamorously cosy within its four cream walls. The window shut out wind and rain and a cloud-burst of climbing roses trellised down the side of the house; and it shut in warmth and puffed up cushion and pillow and the tired body upon the hollowed bed.

Margaret Reisbeck was a thin, nervous woman who had crossed the menopausal Rubicon with barely a variation in her jittery personality – if anything, she was now a little more serene, though her tireless pursuit of culture amongst the arid deserts of little theatre and new art groups would lead one to wonder just how volatile had been her nature in the warmer years of her twenties and thirties. Still, her enthusiasms were infectious for a while until they became tiresome; and the long, cultured horse-face with its incredibly odd barking voice was sympathetic. Moller always suggested irreverently to Helen that she had a black roof to her mouth. Hair wisped and framed, and eyes, hollow fatigued above her brightly painted mouth, explained away the twitchings of bony hands and the restless tapping of feet.

She reached across the breakfast table and absent-mindedly peppered the eggs of the other two before helping herself.

"That's an incredible mine host of yours up at Gungee, Helen," she said. "Is he a civil fellow?"

"He runs a hotel," Helen replied, cutting her toast into three neat strips. "He tries to be all things to all men."

"Oh, my dear! Not really!" Margaret simpered. "I tried to ring you on Friday afternoon before you left, and he went away from the phone for exactly half a minute and came back and said he couldn't find you and that he didn't intend looking. It was gratuitous rudeness, for I hadn't stressed that I want to speak to you. I *had* said a message would do. Anyway, when he came back to the phone I asked him to give you a message." Margaret teased her fried egg into several futuristic shapes and gobbled one of them. "I even made him repeat it after me. 'Please tell Mrs. Striebel' – and he said, 'Please tell Mrs. Striebel' – 'I wish' – 'I wish' – 'she would move' – 'she would move' – 'to a more polite' – 'to a more polite' – 'and courteous hotel' – 'and courteous hotel'. My dear, he actually said the words after me before he could stop himself, and when he'd finished and realized what he'd said, he let out a shrill scream. Absolutely wonderful! I felt it was worth the one and ninepence."

"You tiger," Helen said. "I'll probably find my possessions hurled out on to the street when I get back. Vinny, Margaret is a dreadful woman, and on no account must you be influenced by her."

Vinny giggled into her breakfast plate. Sleep-sated and happiness-masked, her face flushed with pleasure at the inclusion in the adult talk, at being circumscribed by friendliness.

"Mum says Mr. Farrelly puts clerical collars on his beers," she said.

"What an intelligent child!" Margaret barked. "I suppose, my dear, he is a very religious man. Now tell me, Helen, what are your plans for today? I know this afternoon is fixed up, but what about this morning? The rain's eased off. It might be an idea if I run the two of you into town so Vinny can have a look at the shops. Homes of graft and racket, my child, but necessary."

"It's putting you out, isn't it?"

"Not at all. I have to go in to see about the hanging of the spring exhibition for Carya Studios. They've got a basement room in Elizabeth Street, poor things. Shockingly old and depressing. Still . . . a coat or two of flamingo and turquoise ought to pick it up no end. More tea, Helen? Vinny?"

"Well, that sounds pleasant. How about it, Vinny? There's nothing like a spot of window-shopping to make you happy for the wealth of others. There. I'm sounding exactly like Margaret. Two days of you, Margaret, and I've imbibed enough cynicism to antagonize the whole of Gungee."

"Darling, smug little town," Margaret cooed. "I'm burning to see it. One week-end I'll drive up with some of the young things from Carya. They'd adore a sketching jaunt in a primitive backwater like that."

"Oh God! Please, Maggie. That's a prayer. Don't do it to me. Wait until I've left the place."

"But that might be years."

"I don't think I'd want to be there for years. Another one or two, maybe. No more."

"Sure?" Margaret asked archly, who always multiplied a given situation by twice the known number of factors in it.

Helen did not answer, and Margaret smiled, all frayed wickedness over slipping dentures, and looked whimsical and non-committal herself. She helped herself to immense quantities of bread and peach jam, as she did daily without any beneficial effect upon her sparse body. "Well, today is definite," she stated firmly, irradiating breakfast-room and occupants with her compelling smile.

Vinny saw the morning unfolding its colours and tendernesses like a rose. In what gardened acres of mind she wandered, when, having assisted with the breakfast dishes and neatened her room, she went off to explore the rear garden tanging with wet earth smells and sodden shrubberies. As a very small child she had loved sitting under the natural caverns of the leaves, feeling enwombed in their ragged tents of colour, watching greedily the bustling life of the ants and flying insects around her. Even now she found herself eyeing the hollows beneath the mussaendas, with a professional eye. She wandered to the front of the house.

The day had cleared under a toughening wind that scudded along behind cloud races from the south-east. Scattered over the wet blue sky were cirrus shreds torn and ripped into an untidy morning; the river, from where Vinny stood by the front garden fence, was deeply, freshly green, wrinkled into cheeky waves that slapped the launches moored offshore. Each leaf, each blade dagger-held its individual pearl of water. A tram rattled by. Gulls whiter than ever against the deepened colours of the river swooped and plummeted and skimmed above the smaller craft.

Vinny's hand closed round the leather purse in her skirt pocket. Inside it was a ten-shilling note.

"That's all I can spare," her mother had apologized, tucking it in with a horribly over scented handkerchief. "Buy Mrs. Striebel some little thing, Vinny. Not that you'll get much. But it's the thought that counts." Vinny pressed her chin against the paintless wrought iron gate and ran her fingers thoughtfully over the daggers of design that spiked the morning air. She wondered what Mrs. Striebel would like. Her unsophisticated mind sorted over perfume and stockings and stopped dead for lack of experience. It became even more difficult when there was no question of appeasing the goddess, when it was purely a votive offering – the choice was then so unbounded by what would be necessary; it became a gesture that must embody her own necessity as well as the flattery to Mrs. Striebel. She did not reason exactly like this, but the ideas, unformulated as they were, lingered in her mind and moved restlessly, over its surface like gulls on the river. She squeezed the purse into a thin oblong, and then flattened it out and opened it just to make sure the note was still there, stinking and warm inside the imitation leather.

She was perplexed again when, having parked Margaret's smart sedan near the old university gates, they walked back up George Street and then into the city's centre. The back streets had been patterned with wet leaves and freshly cut shadows on the sunny pavements, stamped out replicas of trees. But here, with the Saturday morning crowds, the jangling trams, the cars and the traffic lights, Vinny was too confused to think clearly. Interiors of coffee lounges, murky walls, dreg colour and people-packed seduced the eyes, the wantings – into milk bars youth-stool-cluttered or into frock shops garrulous with feminine facade, all the mendacities of fabric and colour and line. She was still wearing the same skirt, the same rather small jumper from which her overlong arms projected rawly. The violence of her hair against the pale face was very startling; and the pale eyes were nipping with twin-pincered brightness the movement and noise. She marvelled at the numbers and the variety of the faces, the discs of pink or white or red or brown that jiggled past in the mid-morning streets, with looks of purpose or point, lives crusted with assurance. Trams were freckled, too, with faces, but they had more passivity as they swung by, a blankly accepting blindness of the eyes. Helen watched Vinny as Vinny watched the crowds. Margaret had left them a few blocks away in a smother of scarves and parcels and what seemed to be a dozen string bags.

"Well?" Helen asked. She broke the surface of the child's abstraction as delicately as a leaf might wrinkle the surface of a pool.

Vinny said, "Oh, Mrs. Striebel, the crowds. It's the crowds. I can't imagine all these people having different lives. It must be wonderful living in town with so many. All the time. So many. You'd never be lonely, would you?"

"Yes. Terribly," Helen said. She did not bother to explain, she knew Vinny could work out the paradox herself. "Come on, my girl. I have to go in here and buy stockings and all sorts of nonsense."

The counters of the department store imprisoned shop-girls in black. To Vinny they all appeared exquisite painted things, elegant and adult. The prisons themselves clasped like precious jewels, ends of lace and fancy-work, artificial flowers that would make any garden a colourless affair, buttons – speckles of colour, ribbons like paper streamers. The price tags were not obvious. But each sales girl knew the worth of each customer not only from the obvious externals – the declarations of expensive clothing – but as well from the hesitancy which mostly they despised or the arrogance which, peculiarly enough, they seemed to prefer, learning the gestures of it and putting them aside well conned for future use.

Mrs. Striebel was taking so long in her selection at the button counter that Vinny wandered off to a china and crockery display at the far side of the shop. The hideously ornate and the simple battled their themes through ramekins and flower bowls, ovenware, figurines, jardinières. To Vinny the simple looked uninspired. She was only thirteen. Her eyes lit up in near greed at the sight of china roses, flashily glazed horses, shepherdess clocks. She stared covetously. Here was what she wanted. An ornament for Mrs. Striebel. A gay floral tribute, permanent in porcelain, colourful, cheerful, indestructibly complex in design.

A pert, breast-lifted, black-clad girl, only a few years older, looked at her contemptuously.

"Can I help you?" she asked. Not wanting to.

Vinny became pale; her heart pounded with nervousness.

"Yes," she said, gulping her words.

The other girl was taking in with one practised sweeping glance the baggy skirt, the shrunken jumper the mean purse squeezed up between the bony freckled fingers. She hated serving kids, anyway. She half turned, smiled at another girl farther along the counter, and puffed the back of her hair languidly.

"Yes," Vinny continued timidly, speaking to the back of the salesgirl's head. "I want a vase, please. Not dear, though. Not too dear."

The shopgirl turned and spoke without really looking at Vinny.

"What do you mean 'not dear'?" She fixed a point in the crowd with her eye and waited for a reply.

Vinny's discomfiture crystallized into such pain she thought she would cry.

"I mean not more than a pound." She hesitated. "That is – I only have ten shillings."

"I'm afraid you won't get much for that. Not at this counter. All our vases are very good." She underlined "very". "And the cheapest costs twenty-five shillings."

"Please," Vinny said, "haven't you got something? Some little thing? Anything for that much? I don't mind really, so long as it's nice."

"Well," said the other relenting a little. "No vases. How about a small figure? This Dutch boy? Or this horse? No, that's twelve and six. Here. Here's something nice – a little basket of flowers. Seven and nine."

It wobbled slightly and it was all gilt, rose pink, delphinium blue. The salesgirl pushed it forward and put on her admiring face.

"That's real nice. Pretty. Is it for a present?"

"Yes."

"Well, you couldn't get anything nicer. Nor cheaper." Boredom chased the accustomed phrases across the little powdered cake-like face.

Vinny touched the basket gently. It was real nice. She found the shininess of the petals and leaves and china wicker work quite beautiful. She put out one finger grubby and nail bitten, and ran it over the surface. Smooth. Real smooth, too, with little round crinkles.

"All right," she said. "I'll have that." She opened her purse and took out the ten shillings. The stench of scent enfolded the transaction. The salesgirl rang the cash register with the arrogance of an electronic-brain operator. She wrapped the gift indifferently and fastened the brown paper with a sticky tab. Change and parcel were passed across the counter together. The salesgirl was aloof again, hand puffing at hair. To Vinny's diffident "thank you" she condescended a slight curve of her tarty little lips and then stared into a middle distance of boys and fifty-fifty dances and fumblings in taxis.

Vinny found Mrs. Striebel ready to leave. Helen looked curiously at the small parcel but said nothing, and together in stronger sunshine they strolled back to Margaret's car where Helen left her purchases on the rear seat.

"You have a choice," Helen said, smiling up into the jacaranda trees lacing the official buildings and the sky. "We can get a tram home for lunch and race back to the show at two. Or eat in a leisurely fashion here in town and then go straight to the theatre. Which would you like, my girl?"

Vinny's eyes closed in bliss and opened again to the iron fence of the gardens rolling away in greens and yellows of mown grass, down curves as gentle as a kindness to the clumped groves of cotton palms and the children playing in the shifting rags of sun and shade.

"Stay," she said. "Stay here."

So they went through the gates of the park and ate a refreshment room lunch together – which meant nothing in sophisticated eating to Helen but was all the enchantment and magic possible to the child who had never eaten anywhere but at home. She sipped her tea, looking through the lattice of the tea-rooms and watched the pigeons nubbling the grass for crusts. Marvellous, Helen thought, that three thin slices of devon sausage, two triangles of beetroot, and a lettuce leaf could translate anyone into such a condition of pleasure. She, too, sipped her sugarless tea and gazed over the potted plants, the monstera now climbing the side walls, to the older ladies knitting in the sun, in their dumpy browns and angular black, at the women without men and the technical college students cutting downhill towards the river and the Edward Street ferry. Canna lilies burned in the shrubberies, great beds of early zinnias candled the pathways flowing in asphalt streams across the lawns.

There were only a few people in the tea rooms apart from themselves, and now and then a student on the way from morning classes would drop in for a milk shake or a chocolate bar or a pie. The woman at the next table rose and went to the counter. She was shabby and pregnant, each factor seeming to complement the other. Helen noticed Vinny look quickly at the bulging stomach and the shoulders thrown back above the hips to support the weight. Then Vinny turned away to stare out at the lawn dotted with burdenless bodies – girls, young men, and elderly seedless women. They carried no personality but their own, they bore no other body and no other destiny. Pregnancy frightened Vinny. She still remembered three years ago, just before her dad left, her mother talking about the new baby, swelling gently under her apron and her worn out dresses; bulging horribly in the summer months and becoming crosser, and all the rows and then her father leaving and her mother suddenly taken by the ambulance one night, sweating the pain in rivers, in tides, in oceans, and then no baby, but her mother back home again, thinner than ever under the warped timbers of the house, just at the time when the seed pods were splitting open on the cassias. She never saw a tree in seed now without thinking of that time.

It was one-fifteen.

The clock hands nudged them out of the tea rooms down through the swooping gardens under the fig tree basilicas towards the river where it slid olive grey and quiet below the cliffs. The bank on their side gave a steep and tiny plunge to the water and the spatulate mud flats, chocolate shining under the sun. It was too early for the lovers, Helen mused, watching the park seats dotted with old men warming crusted joints or reading their papers. But the day augured benisons for them.

She found the photographer at the entrance where she had always found him, for years it seemed, since she had visited the park, and she made Vinny stand awkward before his tripod and veiled head to partner the mystic rite. Vinny accepted the ticket with a feeling of mixed reluctance and pleasure – reluctance to see herself as she knew herself to be, ginger and skinny and not even waif-life and appealing, just ginger and skinny and dressed in what she called her best and had thought to be all right until she had seen the other girls in the shops and the trams.

But she was pleased to fix this day, to have a tangible reminder of herself grinning up Edward Street through the passers-by and the iron gates. She shifted her parcel up to the crook of her elbow and hugged it to her, while she fumbled the ticket into her purse with the few pieces of small change and the scent.

Moller after tea, replete, unhappy, lay among the cigarette stubs and the dead matches, lay drunken, but not on liquor. Self-pity, retrospective gloom washed, belched over him, flung him into a heap of floatsam in the lumpiest of the armchairs. His relations had gone out half an hour before, crimped like the sand of a low-tide beach, sparkling with knick-knacks and crackling with currency. The over-vacuumed carpeting and the primped, the shaken-out curtains gulped him up.

He thought of Lilian and then thrust the thought back behind his desire for Helen and the loneliness and emptiness of the house. In fifteen minutes he would ring Margaret Reisbeck's. Tea should be over, Helen free for the evening from that damnable little girl. God, he loathed her at this moment! Irrationally he blamed her for the desolation of the seven o'clock news, the seven o'clock house, the Helenless quality of the day. Not that other week-ends had been different from this one, but having made his decisions, having fought past the oranges and the books and the flowers to a little pleasure for himself, he resented not being able to grasp it. He thought of the Lunbecks, the male, the rake – but sly – and the wife suffering gladly for income and prestige and the mixing with the wives of the other professional men in the town. Sourly Moller arranged them in descending order of social importance – the doctor (Jaysus, he breathed), the bank manager, the dentist, the mill owner. Piddling small time.

He lit himself another cigarette and puffed viciously at the family-group photo upon the sideboard, saw Ted and Vera and Lance with dog vanish in a kindly screen of smoke. Findlay must come somewhere near the mill owner, a little above the Anglican parson but well below the bank manager. Tricky, that. He drew a pencil from his vest pocket and scribbled on Vera's telephone memo pad a whole feudal socio-economic system for Gungee. He used little squares for the men and triangles for the women; then, amused, drew lines and arrows and equation symbols for misalliance, sharp business deals, nepotism, and so on. He threw back his head and roared. Where was Rome? He added an insignificant black square well below the town clerk, who was himself below the parson and the itinerant solicitor and equated it with the representative of the law. He could see the upper layer with their bridge-party faces, drinking hard in the privacy of their homes, and condemning the farm and factory hands who spewed their dislike of the day in public outside one or other of the hotels. He saw Lunbeck pawing the hostesses at the intimate little gatherings in one dull living-room after another, getting them to one side of the kitchen at coffee time, holding a breast in one hand and a *canapé* in the other, hiding under the clatter of the women's tongues snapping up and down over clothes and money and cars and clothes and money and was she expecting or wasn't she and my dear her clothes and she is and so on. And the men, big and important in their tiny spheres, carping over their employees: "Sacked him, by God! His eyes were too bloody close together." "Stepped up the production a bit. Snipped a couple of minutes off their morning tea break, and they never noticed."

He saw the town and the rival streams on a Sunday flowing implacably towards their version of Christ revealed one day in seven, leaving six for primitive tribal taboos and ostracisms, for scandalizing and detraction, for the too rare act of charitable restraint. Farrelly stood resigned with his canary-faced wife twittering her aves and paternosters alongside Constable Rossiter. Town Clerk Meerson, abstracted from reality by one of the more fearsome nonconformist gospels, kept his pale, vice-hating face a map of righteousness and dyspeptic texts. The chemist was an atheist – he thought he was daring. ("But are you a *practising* one?" Moller used to ask.) But doctor Rankin and missus doctor Rankin and bank manager Cantwell and missus bank manager Cantwell joined with the Lunbecks and the Findlays and the Talbots in cautious established worship. And the whole town, the simple farming families and the factory workers, all followed close behind, passing through Anglicanism, two sorts of Methodism, and the Lenten sulphurations of Father Concannon with an unprotesting piety.

Moller saw them all and yawned horribly at the ceiling and the family group risen from fire and the clock pointing to seven-thirty. He crushed out his cigarette, and with a forefinger of each hand pulled his mouth corners down and up. His plump face made the Grecian masks of comedy and tragedy, became a Janus, and he reached for the phone, divided in his feelings, and dialled and listened to the ringing in Margaret Reisbeck's empty hall and felt the beginning of union in the sound.

"At last," he said, hearing Helen's voice. "Had a good day?"

"Wonderful, thanks, Robert. Vinny was quite transported by *The Gondoliers*. Poor sausage! The music, the dancing, the matinée crowd had her nearly delirious. We ate an entire box of chocolates and we are very ill and very happy."

"My dear, we are both in love with you."

Helen was silent a moment. Moller, holding the receiver to his ear, could not share her vision of the eager child in the darkened theatre, tensed to such a point of enjoyment she seemed brittle with pleasure, trembling now and again as she sat forward on her seat, her eyes absorbing the light and colour and movement on the stage. Bouncing home in the tram afterwards, still dazzled by the images in her mind. Vinny had watched the neon signs, the trouser advertisements striding on the spot on the facades of buildings, the cigarettes lit up gigantic by the river, the flickering tea pot pouring tea through a dozen bulbs into a neon cup. She had leant forward across the toast rack seat and smiled with such fearful intensity that Helen had drawn back slightly.

"This has been the first day of my life, Mrs. Striebel."

Helen was silent, remembering, then she said, "I don't know whether that pleases me altogether, Robert. The obvious thing, that is."

"Natural adolescent fervour. Healthy in its way. Certainly natural. It will fade in time. Some boy, perhaps."

"I hope so." There was another tiny silence stretched thin as a veil between them. "How was Lilian?"

"As ever. Very ill, but only a little unhappy. Her hospital life and her fellow patients are becoming the real things to her now. Our little cosmos has split, and we find we have practically nothing to talk about. Incredible, isn't it, after fifteen years of marriage?"

"Not really. Perhaps you've reached saturation point."

"A clever woman." Moller shifted his legs over one arm of the chair and leant back against the other. "The explanation of the failure of all human relationships. Are you prepared to reduce ours to the same point?"

"That sounds rather coquettish."

"Nevertheless I'm asking. This evening, for instance? How are you saturated for this evening?"

Helen laughed. "I'm very tired."

"Too tired for coffee or supper? Nothing social, nothing dressy. Just plain natter and coffee."

"If Margaret is back in time to baby-sit. She was due half an hour ago. As a matter of fact, I think I can hear the car now. Yes. There she is booming up the veranda. All right, Robert. Let's say eight, shall we? And where?"

"I'll pick you up if it won't cause scandal."

"My dear!"

He replaced the receiver, humming "*Wie bist du meine Königin*" with syncopated pauses and little batches of mordents and semi-quaver variations that gave the song a nightclub significance. He washed his face, but it still looked greasy and certainly flabby, and then he brushed his nicotine coated teeth uselessly; and after that he put on a tie. The whole effect – the sports coat, the rounded trousers – was not one of being *en fête*, so with a hideous groan he stripped them off and struggled into navy serge, buttoned rather too snugly across his chest, creased a little too sharply on each leg. Still, this was more – more. . . . He went still singing to the car.

They confronted each other in the angle seat of an upstairs lounge with the wary eyes of rivals. Outside the window behind them a vertical neon sign switched from red to green and back again, subtly altering the values of the light about their table. The lounge was filled with drinkers whose talk made barriers of privacy round the two by the window. The pedestrian platitudes bubbled up like froth on beer and settled between the groups in tarnishing rings. A waiter on wheels skated in and out, twirling his drink tray, clinking his gins and brandies, his whiskies and crêmes, like castanets among the fleshy and the fleshless, the hard and the flaccid. The rubber bound bodies of the women bent in their prisons towards the legs-apart-sprawled men using their chairs like saddles. Mouth signalled to mouth over rim, or the eyes were wildly bright and insincere or watery and maudlin above the big and the little noses, the red pores, the powder. In rhythm with attenuated tea-room music pressed from piano and violin by two blasé boys, the washroom doors swung open and shut monotonously, and at each opening Helen glimpsed the stained tiles, a figure re-masking before a wall mirror, the chromium of the taps. And all the time, out here in the large smoke-hung room, the bawdy utterance burst among the red faces pressed together and flung them apart with the bomb of the obscenity into explosions of laughter. Quiet and systematic character-felling went on at tables for two, which stood among the jig-sawed pieces of personality like fortresses of virtue, stone-hurling turrets.

Helen felt the artificial excitement of the setting, the tawdriness, and, feeling it, did not know whether to be pleased that they had made the decision to solve their friendship erotically. The adverb crossed her mind with a temporary embarrassment and involuntarily she lowered her eyes to her gin. Moller was watching her. His heavy eyes said nothing at all, and it was some time before he spoke.

"Tell me, Helen, are you sorry?"

"No."

"Sure?"

"Quite."

He nodded. "Now another question. Did young Vinny hear your end of the conversation tonight, or know you were meeting me? I think perhaps it's unwise that the adolescent population of Gungee should feed on our indiscretions."

Helen lit herself a cigarette. The sign outside the window fell across her in green bands.

"I don't think she could have heard. The phone is in the hall as you know, and Vinny was in the sitting-room with the door closed between us. No, I don't think she could possibly have heard, and I certainly didn't tell her I was meeting you. All she knew was that I was going out for a short time. I hope to heaven Margaret has the good sense to repress her Bohemian descriptions. In any case, Robert, Vinny would hardly discuss it with the rest of her class. She wouldn't get a chance, poor kid."

"Who knows?" Moller said. "This is a God sent opportunity for establishing herself as an oracle. She might use it to make a bid for favour."

"How would that sort of behaviour tie in with the crush on me that you say she has? And I don't know that I like the idea of that too well, either."

"A point. Still, she could be jealous of me. Don't look so incredulous, my dear. Remember the scandalous fate of my predecessor at the school after his idyllic episode with young Crewe. Now, hold hard! I'm not suggesting Vinny nourishes a passion of that extent for you, but you must admit she does worship a little. Who can blame her? You're the only one who is kind to her – unalterably kind."

"Why," Helen asked, "why is adolescence such a difficult time? Why has it got to be so distorted and painful?"

"Mine wasn't," Moller said complacently. "I did all the things boys do at all the normal times. I went into boils in second year, long 'uns in third year, and spent most of fourth studying nature magazines and swotting up unnecessary biological facts in medical texts. I was a charming, natural, unspoilt boy."

Helen laughed loudly and spontaneously. A man at the next table winked. She winked back.

"It's the gin." She explained away her action to Moller who was looking at her amusedly.

"Good for you," he said. "I like to see you unbending. But while we're still sober, a word of warning. We must be oh so circumspect at school. Deny each other more than thrice, my dear."

He said, suddenly sentimental across the tiny wobbling table, "My very dear", and knocked his glass, spilling some brandy on the floor. "They are so full of conscience and God, our village playmates, they would feel it a duty to inform Lilian to make her sickness more unbearable and our happiness less tolerable."

He sighed and finished his drink. The neon sign changed from green to red. The man at the next table swayed across space towards him and called him "sport" and borrowed a match and swayed back. The big clock on the wall above the door leapt five minutes and took the room to nine-fifteen and a higher straining of the voices towards enjoyment, towards packing popularity into fatuities and shallow yap, while the door of the women's washroom swung open and shut upon the blonde and the brunette, all sisters under the liquor, who got pally over the wash basin or shared their waiting discomfort outside the lavatory door with comradely patter from the external sexual warfare. They belched and apologized as one.

"What can we do?" Moller apostrophized the air, ignoring the appetent leer from the man at his elbow. He spoke more softly and leant across the table. "What can we do, my girl, but sleep together? A dull denouement for the warmest of friendships. Hark at my cynicism! But I can think of nothing else." He complained into his third brandy. "I have seen nothing of you this week-end, except tonight, and soon you will have to go, I suppose. I planned this week-end hoping – well, no, of course I didn't hope really – I knew the child was to have the pleasure." He made a face at Helen and took her hand between his sweaty ones. "Go on smoking," he said. "Do it single handed. So, *post hoc*, I have decided that I want an entire week-end of you. Schoolless, Lilianless, conscienceless." A muscle moved with a sudden desperate flicker along the line of his jaw. His kindly, unromantic face looked at Helen's. "I shall take you away," he said, "and we shall don our sanbenitos afterwards."

There should have been a certain fragility about this moment, a suspension of all ambient crudeness, but behind him, sudden as his statement, the washroom door opened like a rip in the wall, and a young and incredibly thin woman in scarlet lurched over the threshold to fall heavily amongst the tables and the chairs. Torn as it were from their context, Helen and Moller watched as her friends lifted her up and carried her from the room, and their real horror was that no one displayed any more surprise than a temporary turning of the head, a pause in the litany of sips. The man at the next table chose this moment to lean his red face across, his watery eyes glistening with apology.

"'Scuse me," he said to Helen.

Moller glared. "Beat it!" he said. "Go on!" He swung his

bulky shoulder between the drunk and their table, shifting his chair further along. "Christ!" he snarled softly. "Christ! I said coffee! Why in God's name did I choose this joint to impress you with? To ease what could be a sordid situation right over the edge. It could be sordid, you know."

"I know," Helen replied, gravely intent on not seeing him. "Very easily."

"The quick extra-marital excitement, the ultimate scuffle, the revulsion. That isn't what I want. At least, that is what it might be, what it probably is essentially, but we must change it with the right props. We must be a little insincere, or artificial, so that we don't disgust one another."

He stubbed out his cigarette and rose.

"Don't even finish your drink, Helen. Quickly. Let's get away from this place. It's like a merciless conscience."

She pressed her bag and her gloves together and looked up at him furtively. Sweat oiled his forehead and his neck. He is neurotic, she thought, and yet who would find him so, punting the ball round the practice yard amongst the boys or fence vaulting or music-listening wrapped in an inner and an outer stillness? It is he who remains most urbane during examination pressure or inspection rounds; he who puts brash Sweeney down with more kindness than he deserves and bothers to talk trivia with Findlay. She followed his large body through the uncaring crowds; she kept close beside him as they passed the piano which was skimming in fulsome glissandos across the barest outline of a tune cartooning the original; she put out a hand and touched lightly with her finger-tips the warm serge of his coat as they went down the staircase laid with hotel-smelling carpet where the darkly varnished walls pressed them together before squeezing them out into a bud of a reception foyer with the closed registration desk, the stale gladioli, the loungers. Queen Street and the trams blazed in at them, yellow and black in prisms of clanking light under the exploding overhead wires, the green and purple dust-ticklings at the tongues of the jolly-poles. The streets were half empty, and in the theatres the crowds sat jammed together in their unreal worlds, cuddling the dark and the fantasy of each other, and sucking toffees and shushing. Oh rapture, thought Moller, hearing the united burst of laughter muffled but still audible from behind the closed doors and the epauletted commissionaire. The shops illuminated their death-faced models draped in silk, the hats displayed on basket frames, the underwear shameless under fluorescent light. Helen took Moller's left hand and tucked it warmly beneath her arm.

He looked down at her in affectionate surprise, and said, "We won't count this evening at all. I hate remembering my failures. I'll plan something a little more tasteful, I promise you. For the moment I'll have to content myself with seeing you home."

Helen found the parcel on her bedside table next morning. There was a piece of notepaper tucked under it, and the edges of the paper were jagged from being trimmed with scissors. The note said:

Dear Mrs. Striebel, thank you for a wonderful week-end, from Vinny.

Helen opened the little brown-paper parcel, frightened of the contents even before she saw them, knowing they would be an embarrassment. She took the ornament out carefully and placed it on the table where it wobbled rachitically under its stuffed burden of roses and violets. The morning sun laid a colder gilt along the falsity of the edges. It stood there, vulgar and tawdry and filled with affection. She braced herself for the insincerity of gratitude, but really there was no necessity for her to pretend emotion, because she was so strongly aware of the effort behind the act, the privation for even such a cheap article, the difficulty of choice.

She took it out to Margaret who was in the kitchen preparing pancakes.

"O God!" she said. "How sweet! And how really awful!"

"Hush! For heaven's sake," Helen pleaded. "It would break her heart if she thought I didn't find it perfect. This must have been the thing she carried round all day yesterday. I remember she hung on to it very carefully, and once when she dropped it in the theatre foyer she went white as death. I know it's hideous, but how lovely of her to do it."

"Changing the subject for a moment," Margaret said, "How's Robert?"

Helen looked at her sister amusedly. "Now what?" she said. "What are you wanting me to say?"

"I think," Margaret said carefully, "I think you might be – pardon the expression – in love."

"Perhaps."

"Isn't it rather brave of you in a town the size of Gungee?"

"What is the reason for this concern?" Helen asked mildly. "Surely I was in at a respectable hour last night."

Margaret paused in her mixing and looked straight into Helen's eyes.

"You look tired – not physically but emotionally." Her face became impish once more. "How will you have your aspirin, honey? Scrambled or poached?"

They both laughed and hushed each other and glanced at the wall behind which Vinny was sleeping.

But she was awake by now, woken when the sun had first splintered the venetian blinds, snug in her cretonne womb, in the grottoed warmth of sheets and blankets, imagining with delicious apprehension Mrs. Striebel's opening of the packet. She had slipped into her room during the night, long after she had heard her come down the hall and rustle out of clothing and into bed, and had stood at her bedside for a trembling moment seeing her, Olympian, lying vulnerable upon her pillow, pale and dream-wasted and not at peace, with her head turning angrily against the lip of the sheet. She had not dared linger and, having put the gift where Mrs. Striebel could not fail to see it in the morning, had gone tip-toeing back to her room. It was a long time before her excitement subsided sufficiently to allow her to sleep. For an hour she lay listening to the stertorous wind outside the house heaving and grunting through the oleanders and shifting the last ribbons of storm cloud farther west. She kept wondering, too, where Mrs. Striebel had been. Perhaps with Mr. Moller. She felt jealous. Anyway, he had no business being with Mrs. Striebel. His wife was sick. She'd heard Pearl Warburton say some pretty mean things about Mr. Moller and Mrs. Striebel. Nasty, sneering little things she wouldn't listen to. Though she had felt last night they might be right.

She burrowed under the sheets and held them up above her to make a tent. It was very dark and warm. She said, "Dear Mrs. Striebel", and put a kiss on an imagined cheek. She raised the corner of her tent slightly and saw the sunlight striping the wall opposite the window in bands of lemon and grey. From the room next to hers came the sounds of someone stirring unwillingly through sleep to wakefulness, plunging her feet into the sea of springtime morning air. Vinny sat up in her faded pyjamas to worship as her goddess paused.

This is it, she told herself. She has seen it.

She hugged her knees tightly against her flat chest and pressed her chin into the hollow between them hard enough to hurt. She will love it, she told herself. She will think it beautiful and keep it for ever. With my note. She heard the sounds of dressing recommence and then Mrs. Striebel going out to the kitchen. She could hardly wait to show Miss Reisbeck, she thought. She crept to the door and opened it, but could hear nothing. So, having waited for a while rubbing one foot against the other, she dressed once more in the baggy skirt and the second of her two jumpers. It was navy blue and larger. Above the depth of colour her pale skin took on a transparency and her eyes a more definite hue. Mirror searching, she loved herself for the first time, where once she had found no excuse for so loving, and with an excess of feeling embraced, as it were, but timidly, the whole house, the silent hallway, the kitchen all pancake-scented-hot, with the morning fragrance of the potted pelargoniums along the sill and rain-wet loam beneath the window.

Margaret's baroque face appeared above the gingham smock as foolishly, misplacedly monkish. She beamed. Helen smiled. The gift stood askew upon the centre of the breakfast cloth, among the canisters and the salt and pepper containers, threatening the day with its implications of devotion and gratitude. During the exclamations that followed Vinny's appearance she became translated to a state of euphoria that prohibited clearness of hearing or comprehending, and allowing phrases like "a very kind girl", "a most thoughtful action", "charming", to monument the moment.

She ate her breakfast, hardly aware, drunk on approval.

All day it was the same.

There was sun and not much wind and a great deal of very blue sky along which boats and buildings battled, pricking and wedging and slicing and scooping with spire or tower or city block or dome. Wherever there were holes in the bitumen, the rainwater puddles glared glassily up at the sky. Gulls came over the city like a drift of flowers sky-planted. The smell of salt was enough to make one cry with a hungry nostalgia for the sea.

They wasted and fretted the morning with talk and tea and household tasks, and in the afternoon, when the thin streamers of breeze blew over the reach, tossing wing and wave and the dried-out tram tickets, Helen and Vinny packed their suitcases into the boot of Margaret's car and got in. She drove them slowly to the Valley and along the tram lines towards the art gallery.

"All set for culture?" Margaret asked. "You know you'd

do much better to pop into Carya and see some real stuff, good strong meaty work. None of your wishy-washy representationalism. Helen, you're too conservative. Next time you're down I'll have to work on you very seriously."

"Next time I'll be your victim, I promise, Margaret. But today you must think of Vinny. Let her see what is normally regarded as painting before you shock her with young – what's his name?"

"Lawrence Reid."

"Yes. His great orange nudes with light-bulbs. Terribly exciting for you *avant garde* types, but I have a sensitive plant here from a more than sensitive village. She mustn't take back any of these extremist notions or they'll be drumming us both out of town."

Vinny smiled, only partly understanding. The dirty blocks of flats angled steps and tiny courtyards to the west and netted the leaves and papers swung in on the wind's tide. Dogs raised legs against telegraph poles, but they were city dogs. Everything had a magic. Dogs, leaves, papers, grubby apartments, the occasional small shop, the Sunday afternoon couples all belonged to a fascinating design.

"– delicious little *gouache*," Margaret was saying, narrowly scraping alongside a tram and just missing a cyclist. Her face, inanely apologetic, swerved to the rider and then back to peer along the roadway. She swung the car down a side-street near the museum.

"Here, dears," she said. "Dust and dullness together. I shall remain quietly on the lawn reading if you attempt to enter this nauseous hole. In fact, I don't think I can even face the Fathers of Australian Art. Just look for me under a cotton palm when you're ready to move on. And don't forget you have to be at the terminus by four."

"Plenty of time," Helen said. "It's only a little after two now. Robert is sure to be a bit late. He so prides himself on being early, Fate nearly always has some mishap lined up for him."

So Helen took Vinny's arm, waved to Margaret who was striding off to a secluded bench down the lawn, and guided Vinny through the gloomy foyer and turnstiles into the main hall of the gallery. They walked slowly through hall after hall in the poor light, where heavy oils loomed over the unvarying expressions of the public gazing up at them. A few young children skittered across the floor and giggled at the nude sculptures. But Vinny was thrilled, even by the mediocrity. She had never been in such a place before, and her knowledge of art was limited to the few pictures at the school and the yearly calendar issued by their grocer. In her immature way she felt that the whole week-end had been a cultural feast – which it had been really for one who had had so little – and impressionable, was demolished by the lovely, the trite without distinction. Helen watched with amusement and compassion her eager craning to read the names of painters and, after observing adults doing it, the standing back from the picture to achieve the right light and distance. Even if the older woman were bored, the girl was not, and tireless for an hour went from gallery to gallery inspecting closely every picture that appealed to her. When they emerged at last in the slanting light on the curved areas of grass they felt as if they were coming back to actuality after a period of time held still.

"How was it?" Margaret asked. She was stretched comfortably along a seat with her back against the arm rest. On her nose rested a gigantic pair of horn-rimmed spectacles. She twinkled when she observed Vinny's startled glance.

"My dear, the wider the rims, the larger the intellect. Actually they have no lenses. They're merely for show."

Helen laughed heartily. "Journalists, bookmakers, and radio types! God bless you all with your corduroy beards and your psuede shoes – the 'p' is silent as in 'pseudo'. Actually we enjoyed ourselves, didn't we, Vinny?" She gave the child's arm a friendly squeeze and Vinny looked up at her devotedly.

"It was wonderful," she breathed. "I can't believe there can be that many pictures all in the one place. The whole week-end has been marvellous. Especially the play yesterday."

"Please, child," Margaret admonished in a kindly fashion, "all this gratitude is bad for Helen. Can't you see her basking in it, getting inflated notions of herself as a cultural fairy godmother?"

Vinny grinned uneasily, whereupon Margaret, seeing the uncertainty on her face, said quickly, "Of course we're glad you've had a wonderful time, my pet. But right at this moment I'm afraid my tastes are earthier than Helen's. What I need desperately is tea – tea and cakes, to be precise – large, sickly, unhealthy cakes. What do you say?"

She swept them unprotesting before her to the car and drove quickly to the place where they had arranged to meet Moller. It was a large sprawling suburban centre, deathly still on Sundays, with its propped bikes, ownerless it seemed for ever, and the empty parked cars and the closed shop doorways. There was one shop of every kind – the newsagent's with the hoardings leaning askew in their wire cages, buckled from the attentions of passing dogs; the fruit shop with the speckled apples and the juiceless oranges; the cash-and-carry grocer's blazing with pasteboard price reductions; the chemist's.

"Surely," Margaret said, "surely there must be something. It's practically the end of the world. Don't they have depots for all you Burkes and Willses?"

She cruised the car slowly up one side of the shopping block and down the other until finally they found a narrow fronted bakery still open and with an "afternoon teas" sign fly-specked in the window.

So in there they sat, knees touching under the unsteady table, drinking weak tea and eating pink and white iced cakes, red cherry centred, and laughing because it wasn't what they wanted, and yet as they sat there became the very thing for each of them.

Through the doorway Helen could see the tired shadows stretching lazily longer under the awnings and settling comfortably down for the evening along the kerbs. She, too, was somehow tired of the sun. With a wonderful leap of the heart she thought of Moller with a spasm of such longing she felt she could not tolerate the waiting. The day was the beginning and the end of a journey. From this moment on, despite the bathos, she would never again be able to eat a plain iced cake without thinking of him. She looked across at her sister and found the frayed art-weary face an unexpected map of tenderness.

"You were right this morning," Helen said. And there was no need to explain. "There is no 'perhaps' about it at all. You were perfectly right."

Four

The mystique, the impedimenta of ritual lay in long boxes on the lawn under the striped foliage of the crotons, awaiting the weekly *agape* that brought together in a select sporting coterie the highest income brackets in the township. Frank Rankin as chief celebrant unpacked a half-dozen bats, an assortment of shuttlecocks, and the long poles and badminton net. It is wonderful, thought Moller as he sprawled under the mango tree with the others, to see the technical mind on holiday, the town's medical practitioner acting just like any ordinary person, smacking a badminton pellet backwards and forwards to other gods all disporting like himself, being human and lovable and decent fellows, and keeping well within their social class. He nibbled the thick white end of a grass stalk and lay flat on his back with his eyes closed. He wondered why they bothered to ask him to their little afternoons, and he wondered why he bothered accepting invitations that so patently bored him. Perhaps the fact that Lilian had been away five months now drew on him the self-conscious charity of his neighbours. "Me betters," he told himself, and giggled with eyes still shut under the dark green shadows of the leaves; whereupon he found his stomach prodded in provocative and playful fashion by a feminine foot and a hard shallow voice as bright as benzedrine saying girlishly, "Penny?"

He recognized Ruth Lunbeck's kittenish tones, the chromatic tonguing of the threadbare thought from a mistress of the suburban phrase. He could not tolerate opening his eyes to that stunted nose, the long jutting jaw, and the eyes stony blue with coyness laying a film over the ruthlessness and the acquisitiveness. She punished her husband's infidelities with regular large purchase accounts at the city stores. Each revelation of a breach of marital trust was followed by a spending spree so outrageous that even Lunbeck wondered if his pleasure were worth what it cost. But in spite of this, in spite of any side effects his treatment of her might have upon her prestige amongst the other women of her group, she clung to the marriage rock like a limpet because it gave her a social standing in the town that she could certainly not have achieved otherwise, being devoid of both intelligence and distinguished appearance. Her body alone was beautifully made, but topped off with that crackling inanity of voice, that striving-after-never-to-be-achieved-but-still-striven-for girlishness, its effect was largely negatived – at least for Moller, who continued to lie very still upon the shaggy lawn.

The toe jabbed him again, finding a tender spot between his ribs.

"Come on, sleepy," urged the kid-sister-let's-all-be-buddies-and-pals voice. "What's the joke?"

She has a quality of persistence, Moller thought, that is staggering. The simplest brain surely would have deduced by this time that I am antipathetic. He was tempted to see how long she would continue to prod with tongue and foot if he remained silent, but another voice, rolling under the trees, rich with elocutionary zeal, made it impossible for him to feign sleep.

"Come on there, Robert," it mouthed. "You look utterly

squalid spread out like a sumptuous bum. Get a racket, you lazy old basket, and partner me."

He gave up. He opened his eyes into the face of a very handsome horse which was bending over him. Its dark eyes rolled under heavy brows that met in slight irritation above the long well-bred nose.

"Must I?" he protested, knowing all the time it would be hopeless to protest. He rose clumsily, slapping the seat of his trousers, and took off his sports coat. Why doesn't she whinny? he asked himself petulantly, but no. No. It's those rounded vowels, those hideous soundings of "utterly" and "too" and "really" and "frightful". Rankin and Talbot, the both, they keep their vowels so open it's a wonder they don't have verbal diarrhoea. He smiled with an effort and held his racket against the sun, blotting it out from himself. He decided he must tell Helen that last little joke, and for a minute was perplexed by her absence. Then he recalled that she had been once and that that once had been enough. When he remembered her embarrassed determination not to accept further invitation, the explanation of his own presence filled him with momentary self-disgust; but this frailty of self-analysis was swept aside in the usual anticipatory pleasure – at five o'clock the doctor, the generous patron, would produce from his steamingly cold ice-box a dozen dewy bottles of beer.

He strolled across the lawn after Freda, still pressing his racket to the side of his head. Garth Cantwell joined them, and a few minutes later Jess Talbot came bounding across, her colossal thighs white as peeled grass husks below her tight blue shorts. Her enormous bust shook with ferocious zeal at all of them, and she gave her racket several practice forehand and backhand drives.

"Oh God!" Moller murmured to Cantwell. "I feel we're going to play a strenuous game. Just look at that enthusiasm!"

Cantwell sucked in the last possible fragrance from his

cigarette – he was not mean, but that was the sort of socially acceptable parsimony that had got him where he was – and smiled and shrugged. His well-fed body slouched now from the effort of years of being successful, which, in his case, meant being on top at all costs; but he still covered it reverently with expensive tussore and tweed, regarding it as something sacred, a temple not of the Holy Ghost but of financial enterprise. He could not whip the money lenders within.

Moller embarrassed him. The fellow never seemed quite *en rapport* with the group and he wasn't sure what to say to him. To agree was rather like letting down the team – his team, the body of people with sporting attitudes and civic conscience who ran the town.

He grunted non-committally and said, "Partner Freda, will you, boy? I don't think I'm on form today either, and that will even things up."

"There's a fine compliment for the women, Freda," Jess said. "We're not only equals, we're their superiors!"

"Jolly well about time!" mouthed Freda.

"Oh Christ, for Chrissake, Christ!" Moller groaned gently into the side of his bat, sibilated as if sharing some esoteric knowledge with the wood and the unresponsive cork surface.

They struck for service and then began playing. While Moller leapt automatically, his arm striking with almost a reflex motion at the feathered ball, he managed to detach his concentration from the game and think seriously of the last week-end in the city, when for the first time he had felt a signal inability to share Helen's activities. Connivance and the acid testing of propinquity had both failed to achieve for him a tolerance of situation, a docility of all the factors that seemed to work unendingly towards his and Helen's eternal separation. Although they had not spoken since of the decision he had made the previous Saturday when he had determined to take her away for a few days from the town, the implications of the spoken word lay at the back of their eyes and startled them with occasional recognition when they passed on the way to classes, or shared periods off, or sat listening to Rowan and Sweeney bickering during the luncheon recess.

The whole of the western sky was quilted with mackerel cloud rippling away behind Bundarra into the Mary Valley. From the front of Rankin's home set on the northern hillside of the town the view of the whole valley in which the town lay opened up its pocket of activity, its crucifix of business, and the neat bungalows pimpling the five exit roads. The afternoon carved its frieze of grouped people, of the white swinging arms and legs and the smack, smack of bat against pellet flying birdlike over the greenness, the five figures under the tree set like Fragonard figurines with all the latent sensuality of careless pose. Already the sweat blotches were dark shadows under the sleeves of Cantwell's expensive tussore, revealed each time he swung his arm. Between the cleft of Jess Talbot's breasts the sweat trickled unpleasantly; her face, white instead of flushed, was beaded with a rosary of water droplets about brow and temple. Moller looked pleadingly at his partner and she flashed him an automatic smile of over-white teeth.

"Serve up," she said, bright and crisp with command.

It was trial by ordeal. Five o'clock came as slowly to him across the gardens as the creeping shadow below the mango tree. When finally the nine of them fanned out around the beer and the sandwiches, the triangles and rectangles of social requirement with the ham and bread leaf-thin among the watercross trees, the sun had begun to tip over the shelf of the mountain in an untidy splash of gold.

"It's going to be a marvellous sunset," someone said.

They all turned to look at the clouds, the hundreds of white islands radiating from behind Bundarra until they flushed a ragged arc half-way across the sky. Lunbeck's thin, anguished face tortured by dyspepsia and sex swung back upon them.

"Lovely!" He smiled agonizedly. "Really lovely. To stay here and see it go down. I feel I must stay. We must, mustn't we, Ruth?"

Ruth shrugged indifferently and then smiled radiantly up at Talbot. She looked down at the splendid length of her brown legs displayed with near immodesty below her denim shorts.

"What about the mozzies?" she asked with the insane innocent of someone in the mid-thirties being childlike. Talbot almost whimpered at her philological tampering, yet with the perverted joy of the flagellant he asked her to repeat the remark.

"The mozzies, Alec, the mozzies," she said, nearly but not quite on the point of nipping him on the arm.

"Heavens above!" he protested. "Say the whole word, Ruth. Not those shockingly inarticulate abbreviations. How I abhor them! 'Mozzies!' 'Cuppa!' 'This arv!' " He consigned them like a papal bull to a bonfire and proceeded to burn them with his wrath. "I work amongst all classes as you know, Ruth, and Welch would bear me out saying this, that never, not even with the boiler hands, do I speak carelessly. I really believe to be careful in speech stamps a man, gives him a definite authority, a standing."

"The Chrysostom of the creameries," Moller murmured.

"What? What was that?" Talbot was weak on historical reference. He swung round, annoyedly prickling like a spinster whose virtue has been challenged. Moller drained the last of his beer, ignoring him, while the others did not know whose side to take vocally – the intellectual or the snobbish – but inwardly, to a man they voted for Talbot, not by reason of his old-maidish preciseness, but because they could not support a cynicism that they could not understand.

"Here! Have another beer, Talbot, old man," Rankin urged, confident within property, amongst the social perquisites. "Where are the Welches, anyway?"

Jess Talbot, happy to see one of the other women publicly chided, smiled like a Botticelli angel, the merest whisper of mirth over an infinite sadness.

"He was needed at the factory," she said, "and Marian went to Gympie for the week-end to play in a golf tournament. Really, I shouldn't say this, I suppose, but I don't know how she can do it, do you, Freda? Those two unfortunate girls of hers are neglected shamefully."

Freda Rankin demolished a small cake in three sharp snapping movements. The opening gambit had been played, and they would be well away soon with their chosen victim skulking pawn-like upon the field of their gossip.

"Utterly incredible!" The consonants cracked and bounced like gravel. The big red mouth munched up mill-wife Welch as if she were a cocktail onion. "Mind you, I admire Sam Welch. Rather common, but he does know how to control things. A marvellous efficient fellow, and in spite of Marian, too. My dear, she's such a bag of poison I don't know how her children survived nine months at the breast. Still, I have to ask her . . . her husband's position. . . ."

Her voice vanished into an innuendo of silence. Making every gesture appear brilliant, she handed round the sandwiches. Like communion breads, thought Moller, like tribal tokens of an infinite ill-will towards others outside the group. The crowd blessed themselves and ate the flesh of their victims with such overt smacking of scandalous lips it was really intolerable. Fragments of conversation, the clichés standing out skeletal, the frame on which the verbose platitudes fleshed themselves, reached Moller's ears as he sat on the lawn. Ruth Lunbeck's voice peppered a long denunciatory story concerning a relation in the permanent army with almost every inanity possible; it came in bursts of static through the cooling air – "deserve horse whipping . . . only a mother could understand . . . supposed to be an officer and a gentleman. . . ." The last filled Moller with an indescribable pleasure; he was later to tell Helen he thought that the phrase had died with the Anglo-Indian novel, but no, here it was vibrant and living in Gungee. He was startled to hear Ruth Lunbeck ask, "Would you like to go to bed with a black fellow?" and felt amused admiration for her ability to reduce such problems as *apartheid* and racial discrimination to such singularly simple postulations. It was wonderful, too, to hear the murmurs of well-bred assent, money singing sweetly with money in a chorus of unanalytical decision. Moller pursed his lips and whistled a little Haydn rondo, hoping to annoy Talbot.

Lunbeck, smiling in a sort of agony, crossed over to Moller and squatted angular upon the grass. Elbows and knee joints, the thin nose, the bony head, all projected their pain against the sky, *estampes* of self-pity, of egotism. He jabbed the air with his cigarette and, about to torture Moller, burnt the flank of the blue afternoon. Moller leant back on one elbow and stared at nothing but the legs of the group, naked or trousered, hairless, hairy, varicose and smooth as oil. They performed all sorts of unlovely stripings across the leafy hedge as they slouched or spread or straightened.

"Have a good week-end?"

Moller switched a wary grey eye upon the ecstasiated profile beside him.

"Fair," he said. He suddenly felt quite cold and curiously cautious.

"I very nearly asked you for a lift on Saturday." (The caution rewarded.) Lunbeck's face became that of a mystic. He smiled bonily, twisting the thin, over-kissed, over-kissing skin of his lips into a dangerous crescent. Moller saw that the orange down on his chin and cheeks turned pure gold in the slanting sun. There was a bracket of fine lines near the corner of each jawbone where the skin stretched even more thinly. The eyes vanished, recessed in smiles, dangerous under the projecting orange eyebrows. Moller looked away to the hill whose trees lashed the summit like hairs all raggedly exposed against the scarlet burning clouds.

"There's your sunset starting," he said.

The sheer torture of the horizon tapered away through the deep reds of heat, through crimson and orange to pink that was nearly white. Each island of cloud – and there were hundreds of them – showed its western edge a glaring gold against the flat bright colour of the rest of it.

" 'Patens of bright gold'," he said, but knew he was not diverting the other.

"Really lovely. Yes. Quite lovely. And no mosquitoes yet." Lunbeck turned suddenly, his face filled with brotherhood, and pressed his points home with the skill of a picador. "Yes. As I was saying, I very nearly asked you for a lift back here last Saturday, but I thought your car might be full up." He smiled dreamily. "Funnily enough I was in Brisbane myself last week-end. Had to go down unexpectedly on Saturday afternoon. I ran out of local anaesthetic and tri-cresol, and Rankin couldn't help me out. I knew I could get some from a friend down there who always keeps far more than he needs. He talked me into staying overnight. . . . No, thank you, Cecily, my dear. Cecily, I'm just telling this old reprobate here how I saw him in Brisbane on Saturday night. He got away too fast for me to buy him a drink." He glowed with the roguishness of it all.

Cecily Cantwell perched birdlike before them, beaking eagerly towards a suspected titbit. The plate of cakes in her hand sloped dangerously, forgotten. She fluffed her feathers, all quivering expectation and chirruped, "Oh Harold! How odd! What a small world!"

"Not so small, really. Not a bad pub that, is it, Herc? You were just leaving when I came out of the bar. I must say Helen Striebel looked pretty marvellous. Didn't know she had it in her."

Cecily Cantwell almost fell off her perch in her excitement.

"Oh, Robert!" she reproved. "And we all thought you went down to see Lilian. And here you are hitting the nightspots! Naughty man!"

The brain of a tweeting bird, Moller told himself. A silence had fallen upon the others, who now turned on him smiles of various kinds. Talbot's wife displayed momentarily a mask of sheer cruelty as if at last some kindly fate had played Moller and Helen Striebel into her hands.

He helped himself to another cake from the plate in Cecily Cantwell's hands, and she glanced down in surprise at his action, at seeing the plate still there. Turning to the others, bright with the moment's revelation, she sensed a mood of excited reproof flying between them.

"I did go down to see Lilian." Moller became angry that he was even accepting the challenge, but for Helen's sake he continued. "She is extremely ill. She will not get any better." Murmur, he told himself, out aloud murmur your concern, your sympathy, but underneath keep saying to yourselves what a bastard the man is, carrying on with his wife so ill.

They murmured their concern; they pressed their sympathy on him. It was all in order. He scratched the lobe of his ear and said, knowing no one would believe him, "I happened to run into Mrs. Striebel myself in town. She'd been to some graduate dinner and we had a quick drink together." He paused to inspect the finger that had been scratching and then added, "Yes, she did look marvellous. Quite surprised me."

No one believed him. But Cecily Cantwell said well there that just showed what a small world it was after all, Harold, who looked at her as he looked at so many women across his wife's shoulder with a "we-two-understand-each-other" look. Oh, the confusion beneath the close trimmed skulls and the regular weekly hair settings with their packing of dried frizziness into close matted unlovely curls! What turmoil of new suggestives churned and spumed around the new victims! Lunbeck stared solemnly at the burning western sky. For a few weeks at least, he assured himself, Ruth's attention would be diverted from his own erotic activities into a between-house-rushing of speculation, of under-blind-peeping, of checking on Moller's hours, watching his lights, listening to the identifiable, accusing, late hour creak of his front gate. Devoutly he offered post-communion thanks. A rush of gaseous wind to his throat made him belch. He covered it up with a social cough and lit a cigarette as Frank Rankin's big blond head, awash with the mental habit of the bedside manner, loomed up large amongst the embarrassment, about to dispel it with a calculated phrase of camaraderie. It was as if he applied a spiritual stethoscope to the heart of the group, listened to its thumpings, and decided on a course of behaviour. Prognosis achieved, he poured beer all round and drew his guests forward to the terraced edge of the garden to watch the sunset. Gerberas starred the borders, massed in lemons and pinks before the great ranks of calendulas whose splotches of crude colour stretched to left and right along the stone-flanked beds. The mass of colour lay at their feet and then the eye was distracted downwards to more colour over the succulents and trailers of convolvulus that welded the banks of earth and stone together. The sea of prismatic light broke in a final wave of intense flowering against the close growing oleanders along the western fence.

Together with the darkness rushing in from the coast, a silence fell on the nine men and women poised above the town that swam below in an orange shimmer, each house splashed on one side with light, iron roofs sparkling unbearably. The sky-islands of cloud spread back towards them in a blaze until they were doused in the faint blue of the sky zenith. Bird echelons, lost as inland gulls, arrowed wistfully across tree and house top. For a moment, together in the loneliness of the evening and the flamboyancy of the sunset, the group felt at one. Husbands, surprised, drew near to wives, and Moller, apart from this coupling, felt a great surge of unhappy sentiment as he gazed down on the sprawling tin roofs of the Gungee Railway Hotel. There, Helen would be feeling the unbearable compulsion of rented room and furniture, the stale jest of clanking goods trains that even now he could see jerking like toys on to the siding, and above all, the dissonance, like some great atonal work, of the upstairs radios braying through three different commercial stations a fanfare of militant joviality in the advertising splurge. He turned half away. The planets of flowers, the asteroids, the constellations, were all drained of colour and bent milkily away from him in the black stippled air. It stretched the finest of nets over the valley. And then quite suddenly the houses lost their golden sides and the sun lurched drunkenly over the world rim.

Behind them on the quiet lawn the insect hum came with the first threatening moistness of the air. Two large planes of white were stamped across the grass as the Rankin's housekeeper turned on the living-room lights. They all turned and went back to the court beside the trees, fumbling in the darkness for the bats and pellets dropped carelessly along the lawn. Cecily Cantwell shivered exaggeratedly and drew away from her husband's flabby encircling arm. The moment was over. Like a signal the radio shouted from the house an unintelligible burst of jazz.

Cecily sidled up to Lunbeck in the dusk. Freda Rankin moved about hostessing pauselessly, guiding to cars, talking through lowered car windows, retesting the slammed doors in an excess of final friendliness. "Marvellous. Yes, of course . . . hardly wait next week . . . certainly will . . . no . . . don't wait . . . it's getting colder . . . yes . . . goodbye . . . 'bye darling . . . 'bye Garth . . . what about Alec and Jess? . . . Oh, with you, are they, Garth? . . . It's quite a walk . . . no . . . yes . . . no . . . yes . . ." on and on and on with the chiaroscuro of the car lights and the garden darknesses becoming more and more evident as the sky purpled over.

Someone remembered Moller.

No one had forgotten him really, all being hardly able to await that exquisite moment when, his soul laid out upon the table, the moral vivisection would begin. It was just that he had slipped apart from them as a member of the group; finally he had disestablished himself by his behaviour, for although this might seem unreasonable when a comparison was drawn with Lunbeck, it followed fairly naturally because he had not the importance of position that forgave these transgressions – with Lunbeck they passed for foibles pardoned, at least in public, amongst members of his own class. Lunbeck was completely unaware that he was a never failing theme of bar-room conversation, that the farmers' wives cautioned their budding daughters and that the young louts set him up as a hero.

But Moller's offence was unpardonable. Ruth Lunbeck would often complain what a disgrace it was when people supposed to instruct the young wouldn't set them a good example. It was one of her favourite topics, aimed, no doubt, at diverting attention from the behaviour of her husband. The group could never forgive, either, his frequent sly gibes at their snobbery, his amusement at their monetary competitiveness, his preference for music and books to racing and football. During the three years he had worked in Gungee he had slowly built up a case for them against himself, innocently for the most part, and inevitably. His relationship with them had only needed one public, one completely unacceptable misdemeanour, and his final severance would be made.

They all knew it now.

There was something of sadness in the farewells they gave him, the unenthusiastic suggestion that he squeeze into Cantwell's car along with the Talbots (the Lunbecks were sorry, old man, but they were driving down to some friends at Cooroy for dinner).

"No," he said, "no, I prefer to walk." And he thought bitterly, you would much rather discuss me before the excitement has worn off; you want to achieve the utmost vicarious stimulation.

Lunbeck leant out of his car. His face worked with an odd mixture of affection and dyspeptic pain. He squeezed the last juices from the evening's grape.

"Be seeing you, boy," he said. "Give my regards to Helen."

When the last car had roared extrovertedly down the east-turning road he said a brief good night to the Rankins and walked out of their double gates and under the hedges of tecoma, still in his sandshoes, swinging his walking shoes angrily against his left thigh. The stars were prickling out. It was quite cool. Trees, houses, shadows, rough road, arpeggios of a chord played too often, rattled away behind him in familiar landmarks, branch road, corner house, light-pole askew near bridge, bridge finally across creek, and the thrumming monotony of the factory on his right as he strode along the road towards the hotel. As if the tonality of the whole town were taken from this afternoon and this afternoon's incidents, so now he did what never before would have occurred to him. He turned in the narrow entrance door and crossed the hard polished linoleum, passing the plant icons; he threaded the stairs to the first floor of the hotel.

Around him, concealed, the animals rustled in their burrows. It was nearly tea-time. The half-light in the corridor showed him Sweeney's bulky frame vanishing down its length to what he presumed was the bathroom. Even as he paused, wondering on which door to knock to find Helen, the shantanlinging of a dinner xylophone beaten into anger percolated the entire building with its rage. Irresolute, he drew into the recess at the stair-head that, harbouring table and chair, served as a writing annexe for guests. Immediately a door beside it flashed open and Jess Talbot, changed by now into skirt and blouse, bounced out and turned left along the corridor. From behind the half-open door came the sounds of her husband fussing through the ritual of dressing, whistling all the time a loud and arrogant version of a Bach fugue. Across the music, within the minute, there came the roar of a lavatory being healthily flushed, and there she was bounding back upon him. Moller pressed against the wall, trapped between Mrs. Talbot and Mr. Farrelly, who was approaching from the other end. Jess's face lit up when she saw him fidgeting under the stair light.

"Ohhhh!" She used the expletive with a special emphasis, always, and a drawing out that gave it all the meaning another might be able to infuse into an oath. It was a little trick of hers. "What are you doing here! Not booking in, are you?"

The laugh accompanying the words was very light and unpleasant. Quite foolishly, he knew, his heart beat dangerously fast and he felt the skin of his cheeks prickle.

He stared back equally insolently at her untidy breasts and thighs, and said pointedly, "No, Jess. No. I'm afraid not. Not even to be closer to you." He turned away. "Mr. Farrelly? Excuse me one moment."

Jess Talbot turned sharply, her mouth tightening with irritation. She went quickly into her room and shut the door loudly. The fortissimo whistling became morendo, accompanying the floating moon shaped pallor of a face that hung lanternwise above the publican's tweeds, his country rags, elderly and respectable to atone for his service to Mammon. Farrelly's watery eyes bulged perpetually, but now they appeared slightly outraged that a non-resident should be found upstairs.

"Yes, Mr. Moller?" he asked. Their eyes fastened on each other's, screwed up with the effort of piercing the curtains of hard yellow the hall light swung between them.

"Would you mind telling me which room is Mrs. Striebel's?"

Farrelly could not conceal his surprise or curiosity. His priggishness jolted him. His head actually jerked and the pear-shaped body rocked on its skinny legs.

"Well, really, Mr. Moller, we don't usually . . . is it urgent?"

"I'll only be a moment. There will be no time for fornication, I assure you."

"For what?"

"Nothing. No time for exactly nothing. And now, please. Would you mind?"

Mr. Farrelly was piqued.

"There," he said grudgingly. "Two down from the landing." He could stomach, in a way, the furtive visits the maids granted to the travellers, the town policeman, the factory boys, because, although he was aware of their happening, by tacit agreement their fact was never brought home to him in this brash fashion. Like all respectable people he could not tolerate the frankness of a self-confessed peccadillo. It made him shudder. It wasn't right. It wasn't . . . respectable, somehow. He felt he might be wronging Moller by thinking there was a base motive behind the visit, but taken all round, he assured himself, school business could be done at school and man-woman business meant only one thing.

He swung round and huffed away downstairs to the thin nervous looking wife who was in actuality as unmalleable as rock, was *the* rock on which the hotel was founded. Biblical. Biblical. And the rubbing of profiteering hands that every day performed the miracle of the Cana transformation with watered spirits consigned Moller and Striebel to their personal wallows of iniquity.

Before Moller could knock upon Helen's door, it had opened inwards upon the furniture duplicated in rooms to left and to right and opposite, inwards like a shutter letting in a wedge of weakly diffused hall light. She swam in it towards him and it etched the surprise of her eyes and her mouth, the hands raised startled, with a curious effect of sheen and shadow.

"May I come in?" he asked.

She switched on her room light again and he followed her inside drawing the door shut.

"There's a very final action," he said.

"A very foolish one," she replied, "and perhaps affecting me more than you."

"Do you care?"

"Not really."

He took both her hands and drew her slowly to the humped-up, narrow, uncomfortable bed. They sat side by side and Moller stroked the side of her cheek and her neck.

"There is no point in being discreet, very discreet, that is, much longer. From now on, *meine Königin*, it is going to be a series of final actions. Final, foolish, and perhaps indiscreet."

She drew away. The oblong mirror of the wardrobe grouped them as four, doubled the surprise, the disconsolate countenances, made their aloneness seem safe among numbers. The room became as crowded as a party.

"You mustn't stay more than a minute. I shall miss out on the shepherd's pie." She grimaced. "Why have you suddenly broken the basic rule?"

Moller smiled with the conscious irony of one about to deliver bad news.

"Lunbeck saw us in town on Saturday night."

Helen caught her breath and said, "But that means nothing. Nothing at all."

"No? My dear, don't think it means nothing to those who want it to mean something. He asked me to compliment you on your appearance, or words to that effect. What a whore-monger! But what is worse, he informed the whole salaciously hungry group. They were all gathered around the afternoon beer, busy with incomes and neighbours, and he lowered this piece of gossip like a baited line. Helen, I'm very much afraid that as far as Gungee is concerned our reputation is irredeemable. I merely want to warn you, prepare you, perhaps, for any snide remarks that might come our way."

"You came here to tell me this?"

"Yes. On a moment's anger. It could have waited, I suppose, but the Talbots mightn't have. Anyway, I seem to have made things worse. Jess Talbot saw me in the corridor. I had to ask Farrelly for your room. They will add all the trivia up, square the sum total and confirm – oh, joy? – their very worst suspicions. By tomorrow surely it will be well on the way to the pupils. Parents miss no opportunity to humble the teaching staff in the eyes of their delinquent offspring."

The pattern, hardly visible, of roses and leaves stared back at Helen from faded, thread-wasted carpet scrap. The water jug, china lilied, rosed and ivied, chipped at handle and lip, squatted whitely in basin. Books lay carelessly along the dressing-table. To the outside commotion of doors opening and shutting, the quick padding of feet between bathroom and stairs, they charted the coastline of this new calamity.

"Perhaps," Helen suggested, "it isn't so bad. After all, it's almost impossible to live in a place this size without causing unfavourable comment. Should I go out with a man we are immediately joined by local tongues into an unhealthy relationship. If I stay religiously in my room, gossip brings men to visit me here. You can't win any way at all."

Moller pulled a cigarette packet from his coat pocket.

"True. Soon we'll be able to draft a complicated set of rules for the etiquette of living in the small country town." He held the opened carton towards her. "There's only one. Want it?"

"No. Keep it. You've had the shock!"

"Good. Thanks, Helen. I really need this." He lit it and drew on it deeply. The lines of worry on his forehead smoothed out a little. "Shall we capitalize on the situation?"

"How do you mean?"

He watched her questioning face in the mirror for a moment. Then he looked away at the books lying on the dressing-table. *Elementary Principles of Trigonometry* caught his eye. He held it for security.

"How about next week-end?"

He could not bear to look at her directly in case she said no. Furtively he glanced back to the mirror. Her eyes, which had been crucifying themselves upon the trellised wanderings of the carpet's flower vines, met his in the blurred glass. This indirect examination of the eyes was not as difficult as turning directly to each other. They felt as if they were watching two other people pushing through one of those rope jungles found at fun fairs.

"Helen, please," he said. "Will it be a beach town? What about Brisbane itself? Or north? Anywhere?"

"You know what will happen if it gets around. We'll be talked about the way the Talbots did about young Allie, poor kid, who's pregnant again. Never mind. She'll be closer to God's right hand than they'll ever be."

Moller looked sceptical. "Yeah! They'll be on it. They're great exponents of the art of getting on."

Helen laughed and shattered the almost artificial atmosphere.

"Next week-end," she said unexpectedly, "next week-end will be very fine. Very fine indeed. I'll think of where tonight."

Moller could not help feeling surprised by her capitulation. The feeling was the very finest of questionings of his sincerity, and that upset him. He later worried at the problem, wondering if he were really the sort of person who hated ever crossing his mountains.

"That was a very quick decision. I imagined there would be all sorts of persuasion necessary."

Helen looked at him with a peculiar expression of disappointment.

"I'm sorry," she said. "Does the easiness of it all make it seem less worth while?"

He pushed his self-doubtings away to an unreality. "How can you ask so conventional a thing?" he said. "Of course not. It makes me far happier. Far happier."

He bent forward and searched the contours of her face

with his lips. The electric light burned unkindly on the rented wardrobe and chair, the satin and cotton eiderdown heaped up across the bed. Helen found tears brimming up in her eyes and rolling down her cheeks. Moller touched them gently with his tongue.

"You're very salty," he said.

"I'm not going to think that this is wrong," Helen said. "Please don't let me think it is wrong or I shall drop the whole thing and I couldn't bear to do that. I've – I've had no kindness for years. Nothing but hotel rooms and commercial travellers and drunks and publicans and baking roads into steaming schools with undisciplined classes jamming the rooms to the windows. I feel defiant. I don't care. I won't. I simply won't. Not even about Lunbeck or the Talbots or any of them."

"There, my dear. What of the Lunbecks? Two frumps in ten squares of timber. The Talbots cannot possibly touch us. Don't cry, dearest, best."

The corridor outside was silent. From the dining-room the clash of eating utensils and the isolated flags of laughter floated up the stair well. Moller kissed Helen again and rose, pulling her gently with him to the door. He jabbed out the butt of his cigarette in the tray on the table near the door.

"Leave it," he said, with a tinny bravado. "Leave it for the maid to tell Farrelly to be outraged and disseminate my latest lechery. I must go though I don't want to."

Their eyes and their bodies met in that intolerable clasp of parting, and then almost brutally he took his arms away from her and went out of the room.

Stairs, potted plants, varnish, hall, bar and dining-room noises. The night air was blue as a plum, and although he was setting out for his home, he felt very much as if he were leaving it.

Five

Played bumble-puppy with a weathered tennis ball springing away on a length of packing case rope; or chipped gum-oozings from the bloodwoods and chewed them until they were so flattened and eucalypt-bitter one couldn't spit them out fast enough; or sprawled on stomach beneath shrubberies driving the ants into frenzies with grass stalk barriers; or merely stood, moving only occasionally, under the cassias, picking the isolated flat yellow leaves away from the green ones, picking the green, opening the pea-shaped flowers and turning them over between the clumsy, marvelling fingers.

Up till that last week-end, Vinny supposed, there wasn't much wrong with that way of spending the Saturdays and the Sundays. Often in the hot September weather it was all you could do, no matter what you wanted. Even in the very hottest weeks in January, Royce would never take her to the swimming hole a mile out of town, because he said none of the other girls went. It was strictly for boys. But she knew, although she never said so, that Pearl Warburton and Betty Klee, shrouded in giggles, wielding their young developed bodies like unsecret weapons, often shoved and pushed and tumbled from the flat, splashed diving rock above the pool – into waves of boys, of encircling arms brown-slippery, to be clutched at, to be clasped feigning resistance, acquiescing. When she thought of it a fierce envy she could not understand filled not only her mind but her body. She wanted to be part of some group; it was the natural urging of her years; she wanted to lose her identity – and there lay the most terrible part of her unpopularity, perhaps: the fact that all the time, contrary to impulse, she was forced to preserve her individuality, to be conscious, day after day, of raw self. To achieve that – to be down at the rock even in the presence of her enemies, leaping off into pools of companionship under the curved brightness of the sky, giggling and slapping with the others, would be a point of contentment.

Since her trip to Brisbane with Mrs. Striebel, Vinny had fed on the memory of it from the moment on Sunday night when her mother asked, "Had a good time, lovey?"

She had dumped the old hat box on the top veranda step and returned her mother's nervous kiss. Electric light from the hall washed right down the steps and halfway along the path to the gate.

"It was wonderful," she replied. "The most wonderful week-end I've ever had."

Her mother wanted to be glad, was glad, even though she felt a nagging jealousy. They went down the hall to the sitting-room, uglier than ever now after the expensive furnishings at the Reisbeck house.

"Where's the others?" she asked.

"Royce's gone down to the factory. He's starting night shift this week, and Rene has gone over to Merlie Passent's place to help her make a frock for the ball next month."

Vinny wasn't really interested.

"You had your tea?" her mother said.

"No. I'm not hungry, Mum."

"You got to have something. You'll get ill travelling all that way with nothing in your stomach. What was Mrs. Striebel thinking of?"

Vinny's loyalty was piqued.

"We had pies on the way back, and some cakes before we left Brisbane."

She slumped into a basket chair with her back against one arm and her thin legs dangling over the other. Mrs. Lalor, routine-bound for ever, resumed her darning.

"I hope you thanked her nicely, Vin. What did you buy?"

Vinny's eyes glistened reminiscently.

"Something lovely, Mum. A lovely little china basket, all full of flowers, roses and tiny blue ones and gold on the edges."

"Gilt, you mean."

"Yes. Gilt. It was cheap too. I saved the change. Two and three." She opened the purse. Inside it she still kept the folded docket for the basket. She lifted it with reverence, and took out the money. Her mother watched the withdrawn eyes and the orange-coloured head, fire-kindled in the artificial light.

"What did you do? All the week-end, I mean?"

So she told her about the trip down, and the rain over the Glasshouses, and the chip-shop steaming through the storm; but she did not mention the singing – she thought it might make Mr. Moller look silly, and after the week-end she liked him a whole lot better. When she came to describe the operetta she found an ally in the older woman who, once a devotee of musical comedy, became in memory the geisha girl our miss gibbs the maid of the mountains was peggylalorneeokeefeinhatslikeplatesandskirtslikesshrubberies. Most unexpectedly for both of them, they found themselves deep in conversation, the first adult one they had ever had.

But of course it could not last, could not withstand the impact of Rene back early from her outing, supercilious under the thick lipstick that halted time upon her sullen luscious mouth. Vinny became the child again, dismissed in a careless hullo, the reject who went truculently to an earlier bed where all the rapture of the last two days played itself over and over against the screen of her closed eyelids.

As she stood beneath the cassias now, two weeks later, the act of the dream with buds and leaves could not hold her interest. She pecked listlessly shifting the shadow patterns across the grass with jerks and pluckings at the springy branches, until after a while there was no fun in it anyway, and she wandered out of the yard down towards the empty back paddock and the road. When she passed the lean-to laundry hanging upon the side of the house she saw her mother through the door bending loverlike over the ironing board. Vinny swung her head smartly so that she would not catch her mother's eye, and ran down past the acalyphas, climbed through a gap in the paling fence, and was out with an incredible feeling of freedom in the hot Saturday afternoon.

"Il fait chaud, il fait beau temps," she said loudly. She broke into a run and yelled *"beau temps, beau temps"* over and over, and leapt up to snatch at overhanging branches or paused to fling stones at Gilham's mangy kelpie. After the yelping and yelling, the stone hurling, the shouting of school-girl French had released some of the resentment she felt, she found herself – involuntarily, surely – walking in the direction of the swimming hole.

Purpose melted the mile into half that distance trodden along the narrow paddock tracks on the town side of the railway line, south through the scrub thickets to the creek. A goods train rumbled north, and long after it had passed her she could still hear it jerking spasmodically and undecidedly at the station. Wondering what made the sound so clear, she looked back from the rise she had climbed to see the township arrow-straight behind her with not a spur or slope to muffle the whistle shrieks. She turned, and to the south the hill s[illegible]ved down into dense scrub where the track was only kept flattened and clear by the feet of swimmers and picnickers. Two hundred yards away the creek ran west below the tall railway bridge and then moved south again in a series of falls and pools.

Vinny gazed all round her. The track before and behind was empty. The sky was very blue, its fathoms of air craft-crowded with huge masses of cumulus, icy white, rolling in on the trades high up. Now and again the bracken rattled as some invisible creature shuddered away, but otherwise, after the track dipped down and put the hill between herself and the town, the humming silence was absolute. She felt excited, and, better than that, she felt daring. She had never before been to the swimming hole in the summer months except one late afternoon a year ago when she had sneaked off without permission and found it empty. Girls around the town who swam there were considered fast, but Pearl Warburton and Betty Klee had managed to keep quiet the fact that they went there, and if Royce had not let it slip accidentally to her she would never had known.

Her blood throbbed like a drum with distant warning. An unaccountable sensation of impending excitement and a peculiar sort of fear that was so nebulous she could have laughed at it made her turn round once or twice to stare back up the narrow scrub track between the white gums and the ironbarks. Shadows that were dirty rags flapped under the trees and dangled from sunlit flags of leaves softly, softly on the lank grasses. Suddenly everything was freckled with the thinnest of fears, and Vinny broke into a trot which brought her to the thick tea-tree bushes at the top of the first fall. It was not very high, about ten feet at the most and now, because of the dry season, was a lean trickle gabbling into the wide pool below. Drought had shrunken this, too, and recessed it from the shores to leave a narrow sandy beach where the boys lay and baked in the sun. The whole place was sheltered, its privacy locked in like a secret, but shouts and laughter reached Vinny where she stood on the outer fringe of the thicket. Softly she began to move forward, her fear of discovery for the moment completely overriding that other nagging quivering fear that kept tugging at her stomach muscles. There was something about the laughter that made her wary, that made her wriggle on her hands and knees a few inches at a time to a place where the scrub thinned and she could peer down through the trellis of branches upon the pool, the beach and the diving rock.

It was three o'clock.

There were three boys in the water when she looked down, but two of them she knew only as workers from the factory, faces seen guffawing in the front stalls at interval, hands palming the orange drinks in the waxed containers, flicking the straws across seats and plucking proprietorially at their girls. And there was another head, a familiar, untidy head, bobbing some yards away. The brown hands paddled the green surface into waves, and Royce's face, with a grinning anticipation on it which she had never seen before, stared hungrily across the pool to the big ledge of rock that jutted out from the lantana scrub upon the bank, right over to the foot of the fall.

Vinny saw the lips of one of the factory boys move as he whispered to his companion, who shouted in immediate laughter so meaningly coarse that she felt the whole centre of that peculiar fear focused upon the three figures in the pool. She hardly dared breathe. She knew, as if she had been instructed, that she must make no sound at all, no sound, but wait for the inevitable moment that clutched the landscape in anticipatory stillness.

The lantana fringing the rock was hollowed into a natural tunnel of deepening green twilight, purple with lost light at its farthest parts. A rustling some distance back made the four watchers swing instinctively towards the sound, and Vinny heard Royce shout, "C'mon there! Hurry up! We can't wait!"

Every outline of every twig under her skinny flanks and belly and every stone beneath her pointed elbows was impressed upon her flesh; the stems knuckled her knees; and even as she eased her body slightly she saw the parting of the last confetti'd sprays of lantana across the tunnel mouth.

Out of the diving rock walked Pearl Warburton, stark naked.

Vinny found the centre of her fear refracted like coloured light on water, broken apart and shaking all around her in kaleidoscopic fashion. She saw only breasts and thighs and the full-smiling mouth and the knees fat-dimpled and the shoulders curving roundly and again the breasts and the thighs and with it all a quiet horror. It was the whiteness and the confidence, the assurance of eroticism attempted and achieved in the amused eyes and the crescent curved mouth of the girl on the rock below.

If there had been the catcalls and the whistles that accompanied the weekly film stimulations, Vinny would have understood, for that was as far as her knowledge of sex behaviour extended – to the rudimentary concealments with their primary reactions – but what puzzled, what frightened her now, was the utter silence, that fell upon the three swimmers, as, oblivious to each other, they guzzled with their eyes the curving body stretched above them.

The moment hung over the trees, the water, the watchers, and the watched, and burst in a fountain of green droplets when Pearl sprang up and sent her heavy smiling body in a dive to the pool. Then followed in the tumbled confusion of the spray the laughter, the snatching, the provocation. Vinny buried her face in the leaves and smelt the eucalypt fragrance even in the dead mould. Shame fired her cheeks. She wanted to look; she longed in a frightening, dreadful fashion to watch the drama played out to a conclusion she sensed though she did not know about it; but the animality of the four people below terrified her. She guessed at a climax beyond her bearing, and found herself wriggling back through the bracken towards the track.

Something made her move silently in spite of her panic, but when she reached the path she flung herself along its security like a mad thing, panting, dry-gasping up the hill and then down towards the town. The rail-motor passed her, heading south. The driver waved to her loneliness upon the hill, and everything, train and houses quiet against the Saturday afternoon, seemed more normal than normal, more real than real. All the way she kept putting the pool and its four scrabbling occupants from her mind, but with the huge horror of nightmare the scene returned again and again, and although she counted it away and conjugated verbs in three different tenses said rapidly with the fury of a fanatic in supplicating prayer, she could not banish it with this simple guile.

Throughout the late afternoon she lay under the cassias behind the side fence and heard her family calling her now and again as the dusk washed up from the valley. And after a while it became quite dark and the stars flowered out quickly in the blue-green sky, and it was impossible to tell whether her face was damp from tears or dew.

At almost nine o'clock on that Saturday morning Helen had walked across the wide dirt road in front of the hotel and had gone up the entrance ramp to the station. There were newspapers curled round the lower cross-bars of the opened gates, sun-yellowed, sun-curled; behind her at the door of the pub the morning's first drinkers, the veterans of high blood-pressure and cirrhosis. The sky bracketed green hills to north and south, enclosed in a loving sweep of blue the township basin. The houses stood without mystery in the high morning sun, boxed-in ochre or brown with white trim, green-blinded verandas all round, or bare as bones and showing the bicycles propped along them and the aged, sagging wire stretchers from the confirmed sleeper out. And they were filled – filled with shopkeepers and their wives, with factory hands or clerks, the women ardent over recipe and preserve, plump and efficient or plump and slatternly or sun-wizened or almost any combination of these things, but present, and for the most part predictable in the behaviour manifestations of the town – in the country women's meetings, at the church socials, the masonic dances, the school concerts; they cut sandwiches and decorated tables and slouched foot-aching behind stalls and sold tickets and cleaned up after their male partners who boozed and betted and carved out a policy entirely independently. They were rewarded with little titbits of gossip garnered at a lodge meeting or an evening's snooker, toned down from its rosy informality at the bar to a cosier family conversation piece. (Lunbeck had excused more late homecomings than he knew.)

There was a knot of people on the station, in best prints and going-to-town silks and absurd serge tight under the armpits and in the crotch, stained across backs and bellies and buttocks. And the heads twisted stiffly to nod as Helen came round the end of the little building on to the platform. She felt her guilt rising like a mountain between her nod and the nods of the others; she was relieved they did not know of the act intended, as bad, she told herself, as the act committed. She bought a return ticket to Gympie and, having crammed the piece of cardboard into her purse, drew her very aloneness about her for protection, and walked out and stood by herself at the far end of the platform. It was a pity she had to be so noticed on this particular morning, but she stood bravely in her one good linen suit and carrying an overnight bag.

Around the southern bend of the line the rail-motor rattled its rust-red length. She stepped forward instinctively and when the end carriage stopped in front of her and she saw it was practically empty, she went, as she always did, to sit by the very last window. The Cantwells got in and waved and she waved perfunctorily herself, shrinking against the hard leather seat, dreading sociability, wanting only to see the houses melt into the trees into the hills, without having to barter worn-out phrases. They sat down a few seats away and she lowered the morning paper that she had raised in self-defence. A short hoot blurted from the front car. Gungee slid back into dust and eucalypt patterns, and then the open paddocks came and the lovely risings of the hills. Town after tiny town stamped its station with skinny farmers and dumpy housewives and urinating dogs across the dirty rain-dust-streaked glass. Now and again when they went through a deep cutting she caught a ghostly glimpse of her own face mirrored on the window, staring steadily into her own eyes; saw the white, wide cheek bones and the full, slightly down-curved mouth and the neat hair in its golden bun beneath the wide straw hat. She asked herself if it were the face of a woman about to betray another, and the eyes swung quickly to the cutting's red walls and the clambering mesembryanthemum and refused to acknowledge the accusation in the eyes. But despite self-recrimminations nibbling like tiny fish at the edges of her mind, she was happy at heart beyond belief, so that she hummed quietly to herself below the racketings of the motor.

It was only when the first slag-heaps appeared like dirty scabs upon the Gympie outskirts that she suddenly feared Moller's meeting her on the platform with Cecily Cantwell's mock-innocent eyes down-tracking and cornering them and transfixing them against the waiting room walls. Cecily, she felt, would love to see them scuffing like bugs behind the ripped hoardings, concealing their twoness under dentifrice and canned-food advertisements, reducing the arrogance of their loving to the flat sordidity of torn posters and scribbled-on walls. The last curve came in with the branch line west, and then the station, and they pulled in slowly under the iron roof to a world of tea-urns and trolleys and the dripping taps outside the washrooms. Helen felt the Cantwells watching her as she stood up to drag her bag from the overhead rack. She gave them shallow smile for shallow smile and, disciplined towards exposure, pulled open the carriage door and stepped down to the platform in the dried-out sunlight.

While the front carriages emptied quickly she searched among the groups along the platform for Moller's bulky form. He was not there, and after the first second of disappointment she could almost have wept at his perception, his anticipation of the predicament of a public meeting in this place. She went into the refreshment room and ordered tea and sandwiches.

The long, stale room was all of a pattern with all the railway waiting-rooms all over the State – the thin and the blowsy girls, hair re-permed over perm, the tired frizz bobbing above the thick china and week-old teacake, the scalding, stewed tea and the slop rings on the counter. She stared, repelled, at yellow buns and silver-papered chocolate slabs, safe and sanitary, and the flies lethargic from too much food crawling over the sandwich piles. Yet with an idiotic determination to extract glamour from detail she felt that even these things would fix the day.

The man on the stool next to hers leant over dangerously and jolted her elbow.

"Sorry," he said, not meaning it, and leered purple and liquor-scented across the steamy air. "Going far? Awful stuff, this tea, i'n't it?"

Helen drew back from the network of veins hovering as if to trap her.

"Yes, dreadful."

"Going far?"

"No. I'm waiting for a friend."

He looked her over. There were old stains down the front of his suit, and it was crumpled as if it had been slept in. He smiled confidentially and the effect upon the tiny eyes was quite horrible.

"Someone's lucky, eh? Us poor travellers don't know what home comforts are. Rocky next stop-off and heaven knows when nex' the missus and me'll meet. Gets a man down."

He blew on his tea and it washed over into the saucer. A piece of bun floated in it, but he rescued it and popped it into his mouth. His lower jaw worked over it busily.

"When's your friend coming?" he asked. He smiled again, with his mouth unpleasantly filled with bun, and winked meaningly.

Helen pretended blindness, deafness. The man placed a hand testingly upon her arm.

"I said when's your friend coming?"

Helen's arm shuddered in withdrawal. Sipping her tea, she said without turning, "Soon. Soon, I hope."

Silence. Then –

"Gent?"

His look sidled all round her, stroked her cosily, interpreted her silence rightly.

"Gent it is. He's lucky, eh? Late, isn't he? Catch *me*!"

Helen gulped the last of her tea and sacrified her sandwiches, shoving the cup and plate back across the counter.

"Hey! What's the hurry?" he asked. "We were just getting matey."

Helen turned and saw him crumpled, stained, unlovely. The tiny eyes stared boldly into her own.

"Boy-friend here already?" He shook his head in sorrow at her deception. His thinning skull waggled foolish reproof.

"Yes," she said. And left.

It was unfortunate, but she seemed to be pursued by incidents that spilt a sordidity over the whole affair. More and more, she felt, the week-end was being turned into a hole-and-corner scramble, furtively undignified. She looked up and down the platform once again, but there was still no sign of Moller and, uncertain what to do next, she turned and glanced through the refreshment room door. The traveller was watching her. He jerked his head with an unmistakable meaning. Helen turned away confused and walked along the platform to the women's waiting-room and entered into the clasp of the brown walls, the unswept floor. One window looked blearily out upon the stacked handles of a trolley pile. She could see a goods train shunting on the far track. All around her in an intense mural effort childish pornographies invited her to gross behaviour through injunction or sketch; name was linked with name in erotic bravado above pencilled anatomies that achieved only yawns. She felt that perhaps it would be better if the government railways arranged for semi-abstract murals by well-known artists to be prepared containing all the monosyllables and drawings so beloved by the bored traveller. If they were added in pleasant burnt orange or sienna or delicate blues and greens as an automatic part of the station *décor* she felt the public would be far more cheered than by these drab reminders of their primary duties. She found herself laughing as she washed her hands at the tap over the filthy porcelain basin. Careful not to touch its sides, she shook the water from her fingers and wiped them on a handkerchief.

It was ten-thirty. Robert had allowed this fifteen-minute interval very wisely. Feeling that he would probably be coming, she went outside again, handed in her ticket, and waited at the head of the concrete stair flight; and then, although she had expected him, his actuality shocked her into trembling as he ran up the stairs to meet her. The sudden touching of his lips to her cheek was almost the first conscious jolt that reminded both of them of the purpose of their meeting. His eyes explored hers. She felt almost ill at the hunger in them.

"Thank you for waiting. I thought – I knew it would be safer. The Cantwells passed me, although they didn't see me, half a block back, and several of the mums and dads as well. The devil, my dear. . . ."

He touched her arm and took her bag.

"Don't say that," Helen said. "I fought a deathly struggle with my conscience last evening. Please. Please, Robert. Let's think of nothing but being happy for a Saturday and a Sunday."

"That's entirely my view. Narrow, exclusive, and cannot be built out."

He said "Helen" and "darling" and squeezed her arm very gently and pulled her against him so that she stumbled slightly, and then they walked in silence down the hill to his car.

He had parked it a short distance up a side lane, and after they had got in he drove slowly down the steep road past the dull houses to the main street with its close-set shops and its tin awnings. Something of the frontier town atmosphere lingered on in this ghost relic of the gold rush days, Helen thought, something so unsophisticated one felt an obligation to stride in buckskin shooting from the hips. She said as much to Moller, who laughed into the dry blue air.

"They were dozens of brawls in the old town's heyday, some of them pretty serious. I don't think a mining town ever lives down its reputation, you know. And of course, although the output is finished now, there's always the stray dreamer who hopes he'll happen on a vein one day."

He pulled in at the top of the town beside the post office.

"Sending off some rude holiday cards to the Talbots." He grinned hideously. " 'Plenty of sights around Gympie!' 'It's breezy up here in Gympie!' 'I've struck rock-bottom in Gympie!' "

Helen wrinkled her nose at him. "If you don't hurry you'll miss the midday sorting. Different, isn't it, from the days when Andrew Petrie ran his dray down to Brisbane?"

She found herself measuring his retreating and returning figure with a lover's eye that discounted shabbiness and the ageing disproportion of the body. She was thirty-two and felt older and at once younger than she would have thought possible, on this burning morning in September. And he was forty-seven, the hair still thick but greying, the face kindly but pouched a little and lined. Yet she felt nothing but tenderness for him; his physical defects gave him a vulnerability in the unkind light that brought her close to tears, so that when he sat once more beside her and started the engine running he was surprised at finding her hand resting across his own. Loving should not be so sad, she told herself, nor seek in the inevitably cruel way it does a sort of nostalgia in fine weather, in days of irresistible blueness and greenness, as if the rain that was not visible in the physical world were gently falling within the mind. Nothing, not even the most pellucid of moments, was ever recalled without a certain misting in the effect, a regret for loss, for the impossibility of repetition. She remembered a winter in the south when she was only a child, and the limned July outlines in plane-tree and elm, in maple, in poplars piercing the cold winds from the west; days when, moving about the house, you stepped with near-sighted care over the ragged papers of sunlight on the floor. Fires ate up the mallee logs at night as you sat with the plate of toast hugged between crossed legs. The changing shapes within the heart of the fire drugged the eyes into sleep. She tried in later years to recapture just the glassy quality of cold of that one particular winter of that bony deciduous season – but it was never the same.

The car swung out along the Tin Can Bay road and Goomboorian fell away to the west as they entered the Toolara pine forests, plunged into breakers of resined air swept up in tides, in waves, on a beach wind.

"*Pinus caribaea,*" Moller said. "Impressed? I am a fund of technical information."

"God! That heavenly smell! How long does this go on?"

"Practically the whole thirty odd miles. Close your

eyes, Helen, and forget school and Gungee and Talbots and Farrellys and just bask. Sheerly bask."

I can look, I can try to imprint these miles and miles of forest ocean on receptive traces of the brain, she thought, but the end of the journey will be here, and the whole week-end will be vanished tomorrow afternoon, and not a thing will be left of it. She gazed pitifully across at the man.

"Nothing lasts," she said mournfully.

"For God's sake!" Moller exploded. He half turned from the wheel. "Helen, get out of those disgusting deeps of triteness. Good God! I'm surprised at you!" He slowed up for a moment and flung her a brief glance of curiosity. He saw the hurt on her face and relented.

"My dear, I'm sorry. But don't say things like that. This week-end has only begun. There will be others. I'm afraid you're incurably female the way you must take mental dips in the past. Try to be a bit male. Live ahead. You'll feel a lot better."

He banged his horn at a curve. A truck coming west swung in savagely close, and was gone before he even had time to yell an oath.

"You see? Not a regret!"

The road closed before and behind, a green cocoon of silence that fell not between but around them. Helen presed her cheek to the frame of the window and parted her lips to the kissing of the rushing air. After a while road and trees became a kind of rhythm, and they spoke little, and the minutes slipped away as quickly as the miles. Nearing the coast they turned east to little Teewah Creek and then curved back north again, and the wide flat waters of the bay surprised them on their right and the first shallow inlets of Snapper Creek on their left. The air was bright, so bright that it seemed composed of millions of separate points – gold-pointillism, dust-stippled and dreadfully alive. Moller slowed the car as they came along the peninsula past the week-end shacks, the stores and the caravan park.

Under the late morning sun in sharp angle, sun on blue water, the broad illumination of the sky, curved brightness, fire and sea reflection met in fathoms of air and beat the yellow beaches like brass. Gulls curved in over the strait following the hulls of fish-hungry craft speckling the sea. There was utter stillness.

He pulled up outside one of the sleepy stores and they bought milk and butter and bread.

"There's a reasonable stove at the house according to the agent," Moller said, "but I don't fancy messing around with fuel, do you? Let's live on tins and the primus."

They called at the agent's home and collected the key; then, having received directions, drove slowly along the beach front until they came to the house. Moller braked and cut the engine and they sat there with the sea wind blowing straight through the car. Scrubby trees along the waterfront, tangled and torn by salt, rested their heads against the sky. A hundred yards away a lonely fisherman reeled in, rebaited, and swung his line gracefully out again across the water. Off shore a motor-boat chugged a diagonal towards the point and the noise of its engine seemed to arch and enclose them.

The house was very squat and ugly and the windows across the front were blinded by fly-screens. A chain-wire fence creaked under the weight of westringia bushes and the front gate swung agape upon sand and tussocks.

"Inside," Moller said, "there will be one bedroom with a frighteningly large double bed, one with two sagging stretchers, and a living-room with a rococo side board and a lino-topped table. I can see it all. The apricot-coloured glass-ware and the two desert scenes above the sofa."

He took Helen into his arms, kissing her mouth for a very long time, and the wind blowing across their closed eyelids felt unbelievably cool.

On Sunday morning they hired a rowing boat from the boatshed farther along the beach and took it across to Smooger Point. The weather was still holding. Big puffs of cumulus floated in the strait and the keel sliced them and the mirrored gulls correlated sky colour with sea colour and wing with fin. The shore-line behind them was a melange of green, grey, and smoky blues, shadow dribblings across white sand and the wet tongues of tidal inlets.

After they had beached the boat they carried their lunch bag up the grassy dunes until they found a hollow, tree-hedged, sea-sound-muffled. Hardly could they restrain eyes or hands from each other's person, so sharp was their present tenderness, their infatuation, though it was more than that really – yet going through the primary process all the same of divining one's own godhead in the other. Lying among their own lunch wrappings, they explored the preciseness of their affection verbally, under a vertical sun that wrung sticky-sweet scent from the grass, made a spikenard as it were of the yellow flowers twisting across the multiplicity of purple bloom on the land side.

"We are too old for this sort of thing," Helen suggested. She picked up a handful of sand from one of the many little lakes of white that scattered about the grove, and let it sift through her fingers.

"You sound like an early Noël Coward," Moller said. He lay flat on his back beside her under the ragged shade of a sand cypress. "Of course we are. At least, I am. Not you, my dear, with your incredibly young body. But you mustn't say it, and certainly not in those reproving tones. Even if we are – what the hell?" He paused. "But it's not a physical oldness that you mean, I know, but mental. You feel we should have grown beyond this sort of thing."

"Something like that."

"Nonsense. What delicious nonsense! I have wanted these two days for nearly a year now. Nearly a year."

She looked across the hollow that held them to the top crests of the ocean-side dunes and did not reply.

He stared into the sky spaces. "Even now that I've explored your body I'm not content. I want to learn it by heart. But that's not enough. There's the mind to learn, and the emotions, and the lovely unreliable intuitions that are essentially female. A week-end isn't enough. Not for all those things. I don't know, Helen, really I don't know."

"What don't you know?"

"How or when I can get all those things. Time does seem limited."

"Yet yesterday you chided me for the same regret."

"Not quite the same. I'm not lamenting what I've had. Only what I mightn't achieve."

Helen looked straight at him as she asked, "Are you content so far with your discoveries?"

He took her hand and held it against his mouth so that she could feel his lips moving against her palm as he replied.

"Content and most uncontent. There's my fullest compliment. Even after these two days, Helen, whenever I shall see you coming towards me along the verandas at recess or in the classroom you turn as I enter, I'll see you as I saw you last night coming towards me for the first time in that tiny bedroom awash with moonlight."

Helen trembled involuntarily. "Not for long," she said. "You won't remember for long."

"At present I think for very long indeed," Moller said. He sighed. "But I know you are right – ultimately. We are too old to be taken in by storybook imagery. Yet really, Helen, it will be a long time before I forget the consolation of your – of your body."

She was silent for a moment and then she said, "After today I never want to see that house again."

He was surprised at the violence in her voice. "Why?" he asked. "Do you find it shameful? Won't it have some sentimental connotation?"

"Now you're being female!" Helen smiled.

"*Touché*!" He was relieved to see the tension on her face relax. "But tell me why."

"I'm frightened," she said, "that both of us might find it tawdry, tawdry enough to spoil it all. Repetition might make more than a joke of the faded orange silk bedspread and the ripped horsehair sofa. You know, I had a bad moment on Gympie station when I was waiting for you."

Moller rolled over and sat up. The anxiety in his eyes was doubled in hers. "Have care with an ageing man," he joked, not really joking.

She told him about the traveller in the refreshment room, and grimy salacity of the washroom walls.

"It was the sudden connection of the idea," she explained, "the harshness of its animality. For a few minutes I was on the point of turning back."

She saw his face. The pain was understandable, but unbearable, too, and she was glad when finally he pulled a face at her and flung his old cynicism forward.

"I'll defend that situation," he said. "You wouldn't have me discount the physical – animal, if you like – side of any relationship such as this, would you? Do you really want me to lie and pretend and excuse and paint it all on a high spiritual plane – 'my-dear-this-thing-is-bigger-than-both-of-us' women's magazine stuff? Do you? Do you?" he persisted.

Helen smiled into his near-angry face.

"No. I suppose it's as you said – we need the right props. But of course I don't discount the physical. You've made an honest woman of me."

"Thank God for that. Why lie to suit the gossips or the prudes that live in the shallows of our own conventional selves? Don't let's pretend that this is all such a beautiful magic we have no bodies. I doubt if there'd be any spiritual affinity between us if it weren't for the primary impulse of our sex. I don't know. I may be wrong. What happened at Gympie was unfortunate, badly timed perhaps. If it had happened a week later it might not even have impinged on your fastidiousness. Who knows?" He rolled himself a cigarette and there was a silence; the hot stillness dripped from trees in the sun to pools of shadow. "But know this, Helen. My body wants yours. Terribly, I'm afraid. And I cannot excuse it. You have an inner comfort and the unquiet in my own mind craves that, too. It's knowing 'flesh in terms of spirit'. *Bist du bei mir*. Good old Bach." He hummed a phrase or two. "Quickly, Helen. I have to kiss you. Bend over me and blot out that light and that sky."

So little things swing bigger ones into scything motion; moments have the vengeance of hours and days and years, even, waiting upon the misplaced use of seconds. A folly to count back through time to this or that as a factor in disaster, but so often the casual movement means seriousness for the mover. And thus it was that Helen and Moller, rowing back to Snapper Bay later than they had intended, timed their shore arrival with that of a smart launch nosing in towards the breakwater.

Helen was leaning sideways over the stern trailing one hand in the wash when she heard an oath from Moller and felt the boat swing as he backwatered on one oar and swung the bows in to shore at a sharper angle. She turned and saw the concern on his face creased into a frown.

"Look away, Helen," he said softly. "The trees. The water. Anything. The launch behind us is Sam Welch's. I clean forgot about their bloody shack up here. Oh God! As soon as I've beached this hulk, head straight back to the house. We'll try to dodge them on the beach."

The boat jammed in on the wet sand, and Helen, holding her sandals, waded through the warm low tide, went up the beach past the scuttling soldier crabs to the shelter of the trees along the roadway. When she turned at last she could see Moller planting the anchor and gathering up the oars to return to the boatshed. The launch dinghy was slipping quietly over the fifty feet of glassy water between it and the shore, and even up there under the listening trees she could hear Sam Welch's shout of, "Hey, Herc!"

She watched him turn in the trap to wave, to smile, to wait for him and to make one of three in an exchange of banalities, while all the time Marian Welch's excited face sought her over Moller's shoulder, reached for her like a gluttonous tapir to where she stood. She half turned to go, and then decided to wait. The breeze came in over the strait stiffening the water into corrugations of green and white; the whole of the bay's craft rocked suddenly in the afternoon breeze, and she saw Moller leave them and come towards her. His face said all she needed to discover, but he spoke sourly as he came up and took her arm.

"No point in your training it back from Gympie now," he said. "That wouldn't disarm anybody. You might as well travel back to Gungee shamelessly with me. As late as we can. They spotted the car yesterday afternoon."

They walked along the peninsula in the shadow of the trees. Helen felt nothing but unexpected relief after all, and she smiled as she touched the inside of his wrist with her finger-tips.

"Just what happened?"

"Apparently they came up by car after lunch yesterday. Up for the week-end. Their shack's farther along the point. Marian told me she saw the old Buick pulled in under the trees, but she said she didn't think it could have been mine. Anyway, they went off early this morning for a spot of fishing up near Fraser Island, and they must have had a good look at my number plate on the way to the beach. I couldn't pretend I hadn't been here last night. I'm sorry, my dear. I really don't know how I kept Marian from you. She was literally itching as she peered up at you."

"They know it's me?"

"Afraid so. They saw you from the launch. Eyes like eagle-hawks."

Their feet slapped the red earth, the sand hollows, the stringy grass.

"Do you mind?"

"Surprisingly enough, no."

"What a lamentable novice at seduction you must think me, Helen."

"No, Robert, no. Not technically."

"Thank you. Thank you indeed."

They both laughed and the long purpose of their mirth brought them to the westringia bushes on the creaking chain-wire and the tussocks and the door warped by sea air and the bedspread of faded orange silk. And it was only when they remembered Lilian that their eyes suddenly sobered.

The costive celebrations of the foursome, the nigglings, the prurience, all festooned the evening from eight until ten when they decorated the sandwiches like parsley sprigs and became garnishings on savouries. A satisfying evening. An evening of unchristian destructiveness at which they all assisted with gossip snippets directed at their two new victims. Whenever the conversation digressed into behaviourisms less spectacular, it was drawn back to its central theme by Jess Talbot who found the topic magnetic.

"I'm interested in people," she explained earnestly. "I don't feel that by being interested one is being uncharitable. Do you?" Her voice was loud and assured and frighteningly well educated. It ploughed through the spontaneous assents. "I can't help it, you know. I make it my business to know other people's business. I feel it all helps towards an understanding."

Her beautiful long hair was drawn back into coiled plaits that shone redly beneath the Welches' table lamp. Alec looked at her admiringly. He loved the simple virtues.

"True," Welch said. "Very, very true." He was a technical college, not a university, man, and he felt slightly resentful towards Talbot with his union tiepin, and his careful articulations. At heart he hated him, hated him for his union tiepin and his careful diction, but publicly could not bring his irritation, his dislike to the point of being rude or even cool. Now and again he exhibited just the merest shade of truculence that exploded in fountains of venom when he talked alone with Marian and the two of them stripped the synthetic social mask aside.

"How long has it been going on?" Marian speculated for the dozenth time. She never tired of flinging this query into the listening air. Titillated by the gossip, she thought of Lunbeck and ogled Talbot, who dropped his church-worker's eyes modestly to his glass.

"Who knows?" Jess Talbot's vowels were at the top of their form. They bowled all verbal opposition aside like gigantic iron spheroids. "Too long, I think. Remember, we do have the effect upon the youngsters at the school to consider if the scandal gets around" – making mental note that it would, that it must. "It's exposing them to moral danger to allow them to suffer such a relationship between members of the staff. Teachers are supposed to be looked up to, surely."

"The horrible thing," Marian said, loving it, "was that he didn't seem a bit ashamed. Not a bit. He actually smiled when Sam asked him if he came up on Saturday. He almost seemed to be enjoying the situation. Didn't he, Sam?"

Sam Welch filled up his sherry glass and leant back in the moquette depths of his chair. Tonight, in some indefinable way, the enjoyment of the scandal eluded him, leaving him with the feeling that the seediness of immorality lay within this assemblage. He glanced round at the three faces, uncomplicated except from the effort of detraction, busy with a liberal transcription of the actions of others. In a moment of astonishing and impersonal clarity he saw, for perhaps the second time only in his marriage, the uninhibited sexual jealousy upon his wife's face, slanting the eyes and the mouth into narrows of unkindness. He saw the oval faces of the Talbots filled up with false godliness, sharpened and lengthened by the shadows of the lamp. Being deliberately boorish, he gulped at his sherry and ran the back of his hand across his mouth. The three of them sickened him, and he felt suddenly that he didn't want to be in all this, that he was sorry for having mentioned the business. Still, he told himself, nothing would have stopped Marian. Nothing on God's earth would stop her when she made up her mind to do something.

"More sherry?" He gestured with the decanter towards Talbot's glass.

"Thank you," the other said, pushing it forward primly.

"No. He didn't seem upset, I must say. Not like I'd be." Welch threw his wife a sly look. "Like being caught with his pants down, wasn't it? Most men would be upset."

He was rewarded by seeing the Talbots wince at his crudeness. It made him happy again.

"What do you think one should do?" Jess asked. "Marian, you have two girls at the school. It must affect you very closely. They're at that terribly impressionable age."

She has nothing to say, thought Welch, and she says it. God, how she says it over and over and over. The sherry was having an unusual effect on him. At the beginning of the evening when the Talbots had dropped in unexpectedly he had been ready to be right in it with them. But now this eternal carping had been going on for nearly two hours and he felt, not sympathy for the victims, but a remoteness from them and their verbal persecutors. The drive back, too, had tired him and he wished above all to go to bed swagged about with liquor fumes, and to vanish into the fogs of sleep. He heaved his stout body round in the chair and glared at her from his creased face.

"Well," Marian pondered, and the intrinsic malice of

her design smiled out with a radiance marvellous to see, "well, I really feel that being on the parents' committee, you know, that perhaps I should just drop a tiny hint in Findlay's ear." She pecked a segment from a dry biscuit and made little crackling sounds.

"That's a bit bloody thick, isn't it?" Welch growled. His half-closed eyes blinked rapidly several times as they all turned to look at him.

"I don't think so, Sam." Jess Talbot dealt suavely with opposition. "I don't think so at all. Perhaps Mr. Findlay might be able to suggest discreetly to them that they are being a bit *outré*." (French, too, Welch thought angrily.) "After all, Alec" – she appealed to him, requiring no assent really; it was merely a public marital gesture – "the children come before the adults, don't they? Every time. The greatest good for the greatest number." She was using her aphorisms like tear-gas to make her audience weep. The meretricious arguments would pile up and swamp charity in a gigantic wave, a tide of adulterated good works. And after all, who could charge the moral worker with being a busybody without also appearing to be in connivance with the wrongdoer?

Alec Talbot's chin quivered. He leant forward, his eyes intent upon his wife. Their communion was complete at moments like this.

"What was that business you told me of concerning the school a few years back?" he asked. "That – forgive me, Marian – homosexual incident with the young maths master? Now there was a case in point."

"Oh, of course! You told me about it, Marian. Remember?"

Jess Talbot was launched. Without hesitancy she plunged down the slipway into a sticky sea of calumny. Her listeners struggled in the wash of words, unable to surface for air under the choking weight of defamation. Welch refused to be drowned. He had had enough.

"You're looking tired," he said unkindly to Jess in the middle of a sentence.

"Am I?" She gave the small smile reserved for fools. "My mind feels as sharp as a razor. I feel quite brilliant tonight. As Alec says, there definitely was a case in point. Fortunately that unhappy man corrupted only one of the boys, but he could very easily have gone undetected and done goodness knows how much damage."

"Corrupted! Terry Crewe! Oh God!" Welch laughed noisily. "What bull! What utter bull! That kid used to hang around the factory at nights when the eleven o'clock shift came off and practically ask for it. He just met a soul mate. I always did feel sorry for Russell. A victim of circumstances if ever there was one."

"You're begging the question," Alec Talbot intervened.

"And you, Talbot, are nothing but a bloody pedantic theorist!"

"Nonsense! Jess is completely right. Poor behaviour on the part of adults, especially those in positions of authority, can set up all sorts of chain reactions in impressionable adolescents. If I were in any doubt before that something should be done, I'm completely convinced now that the best thing that could happen would be for Findlay to be informed. It's indifference of the type you display, Welch, that lets these things snowball until they get out of hand."

"Yes, yes! Frightened Moller will unseat Lunbeck as the town rake? He's not quite classy enough to get away with it, is he?" Welch belched angrily and without apologizing. "He's not bloody classy enough!"

His wife's eyes flickered uneasily between the two men. The evening was taking a wrong turn, and it had all started out so happily, a set of symphonic variations on the one delicious theme. The sunburn, which she felt suited her, shone redly like a lamp through fog under the thinning make-up sweated away by sherry and the warm night, and did not suit her at all really, with her pouched eyes and crisped hair and her forty-three years. She felt she could not bear it if Sam made a gaffe that cut them off from the town's *élite*. Looking round the room, she noted with pride the different objects that implied income, that put their home in a certain class – the expensive radiogram that only ever played aborted versions of musical shows, the china cabinet threatening the guests with its gilt and biscuit-thin cups and saucers, the cocktail cabinet with all the right glasses for all the right drinks. She was home like the sailor, home from the sea of early married stringency, to a harbour of best grade wall-to-wall, of inoffensive landscapes, and a deep-freeze unit just packed with goodies.

"It's the driving," she hastened to explain to the Talbots. "It always affects Sam's nerves. There was the most fearful glare coming back from the Bay this afternoon. We had the sun on the windscreen for miles."

"Don't apologize for me!" Welch was very close to shouting. "For God's sake don't apologize! I feel I'm talking normally for once. For two hours now, two solid bloody hours, you've been on to them. Give the poor bastards a break. Yes, I know! I know I was in it with you," he minced at Jess, interrupting her triumphant and accusing eye, "but can't you just mention the thing and leave it? You never give friend Harold such thorough treatment. But then he's one of the big four! Solid at lodge and lousy with dough! So he escapes!"

"Mind your language, Welch," Talbot reprimanded primly.

"What? What was that? Oh God!" Welch roared with sudden artificial laughter. "She talks of perversion," he said, nodding towards Jess Talbot and turning to his wife. "Her! Perversion! And she's married to such an old woman." He struggled out of his chair and lurched to the veranda door. "I'm going to be sick," he said. "But don't go home on my account."

The Talbots took the sins of their fellows prissily away into the humped night. Roads merged flatly with grass paddocks and the houses were all in darkness. Strung out along the roads were the weak street-lights desolate as the newspapers blown around their bases. However, when they entered the downstairs hall of the hotel there was a light on in Farrelly's thimble-size office behind the bar. They tiptoed past the half-open door, their normal extrovert arrogance subdued by Welch's outburst, but they had not reached the foot of the stairs when Farrelly slipped through the door and called them. The downward stream of electric light exposed the fatigue, the anger, and the puzzlement on his face without mercy. The Talbots raised their well-bred eyebrows interrogatively and Farrelly hated them momentarily for seeing him in braces.

"Have you seen Mrs. Striebel?" he asked. There was very nearly a whimper in his voice. "I've had trunk-line from Brisbane worrying me all week-end – yesterday and now today. They've been ringing every hour tonight since six o'clock. You don't happen to know where she is, do you?"

In the half-light of the hall, slanted across with the shadow of the wide stairs, their eyes searched for and found each other's. In these lacunae of communication they confessed their purpose wordlessly, gave absolution and blessed the intended action.

"Well –" Jess Talbot paused. Her voice sounded very lovely when she spoke softly, and now it had the tenderness of the executioner as well. "This is strictly confidential, Mr. Farrelly, but seeing the phone call is probably urgent I feel I had better tell you. We did hear, Alec and I, that she has been at Tin Can Bay this week-end with Mr. Moller. Perhaps if you rang his house. . . ."

She stopped in a nicely assumed confusion, and Alec congratulated himself, as he often did, on his perspicacity in choosing a wife at once so refined and so unbelievably tactful.

Six

Vinny found the first notice chalked on the inside wall of the girls' lavatory block. It said simply,

MR. MOLLER LOVES MRS. STRIEBEL.

She would never have noticed it except for the fact that loneliness had driven her lately to loitering there, just where the pepper trees branched over the galvanized roofing and made a pocket of shade in the alleyway. The rough white lettering was modest in size, but its categorical finality shocked Vinny with the greater shock that only the dreaded and expected can give. She stared at it a long while, refusing, thrusting back the truth she knew was there; then she took out her handkerchief and tried to rub the words out. Even after she had blurred and smudged away most of the surface chalk the ghost of the message still lingered on the wall. So she wetted the piece of rag beneath the tap and washed away the five threatening words. She knew that according to school rule she should have reported the matter to the headmaster, but some uncanny caution made her first reaction a pausing to sense the intrinsic danger of the statement. She knew it was true.

It worried her all the rest of the day, and when next morning she found the same five words sprawling along the side fence it was with a feeling almost of relief. There was a group of giggling senior school pupils standing alongside it, fooling about before the morning bell. This section of the yard was well away from the main school block and out of bounds to all except the secondary classes. She approached the group diffidently, but their absorption was complete. She could see Howard's smooth and over-handsome face in the centre of the group and hear him singing in a crooner's exaggerated whine, "I can't give – you anything but – *love – babee*."

She could see the Welch girls, too, usually hangers-on, flutterers at the edge of things, now being the pivot of the questions and the sniggerings and the soft replies. Her anger surprised her and she backed away again. No one noticed her go. And by the end of the week the notices had reappeared along the lavatory walls and this time their message was couched in more direct terms, in monosyllables that Vinny had seen before and, although she was unaware of their exact meaning, felt to be unclean.

She did not know what to do. She clasped her confusion tightly within for the first few days and hoped and dreaded simultaneously that the notices would be reported to Mr. Findlay. But the staff continued serenely through the inflexible time-table of each day, the blocked-out forty minute divisions for subjects, unruffled by any undercurrents among the pupils. In class she watched the nudgings and the note passings, the insolent stares that broke out in epidemic proportions whenever Mr. Moller paused on his way out of the room to speak to Mrs. Striebel on her way in, and marvelled at the unawareness that kept their faces smiling and urbane and innocent as they turned to the class during lessons. Innocent? She flogged the little whip of a word about her and was dubious concerning the quality of guilt. She felt she had some sort of personal interest in their relationship after seeing them relaxed and at one on the trip to Brisbane. If anyone must defend them, she decided, she wanted to be the one to do it. And so began a planned directive towards erasing the more public of the notices.

At first the rest of the class was unaware of what she was doing. They spoke with her so little there was really no opportunity for them to gauge her attitude, though if anyone had thought of it they would have been very interested, for everyone knew she had a terrible crush on Mrs. Striebel.

However, the implications of the scandal, the juiciest the school had had since "Sweetie" Russell had lost his job three years before, and since one of the girls accidentally burnt out half a room in the cooking block the year before that, added to the fact that the annual school dance was only two weeks away, completely obliterated Vinny from their minds. Bits of gossip percolated through to the primary school, were not understood, but nevertheless were taken home garbled for reference and handed on to both delighted and horrified mothers who checked and cross-checked the facts with friends until a network of half-truth and half-lies spread over the entire township, a net in which the two fish victims were still swimming unaware.

It was on the Monday exactly one week before the dance that the whole affair, so far lacking any noticeable public unpleasantness, blew up to giant size. The impulse came from an argument between Moller and Howard. At first it was merely the usual exchange of attack and defence over a neglected home exercise; but something in the boy's manner, the smile he gave as he stated definitely he could not be kept in, caused Moller to glance at him more sharply.

"What was that last remark, Howard?"

"I said, sir, you probably know what it is to be busy after school."

"And just how is that relevant to your own detention?"

Howard smiled with ironic patience. He kicked gently at the boy beside him.

"Just like you, sir. Personal matters. I have urgent personal business."

The class gasped with the deliciousness of the outrage, and leant forward, anxious to miss no nuance of this exchange. Moller sat with his body hard against the table edge and with unaware fingers drummed his fountain-pen in the first beats of an intuitive apprehension.

"And just what do you mean by that?"

He knew as soon as he framed the question that he had made a mistake. To liberate the kinds of answer of which Howard was capable was folly in the extreme. He pouted his thick lower lip in annoyance and then bit it.

"Girls," Howard said. "*You* know, sir."

Someone giggled hysterically at the back of the room, but other than that there was silence as absolute as twenty breaths painfully withheld in fear could make it. The telephone ringing in Findlay's office sounded clearly across the intervening silence, and everyone in that waiting room could hear the squeak of his chair as he stretched forward to answer it. His voice floated to them in preliminary politenesses and was cut off by the abrupt closing of the office door.

With his foot, Moller thought irrelevantly. He kicks it shut with his foot. Everything made easy.

He met Howard's impudent eyes with rage, at the back of which lurked uncertainty, a longing to be released from the insolent accusation on the handsome face in the centre of the room. His mind raced over a waterfall lip of tumbled ideas and suspicions. The emphasis in Howard's remark could mean only one thing. The Welches had worked fast – by now half the town must know. He saw the nineteen other faces, and did not see them; they blurred together and separated and they all spelt the same thing; and he knew that he must keep his sense of proportion and a coolness.

"I do *not* know, Howard," he said, "and, what is more, I feel you are being extremely insolent." He paused. In spite of his efforts at self-control, he could hardly govern the shaking that crept into his voice whenever he was really angry. He took his hands from the table, for they too trembled, and thrust them down into his trouser pockets. The quality of the moment in pause showed him as never before wall maps, glass fronted cupboards bulging with out-dated texts, insects in bottles, two suitable landscapes. We have come to a cessation of amity, this place and I, he told himself. This is the point where we start inevitably to turn away from each other. It must be a quick turning.

"Not only will you do your detention, but you will report to Mr. Findlay at the end of this period and inform him of my intention and your disinclination."

Howard's face did not alter. If anything, it appeared more satisfied, as if his whole being sang towards this moment. He had had his public moment of bravura, and later, but not very much later, he would achieve his finishing stroke. He was not sure why he disliked Moller, only that he always had. Perhaps it was a sensing of adult patronage in his manner that worried Howard, who prided himself so on his poise. He had received public humiliation often enough over poor work, too, and the prick of deflated class esteem made him seize this moment for reprisal with a savage acuteness that would have been more understandable in an adult.

The final expression of Howard's malice spelt itself out in chalk letters at least two feet high across the bitumen road strip immediately in front of the school gate. This time the notice left no doubt at all as to the relationship between Moller and Helen Striebel. It was terse, crudely to the point.

It was there at sun-up, and Sid Ewers, driving past in his truck, braked and backed, the better to read it in the thin morning light. He laughed and stuck another fag in his mouth and forgot about it as he drove on. All round the sky limits the stratus clouds lay washed of colour, waiting for the trades to bank them up from the sea. The air was quivering like a water drop about to fall, its totals of suspense piled up into an unbearable charge of humidity and heat that threatened the town swimming in the late September weather.

Vinny, coming early along the road to the school to complete an algebra exercise from the text she had forgotten to take home, sensed it also, even at eight o'clock. The top of the mountain seemed to lean right over the town, its heavy flat blue summit humped dangerously above the forests that washed the town perimeter. Houses held a dream-stillness, dogs stretched vulnerable and panting under shop awnings and in doorway recesses. Along the railway siding a long line of box cars as neglected as tenements squatted unmoving where they had been since the previous night. The footpaths smacked back the shape of her steps into pads of sound that chased away from her down the shopping block past the still unwashed doorways and ramps; past the cough-mixture packets displayed pyramidal in the chemist's window, receiving on their orange and black wrappers the first benedictions of the flies. They were paling along their edges in the bleaching light that already had faded the draper's summer silks and cottons into uneven stripes.

The school buildings piled back up the slope. Vinny felt for them in this early approach, not a tenderness, but a rough sort of affection that was really only a mutation of her dislike. The sun banged like a gong on the tarred road as she started to walk across, and then, in spite of the heat, she drew up short.

Across the road where every child coming to school must see it stretched another sign. The sun motes suspended a dancing net of dust and light all round her, and she felt so hot and sick all at once she nearly fell. To get rid of the terrible words seemed an insuperable problem, for she had only the one tiny handkerchief. In any case it was so public a place that the attention her behaviour would attract would cause further comment. For a moment she hated Mrs. Striebel and Mr. Moller, both, for placing her in this torturing indecision. She still had her homework to complete. It was five past eight. She look away quickly from the words at her feet and ran up the embankment, across the footpath, and into the school grounds.

The whole place was cushioned in silence, padded by the flock of the stifling air. Even the school house lay mutely in the shelter of giant acalyphas and bougainvillea trellised along its northern side. Vinny stood nervously below the primary school stairs and fought her anger and her fear down to a resolution of purpose that made her seize a watering can from near the infant school gardening stand, fill it at one of the rear taps, and stagger off with it down to the road, unwilling, but unable to act otherwise. At first she rubbed hard with a wet handkerchief and after five minutes had managed to erase only three letters satisfactorily. Sweat sprang out like buds all over her white face and she felt giddy from bending in the one position in the hot sun. She straightened and took off her hat. The whole thing seemed so hopeless and she wanted to cry so badly that the prickling was already starting round her nostrils and eyes and the quivering about her mouth. On impulse she bent suddenly and emptied the can along as much of the notice as she could. But it was useless. She had nothing to rub it with and the water rapidly dried off, leaving the words fainter but still legible.

She forgot how conspicuous she must be, how odd her behaviour would appear to a passer-by, and turned in her vicious circle of resentment and unhappiness back towards the school. Her hat hung from one hand, the emptied can from the other, and her eyes, picking sullenly over the complexities of the rocky ground, did not see Mr. Findlay approach.

He found his early morning bonhomie oozing away in the heat, leaving a pebble of annoyance as an irritant in his mid-breakfasting-disturbed mind. His wife had made him look out of the window, had pestered him until he had left his tea cooling in the cup beneath a saucer placed on it to retain the steam, to see in the middle of the road one of his – Good God! Surely not – yes, that damned Lalor child working away with a bucket? He adjusted his glasses. Slipping into his dark vest, he hurried out to the veranda. Vinny had stopped rubbing at the roadway – what in Heaven's name was the girl doing? – and was slopping water up and down from the can. He shut his front gate carefully and went along the footpath towards her.

"Girl!" he said. "Vinny!"

She looked up. Her face was puffed from heat and the pale eyes under the orange hair glared out from the sweat-glow on her face. When she saw who was addressing her the truculence she felt crumpled like a paper fan, became fear, became herself in essence, the shape of unpopularity, the nothingness against the sheer huge importance of authority.

"Yes, sir," she said. There was not even humility left. The annihilation of her personality was complete.

"What are you doing?"

"Nothing."

"The usual answer – nothing. What is that watering-can for?" He felt very cross. His tea would be undrinkable. "Tell me," he ordered impatiently. "What were you doing with the can?"

Vinny did not answer, and the man stared over her shoulder at the blackness of the dampened area in the centre of the road. He strode past her quickly and read the notice. Still Vinny did not raise her head. The few seconds in which he read the crude libel chalked on the hot asphalt seemed to her to stretch over a slow world, to girdle lives and epochs and come back inevitably to this wretched fragment of time with herself wanting but unable to plunge into the springs of tears and with Findlay's voice, cautious and sobered, saying, "It wasn't you who wrote this, was it, and then thought better of the action?"

"No."

"Well now." He stopped, flummoxed, as his mind sifted the implications of the words before him. The milk truck rattled back late from its delivery on the west side of the town, circling wide around them. The driver waved carelessly, but Findlay did not look up. He did not know just where to proceed from here. To show concern would demonstrate plainly to the child the serious quality of the suspicions that were forming in his own mind. True, he had heard fragments of gossip lately, but he had discounted them as being the grievance-formed malice of children. There was a school committee meeting later in the week. Perhaps then a tactful reference or two would elicit any adult knowledge of the matter. Now he felt the main thing was to get the notice removed before morning school. He sighed. His last hope of a quiet cup of tea was gone.

"It was very thoughtful of you to try to get rid of this," he said. "Such things are scandalous and absurd. Absurd," he repeated, hoping his point was being taken. "I wonder if you could clean it out properly if I got you a cloth or a mop. Yes. A mop. You wouldn't mind, would you?"

"No, sir," she replied. "It is absurd, isn't it?"

He glanced at her sideways, curiously, but her face was quite expressionless, her voice toneless.

"Just wait here." He knew she had a peculiar reputation amongst the other pupils. "I won't be a moment."

He took his confusion with him back to the house, mumbling at the idea that had been presented so baldly, pondering the possible and the impossible results of its truth. He couldn't tolerate it, really he couldn't. Quite apart from his own moral point of view, the situation, if it existed, would be a dangerous one in a town like this. He had his own reputation and authority to uphold, even if he did not consider the repercussions on the pupils of such a clandestine relationship between two of his staff, for he could not allow himself to appear as tolerant or in connivance. You are taking it too seriously, he told himself, as he searched in the back lobby for the bucket and mop, pushing aside the ranks of rake, adze, and spade handles. Far too seriously. He could hear his wife, susceptible to the faintest adumbration of gossip, coming out through the kitchen. He intercepted her question with a brisk, "In a moment," and turned the back-door tap on full into the bucket, cutting off speech in the roar. His wife's round unoriginal face watched in a silence that could afford to wait. Ultimately, like a river to a sea, all town doings flowed to her to be filtered as it were by a mind long accustomed to picking over the driftwood of local misdemeanour. He rolled away from her into the hot morning to where Vinny waited by the roadside, receiving the stigmata of the sun in a burning flush upon the back of her neck and on her fair arms.

He panted as he set the bucket down and the water splashed and rocked dizzily against the iron sides. Their eyes met in a levelling of age and idea. Both of them felt it, but only the one tried to conceal it.

"It will only take a moment with the mop," he said. "Hurry."

She dipped it in the bucket and splashed it out again on the tar-bubbling road. He was right. Plenty of water and some hard rubbing at more obstinate marks and it was all gone in under five minutes. Even as they watched the water was drying fast, leaving only the blank, bland surface of the road, innocent as now neither of them could be.

"Thank you," he said. "That was a very kind action. But perhaps it would have been better if you had told me first." They both knew why she hadn't.

"Yes, sir," she said.

"Have there been any others?"

"Yes."

"What happened to them?"

"I rubbed them out."

"All of them?"

"Yes."

Findlay was lost for platitudes. He looked away. "One more thing," he said. Along the road he could see the first early comers to school dawdling in the heat. "Don't talk about this. If I find the child who did it he will be severely punished. Most severely."

"No, sir."

He emptied the last inch of water from the bucket and put the mop handle under his arm. It became part of him, fasciated with the portly limb that pressed it like a rifle. He felt he looked absurd, and that was something his position could not endure. Chauvinism, lack of humour, bigotry, lack of erudition, anything – but never absurdity.

"Run along now," he said.

The morning ate them up, made them a holocaust.

By the time the twelve-thirty bell jangled along the verandas Mr. Findlay, who had wrestled with moral surgings and curiosity all the morning, could contain his impulse to decision no longer. When he saw Mr. Sweeney striding past he asked him to tell Mr. Moller he would be grateful if he could come to the office for a moment. He sat back in his chair and swivelled it with that indescribable release of a decision achieved. He surveyed his room with an inner confidence, the stacked class rolls on the corner of his desk next to the dozens of memoranda chits spiked for reference, the score of well kept, hardly used encyclopaedias, dictionaries, and gazetteers along the wall, the jug of callistemon beside the phone. He was simple and fairly easy to please. He read digests and digests of digests and listened to the lighter programmes of the two national stations whenever static permitted. He worshipped within the Thirty-nine Articles (though for the life of him he couldn't have told you what they said), permitted himself an occasional sherry or beer, condemned gambling with a sonority that brought him notoriety if not respect, and played an insipid game of golf. Altogether he considered himself a pretty all-round sort of fellow.

He sucked at his pipe and doodled on his blotting pad with the red-ink pen. Circles interlocking with more circles were his favourite medium of expression, perhaps his only one, symbolizing as they did the round of each day's predictability, or each year's for that matter, circling about the annual inspection and the possibility of a higher promotion mark.

Moller's large head looked round the door. His face seemed unperturbed, and Findlay stared with a teased-up interest at the heavy dark eyes, the full lips, the greasy skin. No conventionally good-looking lover, he told himself, not here. And his gaze travelled over the thickening body, the careless posture under the worn clothes. But the face, he conceded all in this flashing minute as his eyes reverted to Moller's, the face was intelligent and kind and sensual – and he stopped on the word abruptly and with the puritan's envy and said, "Sit down, Mr. Moller."

He rose himself, agitated, now that the moment was on him and shut the door.

"This all seems very importantly mysterious," Moller said. "Mind if I smoke?"

"Go ahead."

"Thanks."

Findlay sat down heavily and watched while the other man rolled and lit a cigarette. His full lips held it as gently as a kiss.

"I'll come straight to the point, Mr. Moller," he said, swerving from the image. Moller looked at him quickly. He felt he knew what was coming. Anger leapt up, became self, demanding protest, but he forced himself to smile and to keep his nervous fingers still.

"This morning I found an extremely distasteful notice scrawled across the roadway just in front of the school. It concerned you and Mrs. Striebel."

Moller's heart jumped galvanically. He blew out a puff of smoke and tried to watch Findlay calmly.

"As a matter of fact I found one of the pupils busy trying to clean it out."

"Ah! And who was that?"

"The Lalor girl. She must like either you or Mrs. Striebel very much. Or both of you. I asked her if there had been any other similar signs, and apparently she has been busy rubbing them out for about a week."

"Oh God!" Moller said. "Poor little devil!"

"The point is this, Mr. Moller," Findlay said, and paused embarrassedly – but it was a slightly synthetic embarrassment. "The actual words of the message are unimportant, but the implication was that your friendship with Mrs. Striebel is of a – shall we say, non-platonic nature." He paused again.

Moller felt no impulse to reply. Wait now, he thought, for the complication of platitude to follow to entangle his argument.

"Now I am not attempting arbitrary judgments on your personal behaviour. Please understand that. I'm only speaking to you about the matter because I feel such an incident will give us bad tone. Yes. Bad tone." He repeated the words with a near-unction, happy to have lighted on them. "Allowing a thing like that to pass unnoticed would be appalling for discipline, not only yours or Mrs. Striebel's, but that of the whole staff generally, I feel, if the children are allowed to do that sort of thing and get away with it. Not that for one moment I believe there is any truth in the statement." He added this cunningly and took a sly half-glance under the grey eyebrows.

Moller knocked half an inch of ash from his cigarette carefully into the bakelite tray on the office desk.

"It is quite true," he said.

Findlay was not surprised by the truth of the words but by their having been uttered at all. The respectable side of him would have preferred outraged denials. Confronted with an honest reply he hardly knew what to say. At most, he felt, he could bow his head in acquiescence before such open profligacy.

"It is entirely your own affair, Mr. Moller," he said, "but you must agree that it is your duty to see that it remains so. After all, apart from any repercussions your behaviour may have upon you at the school, there is also – forgive my mentioning it – your wife to consider. It is possible that some ill-advised gossip in the town might inform her. Have you thought of that?"

"I have. I've thought of it almost constantly. You know my wife's condition, I think, Mr. Findlay, and I would like to say right here and now that I will not be cajoled either into defining or apologizing for my position. The situation exists. Further than that I will make no statement of any kind whatever." Moller could feel his anger taking control of him like a gale through a tree.

"Of course, of course. I am, I hope, a man of the world" – the flashed understanding smile and Moller wanted to scream with ironic laughter – "but you mustn't mind if I ask you to be a little more discreet. Surely you don't resent that?"

The pleading, Moller thought. He intends me to think I have him in the inferior position, when he knows and I know that as quickly as winking he could have me moved to the end of God's earth. Someone tapped diffidently on the office door, and Moller wondered if, after the person had gone unacknowledged, there would be a small sacrificial offering of corn and oil.

"Later!" Findlay called out. There was the sound of footsteps moving away along the veranda.

Their eyes met across the neat table, and the anger on Moller's face was duplicated on Findlay's, though the latter was trying to appear as unmoved as he could.

"What I cannot understand," he pursued, "is how the children got wind of the business, anyway."

"It's perfectly simple," Moller said. By telling Findlay he would put him out of his agony in somewhat the same way as one might shoot an injured horse. "Perfectly simple. Helen and I spent last week-end at Tin Can Bay and unfortunately the Welches also spent the week-end there. I suppose their girls heard the talk at home and couldn't resist the temptation to buy themselves a little temporary prestige at school."

Findlay twitched. Moller sounded flippant, and the whole thing, this simple contravention of accepted moral code, was so important, especially in this tiny town. He saw, and tried not to see, illicit week-ends shaping themselves round luxury hotels and flats and houses to rent, all coming in the end to that same well wanted, unbearable, mental verisimilitude of an unendurable act of love. He shook his head in an effort to rid himself of the image, and Moller watching him, smiled with sympathy for the first time, sensing the struggle in the man opposite, the battle between his respectable and his carnal impulses.

The edge of silence was serrated by sound as the first ten minutes of the lunch-hour ended and the quietness impelled by the need to eat gave way to the first shriekings and yellings from the primary school. It was hotter than ever, and in the narrow office both men edged uncomfortably on their chairs. Moller took a crumpled handkerchief from his trouser pocket and mopped it backwards and forwards across his forehead and round his neck under the curve of his chin. Findlay couldn't help noticing with fastidiousness that the linen rectangle came away soiled – only slightly, but there it was. On a sudden he resented Moller, resented and envied him his sexual success, although he did not envy him Mrs. Striebel in particular; only in some aching general way that this hot day was making aware he envied him, and resented with a jealousy that took him gaspingly by surprise the physical fallibility of the man, the stoutish body, the thinning hair, the sweating skin with its expanded pores. But again and again his mind alluded to the humour and the intelligence and the sensuality of the face. The confrontation made him shudder in his angry desire.

"Well, we shall just have to be on our guard," he said. "Yes. On our guard." There they come, thick as plums in a pudding, Moller thought. "And if you encounter anything more of the sort, Mr. Moller, I want you to inform me immediately. I shall make a few discreet inquiries among the senior boys, and if I discover who was responsible I shall punish him very severely."

Moller protested mildly enough, "I think that is wrong policy, Mr. Findlay. I think the best thing would be to ignore it. That way the whole business will probably die a natural death in a few days."

Findlay was scandalized to find himself wondering if that were what he really wanted, if his method of dealing with the situation were only a contrivance to prolong it. He hated being opposed and he shut his ears to the obvious sense of Moller's suggestion.

"There is only one sure way the whole thing could die a natural death, Mr. Moller," he said, and his words traced out a cold anger. "By transferring one of you. Let me deal with this my own way, and the other alternative need not be necessary."

"Very well." Moller unaccountably felt bored. He was being pigeon-holed as a problem, his moral competence was on probation.

"If you'll excuse me," he said, "I'm on duty second half, and I haven't had any lunch." He stood up and stubbed the butt of his cigarette so viciously the paper burst and the tobacco splayed out. Findlay, noticing the tension implicit in the action, felt himself moving towards an inevitable decision. There was a school committee meeting in three days' time. He would mention the matter – cautiously, you know – to one or two of the more responsible members, get an opinion. He followed Moller out of the door and, going down the school's front steps, crossed the yard to his home. Annoyance and heat shimmered everywhere and, refracted on the lenses of his glasses, made him stumble blindly.

It was like cornering a rabbit.

Surrounding her, pressing her in against the far corner fence made her seem smaller and whiter and more unpleasant than ever. Howard and his pal, Tangle Davis, drew Pearl Warburton and Betty Klee forward until the four of them held her trapped in a tiny sector of bush-screened shade. So far she had not answered them, but the first terror which had made her speechless was dwindling away now to nothing, to absolutely nothing, and obstinacy hardened her mouth and her pale eyes.

"Come on," Howard repeated, "come on, Lalor. We know you did it. Bert Springer saw you when he was coming in on the run. His kid Joey told me it was you who did it."

The girls watching her stirred in anger. They almost begrudged her this sudden attention. Pearl Warburton leant against Tangle's skinny side. He looked at her and giggled with nervous pleasure and, concealed from the others, she caught his arm and squeezed it with the tips of her fingers. Vinny's glance flickering across the shaken shadow-doubles of the leaves caught the movement of amorous finger-play. Suddenly, vividly she saw again the pool and the bathers and the figure on the diving rock. She had never really been free of the image, for it had come to her whenever she saw Pearl Warburton or Royce. But it always seemed too horrible to be true, smudged in outline even by the passage of a week; yet now the exploring, interpreting fingers proved the image once more and she shuddered involuntarily.

Howard was becoming tired of her stubborn silence. He snapped his fingers hard under her nose and flicked her with them.

"Come on. Tell us!" he said.

Vinny's hand flashed up before she could prevent it and smacked Howard's arm so sharply it hurt her. He drew back, his face crimson with rage.

"Why, you bitch!" he said. "You ugly little bitch!"

"Yes!" Vinny shouted. "Yes, I did it. And it wasn't the

only one I washed off either. I cleaned off all of them. All last week. And every time you write more up, I'll clean them off, too."

She felt crazed with her own defiance. The four faces watching her melted and shifted their outlines. The air was aqueous with light in which leaves swam like seaweed. She hoped she wasn't going to faint.

"She's mad!" Betty Klee said, and giggled. "I always thought she was. Her mother's crazy as a galah."

Vinny did not even hear her. The heat was making her giddy and the tension that had built up inside her until it snapped in uncaring passion had been too great for her to endure.

"And what's more," she added, "what's more, Howard, the next time I see one of your lousy little notices I'll go straight to Mr. Findlay. Do you hear? I'll tell him it's you. I'll tell him it's the four of you."

Pearl's fingers dropped from Tangle Davis's unmuscular arm.

"You wouldn't dare," she said. "We'd make it too awful for you. You wouldn't dare."

"Yes, I would. And there's a few other things I could tell him, too."

"What are they?"

Vinny smiled ferociously. She gripped her belt with her hands and glared across the yard at the distant school. She could see Mr. Moller ambling behind the primary block getting children to gather papers and lunch bags and fruit skins to put in the big green bins. She felt her loyalty to him flare up into the ardour of a crusader. She watched his kindly, lazy body and knew the insanity of personal sacrifice sweeping through her, aggravated by the sudden appearance of Mrs. Striebel and Miss Jarman along the senior veranda. She smiled maddeningly.

"What other things?" Pearl persisted.

"Ah, leave her." Betty Klee dragged at Pearl's left arm. "She doesn't know anything. She's kidding."

Pearl shook off the acolyte hand angrily. There was something in Vinny's face that made her aware of more than bluff, that warned her, usually so insensitive to atmosphere, that there was something far more dangerous than chalked-up libels.

"I'm not kidding." Vinny marvelled at her own effrontery. She looked from one to the other of the four faces, from the oval to the square to the round to the pointed, through meanness and sensuality and flaccid ugliness and good looks, and felt that she had come a long way to find her revenge in this moment.

She looked away then past them and saw the bell prefect hurrying along the veranda to ring the first warning of the end of the lunch hour. She watched him, watched his hand hurl into the air an iron chatter, a monotone clanking of liberation. All over the playground the noisy groups were stilled, ropes and balls caught as it were in mid-flight, the voices struck dumb. Mr. Findlay, magnificently the autocrat, walked along to the stair-head where he conducted assembly with the solemnity of a priest.

"I'll tell him about the swimming hole," Vinny said. Her voice sounded over-loud in this shell of silence. She glimpsed sideways Pearl's plump face, Howard's startled eyes. The sky over the town was filling up with tassels of quick-growing cloud, sud-white and wind-plumped.

"What'll you tell?" Pearl had to hurry with her questioning. The second bell would in a matter of seconds.

"The boys," Vinny whispered, "the boys."

"You'll have to think of your brother's feelings," Pearl replied viciously. Knowing it was useless to pretend unawareness, she tossed caution aside like a rag. Vinny glared into the round face with its full wet mouth and glimpsed her again with curving breast and thigh above the pool.

"You're filthy," she said. "Filthy. And I don't care about anyone's feelings. Not any more."

The second bell rang, a dispassionate arbiter, and

quite automatically the five of them started down towards the assembly lines.

"Mind yourself, Lalor," Howard said, and "See you after school, Pearl." With Davis he loped off towards the boys' end of the senior ranks. Pearl permitted Betty Klee to link her plump arm with hers. She was puzzled. The butt of the class, the butt for so long she could remember no other time or attitude, had suddenly spun a trump before her unbelieving eyes, revealing a situation which she was unsure how to handle. Her excursions to the pool were important to her, not for their sensual reward so much as for the confirmation of her power, the proof that her body could focus and control the desires of men. For a girl of fifteen she was astonishingly old in erotics; and yet she managed to keep her behaviour secret from her parents, who doted on their only child as a consummation not merely of the flesh but of the spirit also. Although she had outgrown the habit of loving them, she was careful not to let them know, because life was so comfortable with their lavished material affection. And for the same reason, the fear that her comfort might be disrupted, she would hate them to learn about her summer outings.

She tugged at Betty Klee and drew her back as Vinny Lalor ran past them down the slope. The bright hair burning, it seemed, with missionary fire, the pallid limbs uncurved even this spring, were lost in the jerking, foot-edging, arm-extending horde of pupils.

"Don't worry, Pearlie." The diminutive was the emotional additive for reassurance. "Don't worry. She doesn't know a thing. Royce must have let something slip, but you know perfectly well he wouldn't tell her. You know he thinks she's a dope. He's always saying so."

Pearl smiled. Sometimes she wished she didn't feel so old. She wanted to shake her fat apostle into an adult apostasy.

"I'll fix her," she said as she slipped into her place in the squad. "I'll think of something."

Seven

"We have been thrown to the Christians," Moller said to Helen.

He took her elbow as they left the school, and pressed it as he helped her down the earth shelf to the road. "I didn't want to talk about it at lunch-time with Rowan and Jarman practically on our laps, but Findlay called me into the office this morning and told me an odd story."

Helen waved to Szamos as they passed the milk-bar. "The Welches," she said. "Oh, Robert, have they told Findlay? We must be costing them a fortune in sherry and biscuits!"

"I don't think so yet, but it certainly will come from that source when they next meet. No. This is allied, but concerning the kids. This morning the old boy spotted Vinny Lalor washing off a big chalk notice on the road in front of the school. He didn't go into detail, my dear, but apparently it was flattering both to my virility and your attractiveness. Poor old boy! He had his departmental face on. All respectable and promotion conscious and keen."

"How can you – no, you're right to be flippant, really. It's too absurd. Bless Marian and Sam. They must have discussed us in front of their two revolting girls. Oh, Robert, what do we do? Now everyone knows or will within the week."

"Nothing. Nothing but carry on as usual." He laughed. "No vulgarity intended. The only thing I hope," he added seriously, "is that Lilian doesn't get to hear. Oh God, I wouldn't want to hurt her. Mind you, Helen, she's well aware that she'll never be out of that hospital cured, and I feel her reason would excuse us."

"And if it doesn't?"

He shrugged. "Wait. The rest of the town will be waiting. We can wait with them."

They walked in silence to the railway yard. Porter McKeith, lounging spread-legged upon an outside bench, fag-rolling in the syrupy afternoon light, nodded at them and grinned, and tongued the edge of the cigarette paper delicately. Two dogs raised their legs upon the far side of a luggage trolley; the milk-cans squatted in silver back towards the entrance gates.

"Here," Moller said – he indicated with hyperbolic gesture the whole circle of the town, the stillness, the scattered shoppers, the pubs with their out-spillings of early evening drunks, the dogs, the lean grasses – "here is the hub of our worry, our punctured self-pride. Why, the nasty, stinking little mullock heap wouldn't even be marked in a Commonwealth atlas, and yet here we are worried sick because we have affronted the guardians of the town. It is ridiculous, utterly ridiculous."

"You can only be important in the area where you move, I suppose," Helen suggested. "Other people's reactions to unconventional behaviour seem to vary in inverse ratio to the size of the environs."

"My little mathematician!" Moller laughed. "You're so right. And it's so wrong that it should be like this. I suppose it's because there is much less distraction, especially of an immoral kind, in places as small. The merest peccadillo –" He spread his hands hopelessly. "I have visions, Helen, of the porridge-pale faces of outraged parents bent reverently over Bibles open at Leviticus and the Song of Songs." He pressed his hands together in the attitude of prayer. Then he said, "Can you see me this evening? We might go for a drive. If necessary I'll carry the car a mile out of town so Lunbecks won't hear me start her up."

Helen hesitated. "Do you think it's wise at this particular time? Did Finlay make any criticism?"

"He did ask for a little more discretion. He's worried about the effect this might have on discipline."

"That's a point certainly."

"Agreed. But I feel he was overstepping the mark when he hinted at a transfer for one of us."

The smile breaking at the corner of Helen's lips and eyes was arrested and twisted into a temporary pain that vanished.

"He wouldn't be so absurd! Punish us like pupils!"

"My dear, it's not absurd really, from his point of view. What is he? Forty-four. Still pretty young in this game. He has a son at an expensive boarding school. He wants to get on. He can't afford to have scandal's hot breath blistering his well laid plans. I know it's absurd looking at it from our side of the situation, but when I look at it from his, I could almost predict to the moment and place just when and where he will act."

"And –"

"First, he'll mull the whole situation over. Has done by now. And then tonight, under a text above their bed reading 'God is love' and another on the dressing-table reading 'Blessed are the pure in heart', he'll talk it over with his wife in their cretonne-cosy bedroom. She'll be the first vote against us. Then he'll take it along – not officially, mark you, but he'll take it along all the same – to the school committee on Thursday night and he'll mull it over with a couple of the boys; and they'll have been worked on by *their* wives and that will be a whole lot of votes against us. So you see, I wouldn't be at all surprised if perhaps he does do something about that threat, and one of us gets a take-off ticket."

Porter McKeith swayed to his feet and rolled away to the signal-room with the half-smoked cigarette saliva-stuck to his lower lip. The afternoon rail-motor north to Gympie was just rounding the southern bend, bucketing along the channel through the scrub.

"It would hardly be you," Helen said. "You have a house here."

"Only rented. There's no bargaining point behind that when you're dealing with clerks in the public service."

"Perhaps both of us will go. A catharsis for Gungee."

"Perhaps. It will hardly matter, will it, once we're parted anyway?"

Helen half turned to leave him and walk down the road beside the lines. She swung round again upon a sudden thought.

"That poor Lalor child! I wonder what made her do it. It's very moving – for want of a better word. I suppose it was gratitude for the week-end, among other things."

Moller grunted. "I gave you the reason once before and you didn't like it. We all have to have a cause – something to worship or work for. And on that trite note I'll leave you until this evening. Please come. About seven. Earlier if you can make it. Come round on the back road and you might dodge the Lunbecks. Or better still, Helen, I'll run the car down towards the pub and you can get in at the corner past the paper shop."

He caught her hand and pressed it very tightly in his own. "You know I'd like very much to kiss you now. Compromise you *con expressione, con moto.*"

Her back was to the sun, her face in shadow, but Moller's burned in the late extravagance of light coming from the western sky. She squeezed his hand in return and briefly placed her other hand over his. "McKeith is watching us fascinated through the signal-room window," she said, and turned finally from him.

She was late coming to the dining-room that night, having spent more time than usual exploring the possibilities of dress, examining her face with a new consciousness that comes to the lover and the loved. Her dress was dark and soft and clasped her body in shadow that strengthened the effect of light upon her hair. It was a study in chiaroscuro. The Talbots glanced swiftly at her as she sat down at the table and she was well aware of their curiosity, their aroused criticism of her appearance. She smiled Gioconda-fashion between the sauce cruets, older for the moment than both the Talbots seated there in the anticipatory stew of indignation – she felt certain they knew about her week-end at the Bay – their juices longing to flow in outrage.

"Something special tonight?" Jess asked. It was an impossibility for her to pay the direct compliment to another's looks. Always the praise was tempered by just that little piece of unkindness calculated to destroy the effect of any pleasure the receiver might have obtained. ("She has a beautiful body," she would say of Ruth Lunbeck. "Really beautiful. What a pity her feet are so ugly!" Or, "Freda Rankin really can look pretty sometimes.")

It was a special skill, Helen told herself. You either had it or you hadn't. She was sure that as a team the Talbots practised their verbal viciousness together. Prick. Prick. Alec Talbot had told her once that Jess and he often corrected each other's speech; it was a game they played, like quoits or darts or skittles, seeing who could detect the greater number of solecisms. How close they must be to each other! Helen shuddered at the thought of this marriage of true minds that admitted no speech impediments.

"No. Not really. Just a morale booster."

Talbot sniffed into his roast beef, quivered above the tissues of cold meat covered with lukewarm gravy, over the unhappy vegetable farrago. Furtively, while he munched, he watched Helen's bosom, or her lips or her hands, but watched without real lasciviousness, merely the curiosity of the welfare worker for the underprivileged, with an almost evangelical interest. Helen perceived his shifting glances and permitted herself an inward smile, thinking how he would, if he could, present her with a tract. His wife viewed both of them coldly, displeased by Alec's behaviour and with jealousy rumbling at the back of her mind in a faint thunder of inference. She always stated, to those of her friends unluckily close enough to be recipients of the intimacy, that she could not bear to think her husband had been anything but virgin when she married him. However, remembering Ruth Lunbeck's amused assertion that Harold had stepped practically from his prefect's study into their hymeneal flatette, and watching Alec now, she was not so sure. She ate her woody potatoes very deliberately, cut them into slabs and small blocks, and pushed them into her prissily chewing mouth.

Since the previous week-end, when the Welches had discovered for them the scandalous relationship between Mr. Moller and Mrs. Striebel, the Talbots found conversation at meal-times more awkward and more restraining than they could have foreseen. Jess was longing to elicit succulent details that would place her conversational value at a premium, but she hardly liked to make direct investigation. At first she had used Mr. Farrelly's agitation over the trunk calls as an excuse for broaching the inexcusable, but all her inquiries, polite or not, met with nothing but a brief explanation that her sister had been involved in a car accident, and was not seriously hurt beyond a fracture of the left arm. All other probings, veiled with the thinnest good manners to prevent her rudeness being charged with indecent exposure, could gain nothing more than, "Yes, a very pleasant two days away." If it had been one of her old school hockey team deliberately bouncing her questions, Jess would have punished her with demotion or detention from sport. Her bust swelled with annoyance as she drew an impatient breath – she would like to suck the two of them in with it, bathed in a faint halitosis that seemed a normal adjunct to such self-consciously militant Christianity.

"Black is always effective," she said, staring hard at Helen's all-black dress, "especially with a touch of white. I think I must wear something similar to our special 'do' next week."

"Please, Jess, not 'do'. Function. Function." Alec Talbot spoke in a kind of anguish.

"Yes," Jess Talbot continued, ignoring him for once because she was punishing him in their own special way. "Yes, Mrs. Striebel, Sam Welch is giving the factory's annual staff dinner on Friday week. This year he has invited the entire staff, engineers, senior office workers and their wives, typists and their husbands, as well as the boiler hands and packers and drivers. We can't help feeling a wee bit worried as to how it will go. A most uncomfortable affair, I should imagine."

"It might be good for laughs," Helen said, with the first touch of real viciousness she had ever displayed towards them.

"Ohhh." Jess paused. "You think we're snobbish?" she asked coldly.

"I do indeed."

"Not at all. I merely think the evening will be a failure with people of such dissimilar education forced upon each other for hours at a time."

"Nonsense," Helen said briskly. She poured herself another glass of water and drank it with at-ease heartiness. "It will do you good. Why keep your tight little university minds in a tight, sacred little university circle? And it isn't as if the senior business staff were university men," she continued recklessly. "You're just making position and money your arbitrating factor there. Personally, I'd rather talk to boiler-hand Perce Westerman and his wife than to Marian Welch any day. Both of them have far more sensible things to say, and if the way they say it isn't contorted with elocutionary garble, who cares?"

Jess was quite white. Her narrow face, furrowed in annoyance, bent forward across the stained cloth and the untidy dinner plates, zealot-keen.

"We care," she said. "Alec and I care for a few of the refinements of life. And careful speech is one of them. You're being terribly unkind about Marian Welch."

"You care for it," Helen said slowly and carefully, "the way chorus girls care about furs. It's a new form of pretentiousness that can hide all sorts of mental bankruptcy. The bray. And as for being unkind about Marian, I would love to know, but cannot conceive, how that is possible. Tell me. How?"

Alec Talbot looked up anxiously into the puffed-powdered-strawberry-sweet face of Allie.

"Two baked custards," he said, he begged. "We've had this out on speech before, haven't we?" he urged them to agree. Placatory gestures were not normally his method, felt apologies were a weakness of character, but he was afraid that at any moment the conversation might swing into a dangerous wood, storm over and under the flying boughs of personal abuse. He only like being rude in whispers or a softly modulated voice. Helen Striebel might shout dangerously and openly.

Helen finished her first course and set the plate to one side. Guided divinely, she rested both elbows on the table and propped her chin on her laced hands. Head supported thus, she gazed down upon them, the very insolence of her calculatedly ill-mannered posture making her relaxed; upon the scaled peak of their enmity looking down into their unhappy faces.

Jess Talbot found only one thing to say.

"You have reason to be unkind, haven't you?"

Helen heard the spoons and plates beaten like tympani by the unsatisfied diners. At the table behind her a quartet of male voices whinnied through last Saturday's losses from start to finish, and the owners gobbled as if they were chaff-bags the uneyed meals in front of them. Heard it all; and saw, in the snipping flash of clear vision that showed her just what the other woman was implying.

"No reason," she replied. "No reason at all. What would make you imagine that I should have?"

"Well, she is rather a gossip, isn't she?"

"Is she?"

"Why, of course. You of all people should know."

"I'm afraid that I don't." (Why wouldn't she state her accusation boldly, come uncleanly clean?) "And I'm sorry for your sake. You seem so terrible anxious that I should be feeling uncomfortable or guilty or anxious. I feel none of those things. Ah! The pudding."

Helen smiled into Allie's face coated like the pudding itself with a seductive cosmetic meringue, iced into the accepted mask of red and pink and black and white. Jess Talbot frowned down at her empty tea cup and then looked across to her husband's rabbit-like face. There was a strange expression on his features, a compound of fear and enjoyment. He really should have been a woman.

Helen felt as if she were poised, leaning forward into unfrightening darknesses, poised about to fly with no bravado at all into clearness; and the utter escape feeling made her see beyond the Talbots to the road and the car and the humped male figure cigarette-illumined in spurts. The Talbots finished their meal with lip dabbings and napkin foldings of technical precision, and left the table. But she did not hear or see. Rather she sensed them gone, and soon so would she be, the cup banging in the saucer, the scraping of the chair, the nod of thanks to Allie half seen in the kitchen, and then up the oilily lighted hall and down first to room to bathroom, back and down and out into the darkness, real, really and truly as they said when they were children and not for ever but capture the moment while you can, crunching on the dry road towards the car.

It crouched in the shadow-jungle of the corner house's crowded mango-trees. Helen's heart beat stupidly fast as she neared it, opened the door, and fell in against body, thigh and mouth. It was endless and ended and he put her gently back, starting the car without trouble for once and smiling, pleased, as the lights raced along the road.

"Where to?" she asked.

"Right out," he replied. "Right out of this town where no vultures rest. How about going down to the coast?"

She nodded and lit herself a cigarette.

"It seems no time since last week-end, does it?"

"No. But, my God, a lot seems to have happened since then."

"The pressure's on," she said. "Jess Talbot hinted at dinner tonight that the scandal has reached her sensitive ears."

"It would be surprising if it hadn't, wouldn't it?"

Off the main southern road the landscape was deep as a well. The car dived into its black bowl and sliced darkness open with yellow light. Along the eastern sky a kind of reflected pallor from the west lay close above the tops of the trees, washing upwards and out into the stippling grey-blue-indigo-black of the sky basin. Road glimmer before and behind took them as unerringly as migratory birds towards the salt-smelling under-moon washing sea. It was only ten miles away due east and Moller drove fast, ripping the black night air carelessly, letting it stream back against the sides of the car like rag.

When they came down to the river and the first lights, the narrowness of the road was a symbolic narrowness they both felt, with situations falling away to one side and sheering up upon the other. It was good that the fever of indecision was over, and it was good that they were committed to each other this night in car and under moon rising suddenly and late and full. But behind this surface confidence was a repressed fear of consequences of the act, of the ultimate feelings each would take away from the relationship if it ended.

The lights sugar-sprinkled the darkness to their left which was north, where the guest-houses and flats to let, untenanted, unlet, squatted along the river-front in out-of-season mourning, longing for the brown girls and the life of the party and the tonsures tomato-toasted and the immodest satin swimming trunks and the honeymooning couples connubially joined for a fortnight by mutual suffering – the sandfly-bitten, red-baked-crackling skin. Under the moonlight the boats showed upon the wide reaches of silver-paper water like pencil strokes, fringing the mournful lines of the jetties where the fishermen sat, blobs of optimism against heaven.

"Shall we go on to the bay?" Moller asked.

"If you like. It's not far, is it?"

"Only another five miles."

He swung the car over the bridge that spanned the narrow stretch of water between lake and river, and they went on again, following the water made magical by bonily outlined tree and casual cottage and the mangrove fingers, sly-sinister with moonshine and shadow, trailing the water. Weyba Creek stabbed the country whitely, and after that was passed the car ran quickly down the last mile to the bay.

Moller parked the car as close to the sand margin as he dared. The last house before the river-mouth curved the beach into a lip stood a hundred yards away. It was so still they could hear the fish rising in the gutters along the river bank. All around, scrub box crowded the moon. He kept remembering the seats under trees facing Moreton Bay and the fish dinners and the love-making of more than twenty years before, and to himself he seemed not the same person at all. Between dances at the great hall, that wasn't really great but the moderns lecture-room, he had stepped into so many arms and eyes and soft meaningless loves that held all the glamour of being young and walking the partner round the kidney-shaped grass plot and between the science schools and the common-rooms. And now, here he was, hundreds of grey hairs later, yearning like a boy on the shores of a nondescript coastal town and turning to the woman beside him as if he would find there the end of the world.

The moon was wrecked on a cloud-bank when they took the car back up the hill and Helen said quite suddenly, "I have a feeling that something is building up for us – we're not safe any more." She was surprised that she did not feel like crying.

"What do you mean? You're frightened of Findlay?"

"Yes, Robert. Yes, I am. I feel he'll break this apart without a care. How could I ever hope to keep anything made of happiness when all my adult life I've failed?"

"You're merely being feminine and nervous. And even if the worst did happen – and please, Helen, please don't imagine I don't care when I speak so casually, I'm merely being as realistic as I know you are at heart – would it ultimately be more than either of us could bear? I always remember back in my student days – it was my final year, and I had a bad case of infatuation for a girl a year behind me. I had a small sports car in those days that made my morals suspect through the whole faculty, and sometimes we used to skip lectures and drive out along the river somewhere, I suppose, where the new university is today. The roads were practically not, and we walked a good deal once we had settled the car safely, and we always seemed to end up in the same little hollow by the water. We went up at week-ends, too, on Sundays in the milder parts of summer, and after a while this particular spot became quite littered with our luncheon wrappers and sheets of the newspapers we took with us. I imagine it was fairly slummy, but we were in love and didn't notice – too busy necking. Anyway, the whole thing fell through. Student romances nearly always do. I went out of town on appointment and she stayed to finish her course."

"How's all this relevant?"

"Wait a moment. We met about six months later. I was back in town during the August vac, and I ran into her quite by accident. Just for old times' sake, and because I'd got over the worst pain of being wiped off, we went out again to the same spot. I insisted. I think, perhaps, I had ideas of trying to patch things up. But here's the rub, Helen. We got there and all the old magic was gone.

Completely. The newspapers we'd left on our last visit half a year before were still there, weathered and dirty from rain. And all I felt, looking down at a place I thought I'd never want to see again because of the pain it held for me, was nothing but a mild aversion. It looked bedraggled, unromantic, and just the smallest bit cheap."

"Did you stay?"

"Only a few minutes – half an hour maybe. And, funnily enough, it was she who wanted to be kissed, to be wanted. But it was utterly impossible. We talked for a while and then left. I never saw her again."

Helen wondered if this were a forecasting for their own affection. She looked at his blunt profile, perplexed, afraid to speak.

"I know what you're thinking," he said, as they entered the township and rattled along the dark streets. "Wait, Helen, and I'll answer you. Wait until I find a place for coffee in this seething town."

He drove slowly along the main shopping block, and on a corner shelved in with dead shadow they found a milk-bar still open, where the ranked eating booths promised a hot meal of some kind. They slipped into one of the green painted pews and faced each other solemnly across the stained table. Moller held the deep-pink menu like a hymn card and read the items for the evening service with a lugubrious expression. They settled for fried eggs with the sullen, the grudging permission of an eighteen-year-old youth. He slouched to the hot range in the window of the shop, slapped grease on it with a spatula, and waited for it to heat up. Then he chopped lettuce laconically and scattered it on two plates with wafer thin circles of tomato. He did not look at his customers again and, while the eggs sizzled in the fat, stared sulkily across a street house-high in girls.

"You're thinking," Moller pursued as they huddled in the privacy of their corners, "you're thinking that already I'm tiring."

"No." Helen smiled. "No. But I think you're trying to prepare me for such an event."

Moller smiled in return with a sweetness quite unbelievable and pressed the fingers of each hand round her wrists. "You fool," he whispered. "You are the only thing I want. But let's not be so immature we enter upon a thing like this, swearing, repeat swearing, blindly, for ever and ever. It is presumptuous even to hope for that, I feel. Helen, we're both adult enough to know that nothing ever stays exactly the same. Something of what we start out with must be lost. But that doesn't mean for a moment that we want it to happen. We just know it probably will sooner or later."

"Sooner, I feel," Helen said pessimistically. This is the second thing, she thought, that he has proved mortal or fallible. Firstly he convinced me of the necessary animality of the affair and now of its transitoriness. Is he disproving the worth of it all for me consciously? She found his next remark discordant with her mood.

"Not till after the school dance," he said with a grin. "Findlay couldn't bear to lose any of his sweated labour until that's over."

"I shan't mention it again. A promise."

Helen watched their plates of eggs being carried from the counter. They were set down in a rough design with cups and saucers and not even an interested glance from the youth who rolled back again behind the till and picked up his sex-magazine and was lost in a limb-wallow. They ate hungrily and drank the stewed black coffee. Helen frowned now and then and pulled her bread to pieces, crumbling it over the plate.

"Still worrying?" Moller asked.

"Not about us. It's young Vinny Lalor. It's absurd, I suppose, but I keep hoping the other kids don't find out she was cleaning off the notices. They'll give her a shocking time."

"She's used to it."

"That's no justification. I imagine they'll think up something really juicy for this. Why does she have to involve herself in our troubles?"

"It's a shame," Moller said, "but it just happened that way. If you hadn't given her that week-end in Brisbane, perhaps her frightening acolyte spirit wouldn't have received the final fillip that made her do what she did."

"Do you think so?" Helen asked. "Oh God! I hope not. I'd feel really guilty in that case."

"This is all nonsense, Helen. You're exaggerating the whole thing. You did the child a kindness. Whether or not you happened to stimulate the crush she already had on you is beside the point, for you had no direct intention of doing so. You can't possibly blame yourself if the kids give her a bit of curry for a few days. It will all blow over in a week as far as she's concerned. So for Heaven's sake cut out this crazy self-accusation. *We're* the ones in the jam – a far greater mess than she'll ever be in, and it doesn't look as if our threatened punishment will have blown over in a week. So please. *Lenta ira deorum*. But it will come, don't worry."

Newspapers rattled past the café doorway in the salted wind off the river. Distantly a dog yelped its nervousness to the floating moon. The kid at the counter coughed phlegmily and turned the pages of his dreams and scratched one cheek absent-mindedly.

We look back, Helen thought, and there we are feeding the swans in the park; or travelling between this town and that, all night, standing in the corridor outside the lavatories because all the seats are taken, and talking, joking most of the way; or at our first dance with the pimply young Jew picking over the sandwiches to avoid the ham; or rolling on the lawn and the pants showing pink, over and over and over. Each moment framed like a picture and distant as a gallery. This particular moment would be added, she knew, and wondered why those times of intense emotional involvement were more shadowy than those of less. I stood off, she thought. I watched myself enjoying the externals, I had not given myself completely.

"It's fun, isn't it?" he said. "Isn't it?"

"Yes." Helen smiled into his face, his begging face. "Yes. The smallest things with someone you love are fun."

"You can stand the inexpensive setting?"

"Please," she said. "That doubting offends me."

"I'm catching that disease you had at the Bay. Hoping that the tizzy *dêcor* won't catch us out. Not for my sake, you understand. I'm worried for you."

"I'm getting better," she said. "Soon I'll be too involved to notice externals."

They edged out of their seats and Moller put the exact change on the check, placing it gently on the counter beside the lounging figure. It merely grunted as they left, ringing in their meal price on the cash register as automatically as a man might make the sign of the cross. Thus blessed they passed into the night-deep street and climbed back into the car.

Moller kissed Helen quickly before he started up the engine.

"Endings," he said. "We're always coming to endings. I feel a bit of your gloom. Don't deny that you are feeling gloomy." He stared out across the black and silver river, into the softness that pushed back the efforts of sight, the softness that was as hard as a wall, impenetrable beyond the few yards that didn't matter. And then inexorably let in the clutch.

He drove fast once out of town and easily up the first slopes. They were both utterly unprepared for the sudden lurch as the car banged into a pot-hole, and the dreadful crunching sound under the back wheels. The car seemed to scrabble uselessly on the roadside shingle and, finally out of control, pitched their terror forward in a long skid to the far embankment that butted the machine viciously and half turned it over. Helen, tumbled against the door, felt Moller's body crushing heavily on her own, and just momentarily she cried out in fear and pain as her arm was jammed agonizingly against the handle. Too stunned to move, they lay clumsily together in the boxed-up space, but after a while Moller pulled himself upwards and managed to jerk open the door. He struggled out and then reached back to seize Helen's arm and pull her after him. They stumbled and almost fell as she tipped through the swinging door into his arms.

"You're all right, aren't you?" he asked quickly. In the moonlight her face was bluish-white. She nodded and rubbed her head against his arm suddenly like a child.

"Sure?"

"Yes. I bumped my arm a bit, but it's nothing."

"Show me."

He turned her slim arm over. It was scratched and blood-scribbled.

"It was the door handle. There's something sharp on the under edge."

He tied his handkerchief round it carefully. "Be brave," he said, "till I see what's up with this ruddy car. I think there's a torch in the far pocket if I can reach it."

He plunged head first into the car again and she could see him threshing the black air like a swimmer. In a moment he wriggled out and by torchlight looked once more at her frightened face. She smiled with an effort to reassure him and he kissed her gently on the forehead.

"You and your premonitions," he said. "Thank God you're O.K. I'll just have a look at the car and see if there's anything I can do. She might only need righting."

Before he even squatted, and as he shone the torch on the rear of the car, he saw what was the trouble.

"Oh jesusgodanddamn!" he groaned. "The bloody back wheel's off and the hub's all twisted. God almighty, what a bastard of a thing to happen!"

"Just as well we're only a mile out of town. It won't take more than twenty minutes to walk back."

"Oh God, Helen! It doesn't matter whether we walk back or go on the rest of the fifteen miles to Gungee. No one's going to fix this damn' thing tonight. It's put paid to getting the car back before tomorrow. C'mon. We might as well walk back to the town and see if there's any transport into Cooroy tonight. You never know. There might be a stray C.T. on the move."

He took Helen's unhurt arm and shining the torch ahead, they trudged downhill towards the river again. The township's lights teased them for twelve minutes before they finally came into the main street.

"Let's have a word with that kid at the café", Moller suggested. "He didn't look a very likely specimen, but he might know a thing or two about the exits."

The long room with its green booths was still empty except for the boy, and entering it, seeing again the shelves stacked with cigarettes and sweets, recognizing the mirror oblongs stamped above each table, the soft drink advertisements sycophantic on the far wall, Helen felt the despair that overtakes the person trying to escape who finds himself involuntarily returned to the same place.

The youth behind the cash register was still reading, but when he heard them come in he looked up from his book, marking the place with a finger, and yawned straight at them.

"Our car's broken down," Moller explained, "about a mile up the road. Can you tell me where the nearest garage is or if I could knock the owner up?"

The boy stared at Moller coldly and then picked at a molar with exaggerated interest.

"You wouldn't get no one on to it at this hour," he said, tossing the words round his probing finger.

"No. I realize that. I was just hoping I might be able to get a lift if anyone's going through to Cooroy tonight, or hire a car."

"Well, Bert Simmons is the nearest. He's just down the road a coupla blocks on the far side. Lives at the back."

"Think he'd have a car for hire?"

"Maybe."

"Failing that," Moller said, "failing that, there wouldn't be a bus, I suppose?"

"First bus in the morning."

"What time?"

The youth yawned again. Even his breath had the stale scent of boredom.

"'Bout eight-thirty. It catches the nine o'clock train up to Gympie."

"Oh God!" Moller said, turning to Helen. "We're trapped. That wouldn't reach Gungee till well after half past nine." He glared back at the humped shoulders, the acne-smudged forehead and chin.

"You don't know of anyone driving in tonight, do you?"

"Look, mister, I don't run the bloody town."

"O.K., O.K." Moller felt testy, too. "Sorry to interrupt your study."

They went out again, a step ahead in time now. At least we are progressing to nowhere, Helen thought. It's possible to progress and be nowhere in this no-town with the long occasional stripes of light and the shadows splitting the river into chequers, with the day cooling off in the saltiest, fishiest of breezes up through the embankment grasses and houseshop alleyways jammed with parked trucks and litter and breathing with the sleeping stray dogs. Unreality was the essence of the minutes in which they moved, and unreality meant no town and no river, no street, no then and no will be and almost no at this moment – that most of all. Disembodied, perhaps, she thought, we will find this garage – as they did – and knock uselessly – as they did – at the darkened house at the rear.

They stood in the deep bays of the garage with its farouche petrol pillars and anxiousness unmasked upon each face sought its fellow and found it. Moller spoke softly.

"I'm very sorry. Very sorry indeed. Not that that will mend the situation, but there it is. It looks as if there's nothing for it but to try to get a room at a pub and go up tomorrow. We can't search all night for possible transport."

"This is twice," Helen said. "Things are loaded against

us. I feel like a child caught out. Imagine Findlay tomorrow when neither of us turns up and then both – both unashamedly entering at the end of the first period."

"Don't worry, Helen. It's an absurd system that can make two mature adults feel like a pair of naughty babies. If that's any comfort. The pub might know of someone going up early tomorrow. In any case we could try to fake up separate entrances, but I hardly think it's worth it. He's not a fool. The Talbots would observe your absence from breakfast, and it would only be a matter of days before he put two and two together – using a copulative verb, my dear." He laughed. "No. We'll just face the thing out. Anything else would irritate him more. In fact, I think the best thing to do would be to put a trunk call through to his house tonight, explain what has happened, and hope for the best."

Hesitancy of the mind, the heart. Moller's feet paused, braked by conscience and his eyes, startled by the shrillness of his thought, caught at hers for safety in the dark.

"I suppose," he said, not looking away from her once, not daring to look away, "I suppose *I* could walk back."

"I don't really want you to," Helen said.

"It would only take five hours or so. I'd be back by about five."

"At sunrise probably. And then what would you say about the car, even if no one saw you come in?"

"That I'd lent it to you."

"Too easy," Helen said. Relief. Relief. The wind blowing from the river dropped and scuppered papers sank into corners, leaves chattered into a final silence. "I can't drive. And Findlay knows it. He and his wife took me for a run up the coast not long after I came and my ignorance of matters mechanical thrilled him. He likes to be the boss in all things. No. No, Robert. No go, my dear."

"You're glad?"

Here at the same time was his wonder and his delight.

The dark air nuzzled their tiredness and they walked faster, their feet smacking the asphalt road, with doors and shop fronts beating back the quickened emphasis of feet on pavement; there was the hand, hard heavy around companion hand, the sudden impulse to look up, look down; and the volubility of their smiling eyes took them dreamlike to the nearest hotel broad-fronting the township with door open, still lit on the ground floor, waiting.

The archetype of all licensees grubbed round in a roll-top desk, looking them over slyly and disbelievingly.

"Broken down?" he said. "That was bad luck for you and . . . your wife, you said?"

"That is correct."

"Mmmmm." He looked at them with joy, salacity achieving, sanctioned. "Ah, yes." Helen noticed irrelevantly that his hair fluffed into a nimbus. "Well, I think I can manage a room."

"Any chance of a lift in early to Cooroy?"

The man behind the desk smiled happily.

"No," he said. "Not a chance in the world. Not from anyone here, anyway. The two travellers staying only got in this afternoon and they booked for a couple of days." He fished in his desk and dragged out a big register. "Like to sign the book?" he asked. "Both of you if you like." He leered up at Helen.

Moller scribbled his name at the bottom of a dirty page.

"Where's your phone?" he asked.

"In there," the other said, pointing to the parlour. He tried an insinuating smile on Helen again. "Bad luck, wasn't it? There's a chair there while your hubby's phoning."

Moller closed the parlour door behind him and crossed to the old-fashioned wall-phone and booked his call. I'm not good at this sort of thing, he thought as he waited. An artificial voluptuary. The phone shrilled its agony across the undusted tables and chairs and he picked up the receiver nervously.

On the other side of the closed door only the faintest sound of his voice came through to the woman in the hall and the man listening behind the office grille. He must be speaking very softly, Helen thought. She glanced over at the barrel of a man totting profits, and was sorry to deny him his scandal. But he wouldn't deny himself, she knew. He would have it in spite of them. And she caught his eye and smiled.

There was a click from the next room as Moller replaced the receiver on its hook. The door opened and he came out, his face unemotional as he met her glance.

"Here's your key, Mr. Moller," the licensee said. "No need to take you up, is there? It's the second on the right at the top of the stairs. Breakfast's at seven and there's no hot water now till the morning."

He grinned as he emptied this cornucopia of information.

Helen followed Moller up the stairs, and they were all hotel stairs, and along the corridor that was all corridors, and into a room that shut them in with each other and the lumpy, uncomfortable furniture.

With the shedding of their clothes they lost their perplexity as well; and somewhere between the long kisses Moller forgot completely the unkindness Findlay had offered him.

Eight

Feverishly Mrs. Lalor joggled needle and cotton in her arthritic fingers, squinting redly and hopelessly in the light from the weak bulb.

"Keep still, love," she pleaded as Vinny wriggled in her being-made-over dress, itching against time, against madeoverness, against excitement in spite of herself. "Only another three inches." The hem submitted to her nervous stitching and resolved itself gracelessly into final folds round Vinny's knobbly legs. Mother and daughter stared dubiously into the mirror.

"You look real nice, Vin," her mother said without enthusiasm, but bravely lying, hoping to be proved wrong miraculously.

Vinny could have wept when she saw herself unsuitable in crêpe, her unformed breasts made mockery of by the suggestively gathered bodice and the two dreadful flounces parenthesizing her bony shoulders. Inwardly she declined despair and proved it like a theorem, until, observing her mother's unhappy anxiety, she forced a tight smile.

"The colour's not bad, is it, mum? This paley sort of green goes with my hair." She shook the overlong skirt out as she had seen Rene do, in order to admire the expensive finish on the black suede shoes she had borrowed from her eldest sister. But it was chilly comfort. Her mother reached over to the dressing-table against the bed wall and produced, as if from a feretory, a tarnished lipstick tube that contained still a creamless, cracked resistance to time.

"Just a touch," she urged, "so as to give you a bit of colour. You look real pale, Vinny, and so you ought, eating no tea and hiking all the way out to Pratten's farm just to get those posies for Mrs. Striebel. Just see if she uses them, anyway. I don't know why you want to run around after her the way you do, even if she did take you to Brisbane."

"Oh, mum!" protested Vinny.

The old jousting, the tourney, the same verbal thrustings, a litany of pale recriminations and tired responses. To divert her mother she took the lipstick and with unpractised finger smeared a little colour across her mouth, noting with astonishment her youth more manifest by the uneven red lines. and so, chrysalis emerged, her mouth barbaric for the first time in her life, she bent forward and smudged a kiss on her mother's cheek.

"Got your hanky and your purse?" Mrs. Lalor asked.

"Thanks, mum."

"And your ticket?"

"Yes. In my purse." She wished she could thank her mother for fixing the dress, but something kept stopping her. She wasn't really grateful because she knew it didn't look much. "I've got to hurry, mum," she said awkwardly. "I've got to get those posies round to the supper room for Mrs. Striebel."

"Oh, those posies!" gibed her mother with a momentary spasm of annoyance, jealousy perhaps, and the constant irritation of the throbbing in her joints.

Merciless for the instant, she watched her daughter run gawkily down the hall, down the steps into the heavily scented garden soft with moths and dew. Then partly because of griefs older than this, and partly because of the impossibility of alleviating the present one, she found, in spite of the violent upsurge of tears within her mind, that she could not weep at all, and set to resignedly to gather thread from the floor, the bedspread, the sewing-table.

Vinny paused beside the door of the sagging toolshed to gather up the tray of flowers that she had left there to retain their freshness in the damp night air, and then went back over the uncut lawn to the front gate and the melting grey night in Duncan Street. Just below in the valley the lights of the station ticket-office and waiting-rooms splashed across the metals and the humped lines of timber trailers delayed in the siding until the Gympie mail passed through. In the house across the road the Gilham boy practised uncertainly the same piece he had been practising for weeks and weeks, and with unerring certainty made the same mistake in the same place. Vinny, listening for it in the darkness, smiled to herself, hugging the tray more closely in her thin arms, smiled because for weeks the irritation of that one trifle had driven her nearly crazy every night. She tottered in the unaccustomed height of Jocelyn's shoes, wincing as pebble after pebble caused her to go over first on one ankle and then the other. The brumous green of fig-trees wearing the evening lateness blurred the road for a hundred yards at this point where the hill's declivity met creek, bridge spanning it, and the main road that lead up over the tracks to the shops and school. Standing in shadow, Vinny removed the shoes and, holding them clumsily beneath the tray, padded along in the powdery dust, her stockinged feet stretching in relief. Ahead of her two figures came in from the branch road and the moth mad street-light at the bridge's eastern end shone like grease on bulbously profiled lips gossip-gabbling of Pearl Warburton's mother and Pearl.

Vinny's empty stomach contracted unpleasantly as she sensed, seconds before she heard, the frou-frou of starched white frock suitably girlish, expertly made, and then glanced down at the skimpy flatness of crêpe still looking made-over in the twilight. Pressing herself back into the bays of the trees, she stood perfectly still, praying that they would not turn and, finding her, clap her in the cage of their mockery. Their voices became fainter. Vinny shuddered in the darkness and, putting on her shoes again, wobbled after them up the next hill towards the town.

When she came near the hall the lights were quite dazzling on the black and the wine and the sea-coloured metal of the cars parked at right angles to the paspalum-rank gutter. There was a noise and an excitement, a scuffing of feet among the paper bags and emptied cardboard drink cartons that flooded her with a rising wonder as she looked nervously in the wide open doors at the dance floor now reverberating to the shouts and skiddings of uncomfortably dressed boys from the senior classes. Around the walls mothers sat in corseted groups eyeing off their giggling daughters, maddening them by plucking at a hem or twitching rebellious belts and sashes. The girls twisted and preened, conscious all the time of the furtive glances of the boys who skylarked in the corners near the stage, smacking back the brilliantine on their hair, fingering the new eruptions on their skin. Streamers, balloons, paper lanterns quilted the ceiling with gaudy colour.

There were no members of the staff visible except Mr. Moller, looking completely different in a dinner jacket. He was on the stage helping the three-piece band shift the piano from the wings. Vinny ducked back past Perce Westerman, loud with an alcoholic goodwill, who was collecting tickets at the door, and went round the side of the sprawling timber hall, down the slope to the basement supper room. Three parallel rows of trestle tables stretched over with cream paper and loaded with cutlery, crockery, and jars of sugar, ran the full length of the room. At the far end a rough work section had been hastily set up near the tea-urn, and round the counter thus formed dodged senior prefects carrying top heavy platters of sandwiches, tomato, cheese, baked bean, from the labouring, near-disembodied hands of staff and school committee. Lost in this crush of effort against time, Vinny felt more confident that her appearance would not even be noticed. She edged crabwise with the flower tray, jostled but strangely happy, especially when she saw Mrs. Striebel calm and golden and untouched by Howard's libels working stolidly over the butter bowl as she pounded milk and fat into an economic elasticity. Breathless, eye brilliant under electric light, animated by noise, dust, and the intermittent bursts of jazz from upstairs. Vinny offered the tray with the sprigs of wattle, the cabbage roses tied with blue silk, the daisies bedded back in maiden hair, offered and was received by a startled Helen as the tray thrust forward impatiently before her.

"Why, Vinny, my dear, how lovely they are, and how kind of you to go all the way to Pratten's! I hope you managed to get home for tea."

Vinny squirmed with love and embarrassment. She dropped her lashes over the shallow curve of freckled cheek.

"Have a sandwich now, anyway," Helen continued briskly, and reached behind her for a plate piled up with triangles of bread.

"Thank you, Mrs. Striebel," Vinny murmured, worshipping. Furtively she looked at Mrs. Striebel's dress, loving and envying. "Who's getting the posies?"

"Not me. I'm not nearly important enough. They're for Mrs. Findlay, the women on the judging committee in the cake competition, and the wives of all the important local men. Sprinkle some water on the flowers, Vinny, from that glass there, and then put the tray up on the shelf out of the way."

How Vinny adored her when she said things like, "I'm not nearly important enough." It was a descending to take Vinny into her confidence, making them equals in the levelling of jocularity. Friends. Almost.

Behind her Pearl Warburton's voice shocked the warmth. "Hullo, Mrs. Striebel. Hullo, Vinny." She paused deliberately. "Got a new dress?"

Vinny swung round to see Pearl, plump, powdered, staring insolently at both of them. She thrust forward a pink hand to touch, ever so gently, the ruching across Vinny's breast and, as soon as she did so, flourished her own beautiful organdie skirt. Her full lips were moist and smiling unkindly. Her eyes wandered slowly over Vinny's person. She smiled again and turned away.

"Anything I can do to help, Mrs. Striebel?"

Incontinent rage swept words of accusation to Vinny's trembling mouth. How dare she? She who had scribbled filth all over the lavatory walls. Only hope that Mrs. Striebel had not even heard of the matter kept her from shouting out the truth. She had not told Mr. Findlay the names of the wrongdoers. She was afraid. She felt with a primitive superstition that it was better to keep that ammunition as reserve, that it would be a permanent form of control over the group.

Helen was angry for a different reason. She had looked on helplessly at the calculated offensiveness of the older girl, and now, feeling the blood refluent once more, as if it had paused in its flow, gripped the trestle edge nervously until her anger had withered away and she was able to speak with calm. Her eyes sought Vinny's indefinite grey ones when she replied, sought uselessly, for Vinny, ridicule eroding all the happiness and excitement she had felt earlier, stood with her face turned away, now the first anger had passed for her too, pale with shame for her appearance and oddly afraid.

"Nothing, thank you, Pearl. Just behaving yourself inside and outside the hall will be sufficient help."

Pearl flung a suspicious look at the bland face. There was nothing to discover. If she were snubbed, her features quickly resumed their mask of enigmatic indifference, her aplomb appeared not one degree dislodged. She stared brazenly once more at Vinny's flounces, said goodbye to Mrs. Striebel, and wandered off arm-in-arm with Elizabeth Turton, who had been giggling foolishly a few yards away.

Vinny's hands trembled as she lifted the tray to the shelf beside the urn. "Leave me alone," she prayed. "Please, God, make them leave me alone the rest of the night." But she knew in her heart it was no use. God only answered Warburtons and Klees and Turtons.

Neither she who was so disconsolate nor Helen who was so angered found continuance of that earlier pleasure in each other's presence, and so Vinny drifted out of the supper basement into the warm anonymous night. The crowds were fairly streaming in now from Murray and Jerilbee roads, in pairs, in trios, in quartets of varying degrees of anticipation according to the age of the person and the propinquity of the opposite sex. Station-wagons, motor-bikes with side-cars, and decrepit semi-utilities were all blurring and clattering down the dirt roads, honking good-naturedly at each other before spilling their occupants, their pleasure offensive.

At eight-fifteen sharp the band whined into life, progressing through hesitant disharmonies towards the intricate pattern of a fox trot. Hulking youths from the outlying farms, still smelling of the beer they had been drinking straight from the bottle in the deserted grass paddock at the back of the hall, swept into motion with grinning confidence, the nipped-in-waisted, high-busted pouters who slatterned out their living in the milk bar, the hotels, the Gympie stores. The drums exploded under Mack Stevens's massive wrists, the saxophone whimpered up to orgastic heights, and the dance was under way.

Vinny slid shyly past Perce Westerman and sidled along the wall to find an empty space. All around her the heavy sweaty serge was selecting with finical caution the tarty nylon, the voile, the stiffened cotton. A few of the older pupils had filtered into the adult group that seemed to dominate the hall, though the dance was run ostensibly for the school, and with over-red faces shamblingly invited their schoolmates to partner them. Vinny watched the girls on either side of her go off, haughty at the favour they were conferring, coldly, not glancing again at their partner once they had assured themselves that he was worthy. She longed, but hopelessly, for someone to ask her, ruining her very chances by looking up too eagerly whenever a boy approached and smiling or saying, "Hullo, Trev", or "Hullo, Johnno". They would look at her for a moment, smile crookedly and mutter backwards, escaping. At nine o'clock she was a thin, isolated figure twisting her hanky round in her moist palm, pretending beneath the bright paper ribbons, the crimson and the tangerine, that she was having a good time.

Moller was standing at the door when he noticed her. Immediately the recollection of what she had done for him stabbed him with its frightening kindness. He searched round the walls of the hall for a likely partner for her, but there was not a boy in sight who was not dancing or busy talking in the middle of a group. He walked from the lights of the hall into the smooth night and felt as if he were entering a pearl. The blackness was richly round and the parallels of mist that had padded out the valleys in the town's centre had merged into a low-lying white sea over which the archipelagoed tops of trees lay holding their branches very still. Muffled giggles and protestations floated to him from the rear of the hall, and he smiled sardonically as he thought how the indentations in the long Kikuyu grass would reveal wordlessly the evening's folly to the garrulous small-town sunrise. The paling fence jettied into the night, and it was here that Moller found Tommy Peters busily chalking short and obscene phrases.

The boy's face was lit up by the glow sifted through the hall's dirty side windows. Moller watched him for a while. Tommy was a study in concentration, his tongue resting on his downy upper lip, his splodgy hands deformed by thirteen winter's chilblains, lining out the words with as much loving care as if he were writing a treatise. Four- and five-letter words were about the only ones he could spell accurately, Moller mused. He hated to interrupt and mar a work of art. Tommy straightened for a minute to admire his statements. Because he was not really dull enough to make use of slander, none of them was libellous. He was merely interested in completing as large and varied a list as he could of all the words he knew drove old Findlay mad. From his pocket he drew a crushed, half-smoked cigarette which he relit.

"Boy," Moller said softly.

The chalk and the cigarette dropped together, but the latter continued to burn in the long grass. Tommy moved a cautious foot to crush it, but before he could do so a mammoth boot smashed down upon it, a steady hand seized his right arm and he was pinioned. He waited for the sarcasm to flay him. It did not come.

"Boy," Moller repeated very gently, and he turned Tommy so that he was forced to look at the fence panels on which he had written.

"Sir," Tommy said uncertainly, and wondered just how much punishment lay in store.

"A lover of Ango-Saxon derivatives as well, Peters. You shouldn't spend too much time in serious pursuits. You'll stunt your growth, lad. Smoking is bad, too." He twisted Peter so that the boy was forced to look straight into his eyes. "Is this your first attempt at sign-writing?" he asked.

Peter winced. He knew about the notice in front of the school gate. He knew who had done it.

"Yes, sir," he said. "Honest."

Moller stared at him thoughtfully. "I think you'd better get in to the dancing. Vinny Lalor is without a partner."

He turned Tommy towards the hall which now throbbed, a prism of gaiety, paned in yellow, busy as an ant hill, the mothers, the queen ants, seated along the sides storing up slanderous impressions with which to sweeten their week-day yokes, the girls flaunting, the boys loud-mouthed, boastful to each other of victories they would achieve at the evening's close. Forcefully he propelled the boy through the door towards the lonely figure on the bench, and then turned quickly away, unable to bear to watch the denouement.

After leaving Peters, Moller sought Helen in the supper room, where he found her weary over the masses of food. She turned to him a face frank with love and fatigue. Because she knew they would soon be unmade as lovers by time and distance she felt she could afford the simple pattern of honesty to reveal through eyes and lips what for months she had been trying to dissemble. This might have been finality, she thought, the aim of all I ever hoped to have, the culmination of a life's love wishes realized in the one person; somewhere beyond these days there lay a trust that all the greener longings of the mind would find fruition responding to a new compulsion of time to be kinder. But, bright as a symbol, the official letter lay within her purse, total in its warning; and although eyes spoke and bespoke passion, lips trembled at what they might say, all she did was take Moller by the arm and walk with him from the parakeet chatter of the women's auxiliary to the jazz-hot-heavy dance floor.

Held angrily against him, she dared to tell him, her voice hesitant at first against the splenetic saxophone.

"Robert." She waited for him to look at her. Sweeney, two-stepping vulgarly past with Rose Jarman, dug Moller between the shoulders, then was sucked into the knotted couples. "Robert, I received a transfer today."

He stopped dancing immediately. She jerked against his arm and clutched him to regain her balance. All about them the grinning faces whirled. Some stared, but soon an island formed round their consternation and at its fringes the ocean of dancers broke and receded in waves.

"Why didn't you tell me earlier? Where to?"

"Camooweal. There wasn't time."

"Camooweal! Jesus Christ!" Moller threw back his great head and laughed maniacally. "Oh, the separation of loving must be secured! We were warned, Helen, but it's hard to take! What can it be? The Welches basically, or Findlay's fear for his job? When do you go?"

"Robert, please. People'll hear you, and I want to keep it quiet until I actually leave. Monday week is the date I'm due there."

"That means you'll have to leave here on the Friday."

"I suppose so."

"Oh God! Helen, I don't think I can stand it."

"Please," she said. "Please let's dance."

He looked at her with gentleness and touched her face with his lips so lightly it could be an accident, then delicately he edged her among the dancers until they were again an ingredient of festivity, solving the complicated rhythms of the band with their bodies.

"Will you be telling the staff before you go?"

"No. No. And I've asked Findlay not to mention it."

"They'll want to give you heat-proof ovenware," he said bitterly. "How cruel of you to deny them the pleasure!"

He hummed with the band. But his forehead and his hands had started to sweat and the assumed nonchalance did nothing to hide the trembling that seemed at first to be a mental thing but that later would take control of his limbs.

"So we have a week left, Helen. A mere week to conclude – is it? – a relationship that has barely started." He pulled her more closely against him and rubbed his cheek across her hair. She could not bear to look up, nor was there need with the verbosity of hand clasped in hand, the devious methods of communion. Where there was no joy left, at least there was pleasure for the flagellant, Moller reflected, the imminence of separation sharpening minutes into tiny daggers; where there was no laughter there was that other most lovely affinity – tears, quick springing, born of hopelessness and so fed. He wondered if Helen were crying and, placing a finger under her chin, forced her to look at him. He had not let her hand fall while he did this and she met his gaze in surprise.

"You see?" she said.

"You cannot dance like that," he said. "They'll accuse me of unkindness as well."

He danced her through the open hall door and into the porch. A great number of people were strolling down the slope to the basement. Helen peered at her watch as they stood at the foot of the steps in the half-light. It was five minutes to ten.

"Feel like supper?" Moller asked with a deathly weariness in his voice.

"Among the hordes?" Helen pulled a face. "No. But I am supposed to be helping."

"To hell with that! The school's had enough sweated overtime out of the staff today. Let's get out of it. Have you a coat or anything?"

"Wait here. I won't be a moment. My things are in the basement."

Helen left him and pushed her way through the stares and the greetings to where she had left her purse and cardigan alongside the urn. She hoped no one on the staff would notice she was leaving, and then quite suddenly didn't care. See me, watch me, she thought and strode arrogantly, slipping her jacket on as she went, her head tilting defiance. Within a week I'll be an old name to smear in this town and a source of unkindly speculation in the next. Poor bloody Robert. She nodded with anguished brightness at Jarman and Sweeney, waved at Millington and his wife and spoke briefly to Mrs. Findlay, curbing the curiosity on the older woman's face with the most unemotional of expressions, and then passed with outward unconcern the ash-grey daubings of incurious eyes whose owners now disowning the sun's anxieties, numb-drunk with night and its connotations, held tomorrow at arm's length.

In the township's one milk bar it was utterly silent. The floor clean-swept, Szamos leaned laconic behind the till reading the real-estate reports, supreme amongst the cheap mirrors and chromium plate, the deeply curved counter with six flavours in its milky maw, and the glass-top sweets bottles. Fortressed by wine gums, bull's-eyes, peppermint sticks, he watched them enter; he was ramparted by chocolate boxes and cigarette cartons, a stack of yesterday's menus spotted by the greasy thumbs of bank clerks, and pay-chits spiked on wire. And he was sick, sick to death of being foreign and lovable and accepted.

He looked hard at Moller and Helen and smiled in oleaginous fashion, but inwardly. The pair of them. Doing it. Under the town's sticky immense nose. He did not know how the knowledge was his. Perhaps he had heard the girls gossiping. But there it was, and in a sly way he admired them for it. For two pins he would come out on their side when the criticism broke and storm-lashed them. Who cares? He wanted to wind up his business, anyway, and spend the rest of his days trolling Spanish mackerel off the Tin Can Bay shores. He rubbed his hands with a gentle warming motion over his obese stomach and waddled round the counter to serve.

"Iffning, Mrs. Striebel. Iffning, Mr. Moller."

He placed his plump fingers fanwise on the laminated table surface and shaped his features into a question.

"Just coffee," Moller said. "One white. One black. Nothing to eat, thanks."

Szamos went off again wordless to the urn near the kitchen door. He lit the gas, rattled two cups on to saucers and poured watery milk into one. While he waited for the coffee to heat he hummed richly, a vibrant nasalization in which the occasional sung word stood out like a plum, and watched the two of them out of the corner of his eye. After filling the cups at the urn he carried them across to the table, wiped off its surface with a damp dish-cloth, and replaced the tea-stained sugar with a fresh bowl. He smiled on them magnanimously. He felt like giving them his blessing.

Helen and Moller sipped their coffee. Each sought in the other's pained face reassurance for what the day had done to them and found only the reflection of insecurity. Insecurity more than grief that, strangely enough, was thin as the washed-down sickle moon scything the crest of Bundarra.

"Do you think," Moller asked when Szamos had left them, "do you think there is any way we can solve this? We will be so far apart. Our only meeting time will be the holidays. Is that enough for you?"

"No."

"Nor me. But what can we do? We could both give up our jobs, I suppose, and go to Brisbane to find some sort of employment. That would be a very drastic action, though. I must – Helen, please understand this if you can – I must consider Lilian."

"Of course." Helen stirred and stirred the coffee in her cup. "There is nothing at all we can do but accept the situation. Letters, meetings – sometimes, and a gradual shifting of our affections."

She looked up from her cup and met his eyes steadily.

"You're too bitter," he said.

"No. I just don't hope for the impossible. It is an impossible situation now. Remember how I dreaded this happening when we were on our way to the Bay that time? Well, here it is. Bearable, really, when it actually confronts you."

"I remember."

"I've always been unlucky."

"You're accepting the situation without much fight."

"And you."

"Helen," he said, "please. What can I do? I have a terrible responsibility to my wife. Successful philandering is the prerogative of the wealthy."

"Philandering?"

"Oh God! I was making a phrase. You know I was only being flippant."

"I know," she said. "I know. But this doesn't seem the time. I'm sorry. Sorry sorry sorry sorry sorry."

"Helen," he asked desperately, "do you think I'm any happier than you? Do you?"

"Men are always involved far less. I love you," she whispered.

"Finish your coffee," he said, "and I'll take you home to the house. You're too upset. We have seven days, Helen, and if you'll allow me I'll make every one of them tell, starting tonight. We'll rise like the phoenix from our burnt-out reputations and startle this stinking little town."

He lit a cigarette with sad hands. He thought of Lilian and then deliberately put her from his mind, and until the following week he was not to think of her again. On the surface of his mind he kept telling himself there would be some way out of the impasse, but underneath it all he knew there wouldn't be. He was buffeted by his love and his confusion. He heard Helen saying, "You may compromise me, Robert, with all my heart," and he watched her finishing her coffee with tiny nervous sips. He leant forward and held her hand as he lit her cigarette and became conscious of Szamos watching them. He sat back. The smoke from her cigarette rose straight upwards and tracking its course seemed to steady both of them. Lapped by a false content they knew that for the next few minutes, amidst the desultory phrases and the glances, they were awaiting with what impatience the opening of the gate, the sound of their steps along the path, the hall, and then the silence of the room embracing them.

As soon as Vinny saw the boy edging along the side towards her, the magnitude of the unhappiness that bravely she had outdistanced for half the evening became too much. Tears scorched under her pale lashes, and in an effort to repress them she turned away to stare fixedly at the stage. Diffused through her sorrow the rostrum lights blurred, fringed, held three melting black shapes that writhed, squeezing their harmonies out, came together, separated amoeba-like, black and gold. The floor whirled giddily, as she, when the clumsy touch came upon her shoulder. Grinning in embarrassment, Tommy Peters stood there, scuffing his large unpolished boots. Words would not come. He felt so soppy asking a girl to dance. Who'd want to dance with him? The over-tight shiny trousers caught him painfully in the crotch and he wriggled from one foot to the other trying to ease the discomfort, furtively dragging at his pants with one hand. Knobbled wrists, red from morning milkings, jutted out well past the cuff-ends of his shirt, and it was at these Vinny first looked before her eyes were raised fearfully to his face. She gaped miserably.

"Dance?" Tommy finally managed to ask.

The hard damp ball of the handkerchief in Vinny's hand was stuffed down the front of her bodice from where it rolled to her waist and stuck out in a funny little lump. She tried to smile, but her jaws, aching from the fixed enjoyment she had forced them to register for nearly an hour, would not respond. She stood and their arms moved unaccustomedly about each other's bodies as they stumbled in and out among the dancers.

Tommy wished he could stop. Neither was able to dance properly, although the knowledge did not hurt him as it hurt Vinny who, foolishly, had thought of her first school dance as a lyrical floating of the untrained feet in patterns of three-four, two-four, two-two. But he didn't dare stop. He thought old Moller would have it in for him good and proper. Cripes! What a belting he'd get if Findlay got on to the notices and the smoking! Perhaps if he kept on dancing with this Lalor sheila, Moller would let him off. Her shining red hair tickled his pimply chin. Not bad-looking stuff, really. He tripped when he saw Pearl Warburton smirking at him over the shoulder of the factory foreman.

"Sorry," he mumbled to Vinny.

The agony in Vinny's mind matched the physical agony of this staggering, tottering motion. Dredging up pride, she said, "I think I'd rather stop."

But Tommy remembered the threat in Moller's voice and dared not take her back to the side bench. He thought desperately.

"It's nearly supper time," he suggested. "There'll be supper real soon. Let's go down and wait."

"Oh, all right," Vinny said. She was beginning to feel ungracious.

She followed him outside and down to where a queue was forming near the side door. At least one-quarter of the crowd was assembled, chattering with that excess joviality that spreads at an assured meal-time. There was a great deal of private chyacking amongst the adults and the older pupils, while the children giggled and pushed and shouted daringly about the staff, drunk with the spectacle of dress-up. Yet Tommy and Vinny were not part of these hungry yelling mobs. They were still too shy of each other, too upset at the poor fish each had netted, to pretend overt enjoyment. Tommy kicked sulkily at stones and kept his head bowed. Vinny fidgeted uncomfortably beside him, watching the actions of his great bumbling feet.

"I've seen you play footie," she ventured timidly.

Tommy glanced across with the faintest show of interest in his puffy eyes.

"Las' week? Las' week when we beat Gympie High?"

"Yes. Then. You run fast, Tommy."

"Yeah. You gotta when you're winger. Gee, they're on to you, though." He stopped kicking to look at her. "You like footie?"

"Yes. I think it's a real exciting game. Like a battle. Remember those battles Mr. Moller told us about they used to have in the olden days? Each side would pick out its champions to fight and sort of represent them. That's what I think football's like, for a school, I mean."

Her eyes shone with the point she was making. Tommy looked at her respectfully for he like being called a champion, even indirectly. Ole Vinny wasn't too bad. An' her hair was real pretty. Pity about her dress. He didn't know what was wrong with it except when he looked at the others, hers looked different somehow. Still, she wasn't bad. Had a few ideas. More than that stupe Warburton or her pal, Klee.

"Gee, I'm hungry!"

He swung his arm to send an imaginary cricket ball into the crowd. His elation was growing. They exchanged grins and even joined in the mocking "hooray" that greeted the official opening of the supper-room barrier a few minutes later. The crowd spread like a sand slide once it was through the narrow opening as couples raced wildly for the seats along the trestle tables. Bannered under school flags and cardboard replicas of the badge with its motto separately picked out in painted wooden letters swinging above the room, they sprawled over forms, grabbing places for their friends; getting near the cakes or the sandwiches or close by the urn for doublings up on tea. Vinny and Tommy found themselves hustled into one of the narrowest angles in the room. But they did not mind. Squeezed affably against each other, their faces moist and genial from the sudden rush and the excitement, they felt an urge to be companionable. Tommy grinned round at everyone, whom he knew by sight if not by name. They were seated with a group of older people who had come in from a pineapple plantation as far away as the Glasshouses. But he still knew them to nod to, for he often went through on his father's truck when he picked up cases of fruit for the Brisbane markets.

Vinny was relieved, relieved to see no critical schoolface near, eyeing her appearance disparagingly. Furtively she glanced at the frocks farther away to note how they were made and mentally to plan one for herself. Cotton, white, crisp, she fantasied, and was awakened by Tommy nudging her gauchely with a plate of sandwiches.

"Tomater," he said. "Lovely."

His jaws worked with gusto. His eyes gleamed. Vinny took a sandwich and found she was enjoying herself immensely. The adults at their table ignored them after the first nods and reciprocal smiles and she listened to them plunged into technicalities about cars and later a horse one of them had interests in for the Doomben. So thrown back on their own conversational resources, at first the boy and girl were hesitant, but later, mellowed by cake and an anaemic fruit syrup, they fould themselves contentedly swapping hatreds for their several teachers. Vinny had searched the room for Mrs. Striebel and, not seeing her, felt her absence with a pain only one so young could feel.

Shyly she volunteered, "I went to Brisbane a couple of weeks ago with Mr. Moller and Mrs. Striebel."

Tommy gawped at her and dropped a blob of mock cream on his trouser leg.

"Whaffor?"

Vinny giggled as she wiped the cream off his trousers with a paper napkin. "Mrs. Striebel took me to a matinée. It was beautiful. A play with singing and dancing and lovely music and costumes. And afterwards we had tea at a real posh place with lots of knives and forks and chicken rolled up in bacon. Kromeskies, that was called."

"Gee! Where didja stay?"

"At Mrs. Striebel's sister's place near the river. Ooh, at night the lights on the water and the boats blooting were marvellous! And I saw a big liner come in Sunday morning before we drove back. I had a lovely time."

"I'll bet." Tommy looked at her admiringly. "Howju keep it secret so long?"

"Mrs. Striebel asked me not to tell anyone so people wouldn't think she was favouring me."

Tommy nodded. He had nearly told her what the boys were saying about old Herc and Stree, but thought better of it. He did not know that she knew, and, seeing she liked them a lot, with a precocity of finer feeling he did not want to hurt Vinny.

"That was real decent of her. To take you," he said. "I bet you like her."

Vinny glowed. Just for a moment her plainness vanished behind a front of pale skin and intensely sparkling light eyes. A small red patch of colour spotted each cheek-bone. But the magnificence of emotion was far too private to allow revelation.

"Yes," she agreed. It was all she could permit herself to say.

"I went down to Brissy last year," Tommy said, "but we came back the same day. I was helping Dad run the truck down with a load of bananas and on the way back he let me drive her for a while. It was beaut, too, till I stripped the gears and Dad walloped me so hard I thought I seen stars."

"Can you really drive?"

"Oh, a bit. Drove nearly all the way back, like I said."

He swaggered with braggadocio and gazed nonchalantly around the supper hall. The crowd had thinned out a great deal and they could see two or three of the staff drinking tea at the far end of the room. Overhead renewed thumpings of the jazz-angry feet compelled the band to more intense effort. Tommy's watery blue eyes met Vinny's grey ones. They both looked away in a confusion of warmth.

"I have to go after supper," Vinny said, tricking her fingers into a pattern laced on the green crêpe dress. "I told my mother I'd be home before eleven."

"I'm going, too," Tommy said. He thought for a minute. "I live past you. I'll double you home on my bike if you like."

Outside the hall the smell of the dew-wet grass and the geraniums clumped along the hall front was sharp as a dream. Water-clear the sky had rolled its mists back, and the star-islands floated in fathoms of black air. All the roads leading out of town were palely definite until they washed away under the shadows of the stringy-barks and ironbarks, the spotted gums and bloodwoods that clustered along the very margin of the dirt tracks. There were couples smoking near the doors and near the cars, and talking more quietly now the later evening hour amplified voices, gave them a crystallinity.

Tommy dragged his bicycle from under the side of the hall, and then, with Vinny walking beside him, he pushed it slowly up to the road. After some false starts, collapsings and laughter, she was finally seated uncomfortably on the bar while Tommy held her firmly in the skinny parallel of his arms and pedalled heavily. When they had ridden down the main street they coasted right past the darkened pub on the near side of the line and under the railway bridge. The goods train was still in the siding, but a red lamp moved along it as one of the station hands walked down the tracks to the northern end. The hill on the other side, once they were past the creek, was too steep for riding, so they dismounted and wheeled the bicycle side by side past the last town lamp. Vinny sacrificed her pride for the second time that evening and, having removed her sister's shoes, hobbled along the road with her sore bare feet.

For her the night had been a turning point. Until this moment she had been conscious, frighteningly so, of having one friend only. And yet she could not really call a mature woman twenty years her senior a friend. The pupil-teacher relationship made that impossible. She did not include her family in her estimate of what made understanding and amicable companionship, because always there was the fear that love was displayed through duty, that concern was parental conscience. Her reasoning was not evolved in those terms, but it all came down to the same tiny meaning. Yet now, at this moment and under the slow saraband of tree-shadow along the out-of-town roads, she felt she had won what for years had been absent from the purpose of her day, a friend who liked her in spite of her dress, her face, her clumsy manner.

It was cooler suddenly as they neared the crest of the hill. When Vinny shivered, Tommy unexplainedly put an arm across her shoulders and gave her a timid little squeeze. And a strange silence fell on them both. His feet scrunched, the rubber tyres hissed through the dust, and the darkness of the figs filled in the road ahead and wrapped them like a greatcoat. In the black paddocks behind the fences the sound of cattle moving quietly came comfortingly to them, and at the top of the hill Lalor's picket fence grinned greyly into the mosaic of leaf.

"Home," Vinny said.

As if by consent they stopped where the frame of a giant casuarina threw a ragged phantom double across the roadway. Under the purple-grained twilight the children's eyes shone with quiet anticipation, and Tommy, letting his bicycle slide into a tangled heap of wheels and handlebar, put his untried arms round Vinny's shoulders and his soft boy lips on her shaking mouth. They were not certain what to do, and after their mouths moved apart, Vinny rubbed her head like a young animal against the breast of his serge suit. He smoothed his hands tenderly over her hair and she felt the tears spring sharply into her eyes. She did not dare look up, and her voice reached him muffled not only by serge but by years and years of loneliness.

"I had a lovely night, Tommy."

"Me, too."

They dropped their arms from each other and Vinny, tremulous with love, with tenderness beyond bearing, walked past him to her front gate. She watched while he picked his bike up, watched while he kicked down hard with his left foot before swinging his right leg over the saddle, and long after he had waved and wobbled down the stony road into the darkness, she stood there crying for very joy.

Nine

Tuesday morning unfolded its leaf in sudden gentle green. Coastal breezes played the sun-rays like guitar strings, plucking the aridity from the morning and touching off plangent monotones as the loquat-tree whacked against the half-empty water-tank. It swung Vinny through the last tumbled dreams tossed about like hay, through the hurtled bedclothes of a restless night, to run near-whipped by the drumming tree to the mirror slivered down the wardrobe front. She touched her lips with gentle fingers and pressed the pads at their tips to her mouth as softly as another mouth. Her whole body tautened with pleasure.

As if through a score of yesterdays she could hear her mother calling her to breakfast, and in the same mesmerized way she put on her dressing-gown, handed down, ripped under the armpit, and went along the hall. As she knotted her girdle, she knotted last night into place, safe and concealed from the breakfast ritual.

There they were, above the cracked china and the open packet of cereal, the sugar brown-lumped from wet teaspoons, and the milk still in the bottle streaked from the front-gate grass. She saw them as if they were all impelled by the wind to lean one way and she another. As they were. Above the stains, the gnarled cutlery, their faces still sleep-crumpled surprised hers in a smile and they racketed at her with laughter and questions.

"How was the dance?"

"You must've had a good time! You came in pretty late."

"What'd Mrs. Findlay wear?"

"Say, sis, who was the boy seen you home?"

Vinny stopped grinning. The hungry pulp on her plate soaked up the milk as she stared back at Royce, holding her spoon in mid-air with the sugar grains tipping over the side.

"What you say?" She still hated him. She looked away. She thought she always would now, after that Saturday afternoon. Just looking at him made her want to run away. He kept at her, probing with his eyes, until she returned his look.

"You heard. Course she did, didn't she, Rene? I said, what boy seen you home? It's no good saying none did because I heard you say good night."

"Ooh! Our Vinny!" Rene moved her scarlet mouth into the shape of well-bred amusement. "Aren't you starting a bit young? We'll have to watch her now, Ma."

Vinny shifted her gaze past all of them, out of the window and down the lawn to the mango-trees. She felt that if she did not listen they could not intrude their hatefulness upon last night. They could not snip away even the tiniest bit for spoiling.

"Leave her alone, you kids," the mother ordered. Her hair sprayed untidily from its loose bun. Her eyes were hollowed from lack of sleep, for she had stayed awake worrying at the darkness, counting bills like sheep until she had heard Vinny come in.

"Eat up your breakfast, love," she said to Vinny. "And try to put some weight on those bones."

Not even you. Vinny pushed the mash angrily into her mouth. Not even you or you or you. I am quite happy alone, bending one way and all of you another. Rene has her boy friends and Royce has Pearl and Mum has Rene and Royce; but I have Tommy now, and Mrs. Striebel who is always kind and who has my present to remind her and who smiles when she speaks to me.

She finished her breakfast, the butter-smeared toast, the strong tea, hearing the words of the others fall about her like rain – the repeated anecdotes about the older married sister living in Gympie, the scandals from the butter factory where the foreman had a grudge on Royce, Rene's titbits about the orthodontia of the town – it all blew past her angry mind mistily.

She shoved her chair in with a bang and went back to her room to pack her school-case. The books lay where she had scattered them along the dressing-table, and now she clumped them into an awkward bundle and dropped them in the battered bag. She could hear Royce saying, "What's bitten her?" and her mother hushing him. She dressed slowly, thinking all the time of Tommy, of his long thin face, his slightly pop eyes and his grinning mouth. She looked in the mirror at her own freckled features and decided that perhaps he mightn't mind her freckles so much, seeing he was covered with them. She did not yet know it was the duty of her sex to be perfect, to offer to the male, no matter how insipid he might be, an unblemished appearance. . . . For the first morning for months she brushed her hair very hard, and then, on an afterthought, picked clean her finger-nails with an opened-out bobby-pin. There was not much else she could do, she thought, not after she had gone to the bathroom, scrubbed her teeth, and washed her face.

And yet, these preparations done, she still looked the same except for the expectancy, the hope in the eyes.

Half-way to the gate she remembered she had not said good-bye, and on the point of turning back she scowled fiercely into the sun and walked determinedly ahead. The casuarina-tree was stripped of its magic in the clear light. It washed backwards and forwards, seaweed in the wind currents, and not the shadow of a kiss seemed to remain under its leaf-roof. But she paused and ate it up with her eyes, devoured it with tenderness, and stood there concealed from the house for five minutes at least watching the shadow rhymes swing across the fence stakes. What had happened to her last night was in no way related to what she had seen at the swimming-pool two Saturdays ago; young as she was, she could distinguish the gentle from the cruel in this basic relationship. The two actions to her were as far apart as north from south. She picked a small branch before she moved away, and she held it with adult sentimentality all the way to school where, superstitiously fearful of throwing it away, she thrust it into her suitcase underneath the pile of exercise books.

It was early again when she arrived, but she went up to the girls' lavatory block and sat there in one of the cubicles quite a long time until the crowding of ankles seen below the door warned her it must be getting near bell-time. She went outside into the talk and the laughter, but no one noticed her. Pearl Warburton, combing her hair before a small propped-up mirror deliberately turned her eyes away as Vinny approached.

I don't care any more, she told herself. Not any more. Tommy likes me. Not you, not any of you, but me, and he kissed me to prove it. She put her fingers once more to her lips and out in the harsh sunlight seemed to feel the tenderness once more upon her mouth.

Morning classes were a stale reaction from the excitements of the night before. Most of the senior pupils were tired and dark-eyed from lack of sleep and they yawned openly during lessons. An unsmiling and worried Mrs. Striebel hardly looked her way once during the period. Vinny kept glancing over to where Tommy Peters sat by the window, but he did not seem to want to see her this morning, and once when she did manage to catch his eye he only gave a quick embarrassed grin and then looked away. When this happened the whole day collapsed in sunlessness, though outside the window the sun was shining just as brightly on the hard trampled earth of the playground, and she kept hoping to herself in dozens of ways that perhaps he hadn't really noticed her, he was frightened of being caught talking in class, he didn't want the others to guess. Oh, that was it! It was preciously secret, theirs, personal, belonging to no one else.

She looked up from the patches of figures on the paper in front of her with such visible extension of relief brightening her face she immediately invited a question from Mrs. Striebel, who was poised upon the intricate escarpments of quadratic functions.

And so the day moved on, an ordinary day really, but to a few of them a *dies irae*, surface bubbling from undercurrents of anxiety that flowed endlessly. The large pendulum clock in the senior room ticked indefatigably towards twelve-thirty through the murmurousness of classes at work, the throbbing resonance of the cicada-swarming trees. Sticky heat and sunlight gummed the landscape together like glue.

Vinny took her lunch up to the pepper trees west of the lavatory block. It was quiet there, and she could eat and read a school library book as she sat with her back hard against a tree bole. She munched and idled with a few paragraphs and then, indulgent to her fancies as never before, sacrificed herself utterly to the nostalgia of the previous evening, moving ecstatic through imageries that could not see at this very moment, Tommy Peters, freckled and eager, boasting of his night out to a group of the more unsophisticated boys.

They lapped it up. The story was saucered cream. He added a little here and there and they stared at him with widened eyes of admiration and comments of "you never", "come orf it", "you beaut", "she can't be such a dope after all". He didn't do it because he disliked Vinny; he felt a liking for her that worried him. But he resented having given way to a soppy impulse to kiss her; he felt that by boasting he could square the situation with himself.

It didn't take long for the story to spread. By the time the first half of lunch was over there wasn't a boy in the senior class who hadn't heard it, garbled by now beyond recognition but with its two participants glaringly, oh humorously there. Howard told Pearl Warburton beneath the senior veranda near the bubblers, told her with the supercilious amusement of the sophisticate. They giggled unbelievingly, unenvyingly together.

The clouds kept rolling up from the coast above Bundarra. One felt that if the day became any hotter it would burst like a bomb. Vinny sat in the privacy of the trees with her tunic pulled well up above her knees, shifting her legs now and again as they glued together in the heat. She finished her sandwiches, her two biscuits, and then nibbled an apple right down to the core. She picked the shiny brown seeds out and flicked them with thumb and forefinger, and then she wrapped the core up in a tight screw of lunch wrapper.

Sitting under the trees, freckled over with shadow, she knew contentment. Shyness prevented her from seeking out Tommy and an innate caution dreaded rebuff; so that she was happy enough to sit there and merely think about the dance and the dancing and the supper and the secret held by the casuarina-tree. If she had been asked to do so she could not for a moment have probed the pain she once felt in crueller months: the time when she was seven and had lice in her hair and had to be sent home for a week, coming back with skull shaven beneath an old navy beret, martyred under the nudges and the giggles and the spoken taunt; or the time she had sat next to Betty Klee and Betty had kept moving ostentatiously away from her. "You smell," Betty had whispered, and she had known it was untrue; but the other girl had kept it up so long it had worried her, and for weeks she bathed herself with exaggerated care and burned with self-shame as her enemy, amused by the success of her campaign, spread the lie amongst the others till it was a byword when she passed, a constant prick to her wretchedness – when they all tired of it as suddenly as they had begun.

Time tortures less and less, Vinny thought (though not in those words), and she wondered if the period of sufferance in which she had moved for most of the year was because they were all growing older. She even loved her enemies this day, in spite of the heat. She felt towards all of them the overwhelming charity of the unexpectedly successful.

And so it was quite unbelievable when she found herself staring up into the victim-hungry face of Pearl Warburton, who had come upon her swiftly under the avenue of the boundary trees, cloistered like an angry nun among the groves, and on the thicker more silent grass of the fence margin. Behind her Betty Klee moved up from the hot yellow walls of the lavatory block and joined Pearl beneath the pepper trees. They both looked at her in silence and Pearl's face bore the cruellest and tiniest of smiles; she licked her full lips and the moisture shone like oil in the light.

"What did you mean," Pearl asked, "by threatening me last week?"

Vinny's fingers tightened nervously round the library book. Out of anger she sought desperately the courage that had carried her over the wild rapids of bravado and challenge that other day. Her eyes flickered from Pearl's face to Betty Klee's malicious doughy one. Her stomach quivered with sickness as it had always done when she was being attacked. She tried to flesh within her mind the shadowy figures of Mrs. Striebel and Mr. Moller to stimulate her crusading urge. Nothing came, nothing but Pearl's voice niggling at the same question.

"Nothing," Vinny said sullenly. "Nothing. Nothing." There was nothing she would do to harm anyone, could or would do.

"That's good," Pearl said. "It's good, isn't it?" She turned to her friend. Their faces seemed enormous, ballooned in the heat. "From what we hear, we could tell a few things about you."

"What things?"

"Ah! That's just what I asked you, and you wouldn't say. Why should I?"

Betty Klee became the apostle bound by indissoluble ties of envy.

"Yes, why?" she asked, she echoed.

"I've never done a thing," Vinny protested, her skinny body trembling with pique. "Never. You and your boy friends. I've seen you at the pool, do you hear me? Seen you. So there's nothing you can say about me."

"Oh yes, there is."

"There isn't!" Vinny shook her head. She felt oddly uncertain. "There isn't. There isn't."

"What about last night?" Pearl asked. "After the school dance? What about that?"

It was the raping of privacy, the shattering of personal stillness into laciniated fragments of the intruded self that shocked Vinny most. Without being aware of doing it, she had sprung to her feet to stand with her back pressed against the rough sliprail fence. Her school-case fell open on the ground, the lid hanging askew to reveal the grease-spotted interior with its brown paper lunch bag and grubby textbooks. Looking down at it she was ashamed, even in this moment of anger and fear, and she tried to kick the lid shut.

They could only know Tommy had kissed her because Tommy had told them.

The same tide of despair that flooded her mind when she knew of Pearl's intimacy with Royce swept her away again, floundering and plucking at air. Everything around her had a liquescence, was melting away.

"Nothing happened after the dance. I jus' went home."

She could not help denying. The situation was compulsive to denial. She saw Betty Klee move forward, saw her lips shape words, and with an effort made out her question:

"You just went home with somebody, didn't you?"

"Who?" Vinny asked, challenging her.

"Tommy Peters, that's who."

Nothing had any importance any longer. The dance, the day's contentment fell away like leaves from the branches of her mind. Her blood beat faster along its rivers and she felt the sweat-beads star her forehead.

"What if I did?"

"Ooh!" said Betty. "What if you did! I hope your mother doesn't find out what you did!"

Pearl watched them both intently, still smiling slightly.

"I didn't do anything."

"That's not what Tommy says!"

Vinny sensed the tears trembling under her eyelids.

"You're all a lot of liars," she whispered. "A lot of liars."

Betty Klee giggled and swung her arm through Pearl's.

"We're not, are we, Pearl? You just ought to behave." She was struck by a sudden delicious thought. "You'll have a baby," she giggled. "That's what'll happen to you. You'll have a baby."

Vinny's bright-white face, dark-stippled by ginger freckles, shone its horror back across the little space between the three of them. Her stomach felt as if someone were squeezing it up very small. The arteries in the crook of each elbow tingled in a loose uncontrolled way as if they had no purpose of flow. Her mind exploded into dozens of thoughts tiny as matchflares, huge as neons, that said "nonsense" and "perhaps" and remembered her mother's sweating eight-month pregnancy and the fat-bellied, child-heavy woman in Brisbane. A tiny squeezed-out sound came from her throat and fluttered uselessly as a white moth over the heads of the other two.

"I won't," she said. "Oh, I won't! I can't. You don't know what you're talking about."

Betty Klee was delighted. Quite by accident she had discovered a very fine torture. She called Pearl in for support.

"Yes, you will. And your stomach will get big and you'll vomit. Oh, you were silly, wasn't she, Pearl?"

Pearl, with the eye of the practised voluptuary, took in the undeveloped body retreated against the fence, laid her glance in an unflattering caress upon the breastlessness, the no-thighs, the uncurved mouth.

"You'll have to leave school," she said deliberately. "Everyone will know. You'll have to leave before people start talking about you."

Vinny searched their faces uselessly for some relenting, a seed of kindness, perhaps, and found none. With the strange irrelevance that comes to the mind confronted with a dangerous situation, she remembered dandelions yolk-yellow in paddock morning grasses and the oleander bushes at one side of the house double-puffed pink above their poisoned leaves and the darkened theatre with the orchestra-pit glowing like a camp fire below the moving peopled stage – all the lovely things – and the basket wobbling with the tenderness of giving – and none of these things had any importance any more. The giant hideous accusation towered over the day, spread across the sky to meet the angry nimbus piling up in the east. The motionless air around them shivered suddenly into wavelets amongst the branches of the pepper-trees in the swift chill breeze that moves in before a storm. On the ground at her feet one of her exercise books rustled open in the wind and they all looked down as page after page riffled back through careless ink-working and scarlet correction symbols.

Vinny could not force out a reply to their charge. Trapped in this cocoon of time, she would prefer to remain statue-still watching the days, the weeks, whipped back like films in the moving air that coursed her arithmetic book. The other two watched her, neither annoyed by her silence nor satisfied. Something instinctive assured them that they had achieved the effect of shock, but the more sadistic sides of their natures desired protestation, ripe panic burgeoning in tears, the wild white flower of hysteria.

"Don't you care?" Pearl asked.

The bell rang with a surprising loudness. Vinny bent down automatically and began stuffing books and papers back into the bag. Then she banged the lid shut. She had trouble with the catches and while she struggled to press the levers into place tears rolled from her eyes down the gentle curve of her cheek.

"Don't you care?" Pearl persisted. "Don't you?"

She could not bear to look at them any more, and she picked up her bag and pushed past them unseeingly. She ran through blindness and deafness down the slope of the yard to the marshalling lines.

But the matter did not end there.

All the afternoon Vinny sat uncomfortably in class imagining the others were staring, were whispering the hideous thing, were broadcasting it in notes passed behind book-covers or palmed stickily along forms. Several times during the last period she caught Betty Klee and Pearl Warburton watching her, and Tommy Peters looked her way, but she immediately lowered her eyes to her text.

Outside the sky was bruised with storm-cloud rain-black and pressing down upon the mountain and the town in indigo seas ready to break into torrents of streaming water. An unnatural radiance, yellow as sand, hung over paddocks and trees, washing them into a brilliant green; the houses stood cubed, projecting uncannily from the normally flat landscape. Depth made everything appear much closer. In the darkening classroom Mr. Moller lounged gloomily beside the window, staring with a kind of dispassionate curiosity at the storm moving towards them. Towards the coast the first thin wires and fringings of lightning danced above and along the horizon, and definite as drums the thunder tumbled in over the town. The first rain droplets were heavy and scattered, tapping berries of water upon the tree foliage the resonant iron roof of the school and the dusty yard. After a while the class-room became so dark they could scarcely see the blackboard, and all down the length of the school buildings the lights were switched on and the bare bulbs glimmered as uselessly as stars.

The down-burst of the rain came from a dramatic crash upon the roof, leaping upon the iron like gravel, bounding sharp as rock-pellets from window-sills, veranda rails. At three the school surged out of the rooms in noisy hordes along the wet verandas and down the dripping steps. In a jostling press of damp clothing and hot perspiring bodies they packed the cloakrooms where their hats were hung, waiting for the rain to slow and the school buses to come in from the coast run.

Vinny shrank back in a corner and squatted on her bag. All about her the artificial camaraderie induced by the situation played itself out in giggles and chatter and jocular horse-play. It was twenty minutes before the initial violence of the storm passed over, and after the crowd had thinned Vinny squeezed past the others to the steps. Stumbling, her head down, her hat held flat against her chest, she raced to the shopping block, springing across the gutter freshets to halt panting in front of the chemist's. In a slice of mirror let in behind the carton displays she saw herself with red hair flattened and darkened by rain. Her pale double stared back at her and for a second she wondered if she did look different, if she were.

"What are you going to call it, Vinny?"

The Welch girls moved in behind her out of the rain. The older one laughed.

"Tommy of course." She leant and whispered in her sister's ear. They both shrieked with unpleasant laughter. Vinny felt trapped and quite hopeless. She kept running her broken pocket-comb nervously through her hair. The very faintest of tremblings had begun in her hands.

"Ooh you are awful, Rhonda," the younger one said. She lowered her voice. "Rhonda says it will be company for Mrs. Striebel's."

They both collapsed with laughter, holding on to each other to support their mirth. The nightmare quality of the day began to obsess Vinny. In an effort to cling to the substantiality of things about her she watched the gutters jammed with paper flotillas, the trees in the little lozenge of park where the war memorial stood, weeping steadily down the honour roll. The Welch girls eyed her as she looked beyond them learning the detail of the rain-swept kerb. If they knew they were hurting her they were determined not to show it.

"Will you nurse it yourself?" the older girl asked with imitative sophistication. She and her sister had to hold each other's hands to tolerate the exquisite daring of the question.

"Stop it!" Vinny shouted suddenly. "Stop it! Stop it! Stop it!"

She was not certain what they meant. She felt sure it must be something unpleasant, something not spoken of. For the second time that day she was driven into flight, out from the shelter of the shop awnings, out into the stripes of rain. The vertical shutters of water closed in round her and she did not care.

When she arrived home her soaked clothes pressed a second skin against her thin body. Sullenly she changed and then stayed in her room fidgeting with her homework, her few books. Her mother thought she seemed pale and more glum than usual, but Vinny often had moods like that. So she asked no questions and after tea lay back in the drab settee where sleep took her away from house chores into dreams of even larger wash-ups all tangled with visions of the luxury-hotel holidays she would never experience.

Vinny went back to her room, twisting her huge knot of unhappiness and worry within herself, and after she had undressed and switched off the light she lay on the bed trying to probe, not her unpopularity, for she had learnt to accept that years ago, but the terrifying future that had been flung at her. She knew nothing of the physiology of sex, and her mother, tired beyond belief from child-bearing and rearing, had become too cynical, perhaps, or too weary to see that any form of sex education was given to her youngest child. All the others had found out, some way or other, and she herself had added veiled and puritanical hints to the collated hotch-potch of physiology and eroticism and sheer nonsense that they had built up from conversations with their friends. Of the three children still at home, Rene had seemed wise even in the womb, and boys . . . well, she consoled herself with the age-old misinformation that boys always managed somehow.

Vinny knew nothing, nothing at all beyond the baldest fact that the baby grew inside the mother. She associated this with all forms of spiritual and physical unpleasantness, with family rows and vomiting and fathers leaving home and great swollen bellies and adult hatred. How the baby came to be inside the mother she had no idea. She had thought vaguely that it was just something that happened when you got married – automatically, like wearing veils and having rice and confetti and glory boxes and best men and bridesmaids. Now she wasn't so sure that you had to be married. She recalled dimly the hearing of scandalous fragments about the various girls in the town who had "had to go to Brisbane to have it", little snippets – "they never said who the father was". At the back of her mind swinging like a pendulum was the foreboding that this thing could also happen to her.

She twisted over on the rumpled eiderdown and tried to push the thought away by burying her face in the stuffy, sneeze-filled kapok pillow. But it was horribly persistent. It would not leave her. She kept telling herself that it could not possibly be true, but the tiny fear remained. Perhaps kissing gives you babies, she thought wildly. Or perhaps it's how you feel when you kiss that does it. If you feel love or tenderness. That might make it marriage. Illogicality took over the panic-routed remnants of her sense and she wept gently and steadily into the made-to-receive-tears softness of the pillow. Down the hall the pendulum clock keeping time regularly fifteen minutes ahead struck nine-fifteen. She heard her mother creak slipper-comforted and stayless out of the cane-settee and shuffle to the kitchen to make the supper chocolate. She felt she could not discuss her tragedy with anyone: if it were true the shame would be unbearable. Certainly she could not face speaking to her mother. The mutual embarrassment that often makes frank discussion between parent and child virtually an impossibility was here so great, augmented by the unhappy home-life of her parents, that she could not bear her mother to get even the slightest hint of it.

It was her loneliness that made her so afraid.

In the darkness she placed a hand upon her stomach. Was it any larger? She ran fearful fingers across it, palpating the hard little belly. It was the same. Or would one know? How long was it before the swelling made the old ladies turn and boys on bikes yiack to each other? The very thought caused her to prickle with fright. She curled up on her side, knees drawn up to her chin in the eternal position of the embryo. The bed kennelled her in its warmth.

Her sobbing was less now. Fatigue closed her pale lashes over her pale eyes. Outside, the rain puttered steadily on the tank roof and all the time there was the trickle from the guttering emptying into the tank.

Rene opened her door to call her out to supper, but she pulled the sheet up quickly over her head and pretended to be asleep.

Ten

Somehow next morning Vinny felt a nagging reluctance to go to school.

When the first skins of sleep peeled onion-like away from her mind, she was conscious of nothing but bed-warmth and the ease of legs stretched out relaxed under the sheets. Half awake, she rubbed one foot lazily along the shin of her other leg, feeling the scabs of a recent graze, and watched the trembling lights on the unpainted pine ceiling.

Then suddenly the memory of yesterday hit her. Her stomach knotted in fright and she sat up, pulling aside the bed-clothes to inspect her flat belly. It looked exactly the same. She felt the same. She pushed her red hair away from her face and slid out of bed. But the thought accompanied her to the mirror, and through her dressing, and all through breakfast it chased around with a phrase she had heard somewhere – "eating enough for two" – and she could hardly eat a thing. "I am the same," she informed herself, sulkily pulling at cold toast. "The same." And the little doubt persisted, winding in and out the half-heard conversation of the others until everything was confusion in her mind.

Although she would have liked to pretend illness, she

left as she always did, turning slowly down the road past the casuarina. There was still a drizzle of rain, fine as cotton, from the cloud-covered sky, that flecked her face, her hands, her shiny black raincoat that had been Rene's and the sou'wester that was actually her own. Some yards beyond the crest of the hill a track led off into the bush fringe before the paddocks of Rhodes grass swept away to Pratten's farm. Facing the track, Gilham's gaunt timber home stared with its over-polished windows at the monotony of the ironbarks. She could hear Ray Gilham practising the same piece. It was a keen edge to her unhappiness hearing that melodic line with its inevitable discordant mistake, reminding, thrusting in the daytime dream of two evenings ago. "No," she said aloud, and pushed her worry away. But it bounced back with rubbery insistence and she found herself glancing down at her stomach, suddenly afraid it might be bulging below her tunic belt.

Standing in the shelter of the dripping leaves, she paused at the entrance to the track, hearing across the road the piano whimpering untuned over its twenty-note treadmill. If I sat a long time by myself, she argued, if I didn't go near the school, perhaps I might be able to think this thing out better. She thought of the nineteen other faces of the class asking her about the baby, telling her about it, threatening it, and she knew she could not go near the school that day. Instead she went quickly down the path packed with sodden earth-smelling leaves, her tunic brushed by the wet bushes. Irresponsibility flooded her mind so much that she overcame completely her fear of the punishment that went with truanting and her apprehension that the pretended reasons she offered the next day might be found out. In fact, she pushed next day as far away as next year, and lost herself under the trees and rain. After some time she found she had come up from the north upon one of the outer and now disused sheds belonging to the farm. The door hung askew on its shrunken timbers, revealing the trodden earth floor, and opened in on a small dark place of cobwebs and heaps of broken boxes. She went in pulling the door wide open so that she could see over the paddock undulations to the farmhouse cresting the green wave of the hills, flung down under a foam of trees. She propped the door open with one box and sat upon another. And so for a while did nothing but stare, unthinkingly at last, across the paddocks and the fences.

Often when the mind endeavours to determine its problem, and remains, as it were, still, thrusting aside everything extraneous in order to see this one thing in a blaze of light, all the extraneous things keep creeping back so insidiously that the primary problem is obliterated entirely. It is like a man trying to photograph his family in a public park – constantly across the eye of his camera, cutting the corners, streaming between him and his object, come the lovers, the ball-chasing children and the dogs.

Vinny gazed up the hill, alive with her worry, knowing in the darkest and tiniest place in the forests of her mind that the thing wasn't, couldn't be true, and yet fearing, dreading that it might be. The clash of possibilities made it worse. One of the Pratten boys ran down the back steps and slammed into the outside privy. She could see old Mrs. Pratten wobbling under the fruit-trees at the side of the house, and faintly, faintly, the heartiness of a radio programme wrapped up the morning and its problems like a jujube in Cellophane. . . .

Her mother had met her at the back door that afternoon in May, concerned and fussing.

"Are you all right, love?" she had asked.

"Yes," Vinny answered, puzzled.

"You didn't feel different, did you? Not sick or anything?"

"No. Why?"

Her mother took her inside gently. This tenderness was unnerving. She led Vinny into the bedroom and showed her her pyjamas. Vinny looked at them with a peculiar feeling of panic.

"What is it?" she asked. "What's happened?"

Her mother pressed her child's thin arm between her hands.

"Please, love," she said, "don't worry. It's all natural. I should have explained before, only I forgot. Mothers do forget how old their babies are getting." She ventured a half-smile, trembling with the guilt of her neglect. "I was frightened all day you might have been worrying what was up with you. I only noticed when I was taking the clothes out to wash."

"I never noticed anything," Vinny said. "I felt all right." She resented having to feel different, to adjust herself.

"It happens to all girls when they reach your age," her mother said, explaining insufficiently.

"What does?"

"This. This does Vinny. You can't have babies unless this happens. All this means is you're a normal girl and you'll be able to have children of your own one day."

Vinny contemplated the floor. She felt ashamed. She could sense her mother's embarrassment and she felt embarrassed on her behalf. But her mother was talking on. She urged her daughter to the bed and sat beside her, fiddling with the yellowed fringe of the quilt.

"Every month it happens," she said. "Perhaps not now for a while but later. You're only starting to grow up."

Vinny was startled at seeing her mother's mouth jerk with feeling.

"Does it happen to everyone?"

"Everyone."

"Don't they mind?"

"No. Why should they? It's part of being a woman."

"I hate it," Vinny said. "I hate it. I'd rather not be normal. I wish I were a boy."

"Now don't be silly, lovey." Her mother was concerned because she had omitted to prepare her youngest child for the shock of puberty. "There's nothing wrong with it.

It's natural. It's like seasons in your body. A sort of ripening." She fumbled around the idea and then gave up, timid of her own imagery. "And, anyway, it stops again when you're forty or thereabouts."

"Can you have babies then, after it stops?"

"No," her mother said. "Not ever."

"Well, I wish I were forty."

"There," her mother said, and patted Vinny's arm awkwardly remembering she had felt the same way thirty years ago. "There. You won't feel like that always. Even next time you won't mind so much."

But the next time had not yet come to Vinny's immature body, and after a while, indeed, she had forgotten all about it. The day became a signpost, but one so distant she could no longer see it clearly.

The conversation of that day flickered across her mind in a tentative manner as she sat now kicking the door unrhythmically, hating and enjoying at the same time the long screech of its unoiled hinges. Certain of her mother's words assumed a looming importance when taken from their context. What had happened then proved she was normal, that she could have a child. This realization made her feel so ill she bent forward to squeeze her stomach into a sense of firmness rather than this horrible feeling of emptiness. She could not analyse fear; she knew nothing of its processes in the body, that these visceral disturbances were a natural sequence to a day of shock and continuing unease of mind.

She tried to line up the incidents of the previous twenty-four hours and, after reviewing them, to see their folly; but all her efforts were reduced to Betty Klee saying over and over, "You'll have a baby", and Pearl Warburton silently consenting to the statement. If only she knew how you did have babies. Feeling that surely Pearl must know, she could not believe anyone could make so serious a statement out of pure malice, and concluded consequently there must be truth in it somewhere. Oh, all the horror of the possibility clutched her! The shame. That was it more than anything – the agony of the shame of the heads turning, your own eye dropping, of the unknown quality of bearing another body within your own, the sheer high-pitched terror of having to chart such strange country.

She found to her amazement that the tears were running freely down her face. When she had rubbed them off with the sleeve of her blouse she mournfully opened her school-bag. All the familiarity of the interior, the corners plugged with crumbs, the name "Vinny Jean Lalor" painted across the inside of the lid, flooded her with a further uprush of self-pity. She unwrapped her lunch, and the bread packing the cheese and lettuce into thick wedges grew moist as she nibbled slowly and without hunger along their edges.

Time loafed along.

They were sweeping up at the farmhouse now, and the older Pratten boy was driving the family milker back to the western paddock with the rest of the little Jersey herd. Vinny scrambled to her feet and fidgeted around the outside of the barn, sheltered by the whips of willow woven across the morning. Already she was becoming bored: the hours were slow to crumble away and she was keenly conscious of wishing the day were over. However, even as she wished it so, she remembered that often in her short life had she longed for a lunch-hour to end, a schoolday, a week of schooldays, a term. Perplexed, she wondered if others ever felt this way. She couldn't imagine it, for all her contemporaries were constantly being assured by adults on school speech-days that childhood was a wonderfully happy time, a period of interest; how lucky they were to be young, the politicans and the church ministers told them confidently, with all their lives ahead of them.

She wished she had found a friend the way the other girls had. It was all very well loving Mrs. Striebel, she considered resentfully, but with her she could not stroll, arms encircling, heads close in glorious secret whispers, sharing the sweets and giggling together at the pictures on Saturday nights. If she had someone she could talk to about this present horror, that would be the biggest help of all. It was not being able to discuss it that made it so dreadful.

On impulse she slammed her bag shut and went downhill, deciding to go to school after all. She could tell some story, say her mother was sick. Mr. Moller was pretty easygoing and after he'd asked for her absence note a couple of times he'd probably forget all about it. She wondered if the others would persist in their persecution, yet, intelligently enough, she thought that would be better than sitting there thinking about it.

When she reached the gates the grounds of the school were empty, but from the infants' section she could hear Miss Rowan in priestess frenzy presiding over rote spelling. Through the senior-room window Mr. Moller's shaggy grey head and shoulders were visible as he stood behind the class. Now and again he disappeared from view as he bent over a pupil's book, and Vinny imagined the neat red-ink marks he would be placing upon exercises, the trim underlinings, the occasional sarcastic comment in the tidy handwriting. She went to the rear of the school and had a long drink at a bubbler. Her mouth was very dry and even after the drink there was a strange thick feeling in her throat. Braced like a diver, she plunged into the actions required of her – the hanging up of the hat, the limp excuse to Mr. Findlay, too busy to listen properly and egotistic about knowing his scallywag mark, the timid knocking on the class-room door. It was almost a relief to see the grins signalling across the room when she appeared, to sense the rustle of interest as she went to her place after handing Mr. Moller her late slip from the office. She kept her head lowered and her eyes fast upon her text during the lesson that passed slowly as a church service, though there were only fifteen minutes of it left.

After the room had emptied for lunch, she hurried outside, but not fast enough to avoid her enemies, who were upon her in a wild dream of voices, of questions, digging into her privacy. She tried to push past the little group, but Pearl Warburton caught her arm.

"You tell her, Betty," she said.

"No, you."

"No," Pearl stated firmly, and then she giggled. "No. You must tell her."

"All right," Betty Klee sparkled maliciously. "First of all though," she said to Vinny, "why were you late this morning? Not sick, were you?"

Vinny's face was blotched with fear. She trembled a little and kept swallowing at the dryness in her throat.

"My mother. . . ." Her voice trailed into a limbo of lost utterances.

"Your mother?" Pearl seized on the phrase. "You haven't told your mother? Bet she'll take a piece out of you."

"I wouldn't dare tell mine if I was going to have a . . . you know."

The Welch girls simpered. Eyes looked meaningly at eyes.

"My mother was sick." Vinny started to shove her way through the knots of girls on the veranda. "Let me down. I want to have my lunch."

"Got to keep your strength up," Betty Klee said. "Think of baby." She caught Vinny's arm. "Not so fast. Do you know where Tommy Peters is today? You seen him?"

"Maybe they were getting married or something," Rhonda Welch suggested.

"No. They couldn't have done that," Betty Klee said. "They couldn't possibly have done that, 'cause Tommy's in real trouble."

Vinny was interested. She could not help it. She wanted desperately not to be, but her love and her hatred tangled each other like tree and parasite vine, and she kept her eyelids lowered quivering over the questions in her eyes and stood in a waiting silence. Betty Klee gave her an irritable little shake.

"Tommy's gone to Gympie," she said. "He bust his father's truck late yesterday arv. He took it without permission and skidded on the wet road into a whacking great tree. It's a real mess now and he wasn't game to see what his dad said, so he hitched a ride up on Sid Ewer's van and said he was going to get a job."

She paused to watch the effect these shreds of violence might have upon the other. They flickered a colourless lightning ominously through Vinny's mind. It's because of the baby. *Can't give you anything but love, baby, babee, babeeohbabee. . . .* She jerked viciously away from the restraining arm and swung past them, past Rhonda Welch who saw fear scribbling its furrows on Vinny's face.

"Ooh-er!" she said triumphantly. "Ooh-er! Bet I know why he was glad to go!"

How quickly the others seized the point. Betty Klee gobbled the feed line and spat it back nastily.

"Didn't want to see baby Tommy. Bet he staged the whole thing."

Vinny found herself crying, unable to stem the rage and shame that poured from her eyes. A violence of emotion took her away from them and she was free at last in the yard, hunted and doubtful where to turn. Finally the rabbit she had become crept to a lonely place near the woodwork block and sat there in the warm sunshine that had broken through the clouds. She sat there for the remainder of the lunch-hour, a geometry book open on her lap. And she did not read a word.

They left her alone for the rest of the day.

Home took her in with a union of safety and non-safety to the steady things, the reliable bladebone stew, the dried apricots soaked overnight and stewed ragged in too much sugar, the sweetened white sauce in the brown jug. All the things that had given the security to home for years and had gone unnoticed, now blazed their unalterable ordinariness across the fear-filled blank of her sky. She felt despairingly she could no longer touch or taste or enjoy these things in ever the same way again.

"You're not eating," her mother said. "You must be a bit off-colour. You haven't eaten properly since you went to Brisbane."

"She's in love," Royce said between enormous bites. The words were chewed up with the bread. "Yeah. Know the symptoms. Good ole Vinny's got a sweetie."

He hacked at her ankle jovially with his foot and couldn't understand it at all when she suddenly burst into tears.

"You're always at her, Royce. Let her be. What's up, love?"

Vinny could not reply. Perhaps she was ill. She certainly didn't feel like eating. She felt more as if she was going to be sick. She rubbed her fists into her eyes with a final action and got up from the table.

"I think I'll go to bed early," she said.

But instead she went to the front sitting-room they hardly ever used now and routed round amongst the old books on the shelf behind the door until she found the one she wanted. It was a plump medical tome for family use, suitably pruned of anything liable to stimulate unhealthy adolescent speculation. But it did so, all the same, with a minimum of factual information; and though all the family had been forbidden to read it as children, nevertheless it had been well thumbed by them at one time or another. Vinny slipped it under her cardigan and crossed the hall like a thief.

When she had got into bed she went quickly down the index to "Pregnancy" and turned to the section named. She was the only one who had not yet made use of the book, and now she read avidly, morbidly – but was not helped. The only thing it achieved was to give her a deepening dread of what might be happening within her, it did not tell her how conception actually took place. It was one of those soft-pedalled, broad outline books that omit half the relevant symptoms of even the more pedestrian complaints and keep all their human structure diagrams completely asexual. Her search, in fact, did nothing but accentuate her fear. It in no way relieved it. In spite of herself she read fascinatedly on, touching lightly on puerperal fever and post-natal haemorrhages. She felt deeply knowledgeable about the entire process of parturition except for that one important factor.

So much for that, she reflected bitterly. Tomorrow would be Thursday and she had lived through Tuesday and Wednesday. But time in this instance would be no softener. Time would bring the ultimate shame only closer. She slept finally, and she slept badly, opening the doors of one queer dream after another, gobbled up by situations that were terrible in their shapelessness. In the morning she felt as if she had not slept at all, her mental and physical fatigue crushing her under an immense weight. At first she lay drowsily, all thought of her problem gone, yet with a puzzled non-comprehension of her exhaustion; but as consciousness widened her eyelids and her mind it sprang on her tiger-fierce, more overpowering by its contrast with that one moment of untensed being.

It was worse that day.

They made signs as well as comments. Betty Klee kept patting her stomach and thrusting it forward whenever she passed Vinny, so that she could have died of shame. All the senior school seemed to know; they giggled when she looked at them, and every pair, every trio, every quartet, she was sure, was discussing her and her agony.

The nagging worry, the fear hardly left her now. If it paused when she became involved in French translation or a geometry rider, the engulfing way in which it raced back was frightening. She felt really ill. Fear, loss of sleep, and hardly any food for two days were beginning to force a physical reaction from her. In the lunch-hour a sudden nausea forced an attack of dry retching that continued for nearly ten minutes. When it was over and she had the spasms under control she was too ashamed, too frightened to emerge from the lavatory, in case the accusing and meaningful eye of a classmate met hers. She sat there for the rest of the lunch-hour, pressing her foot hard against the door when anyone tried to open it, sweating heavily in the heat and becoming weaker and weaker.

She thought the lunch break would never end. As soon as the bell rang she wobbled to the lines, white as chalk, swaying slightly from dizziness. The others were watching her, but she was too ill to care; and, in addition, the fact that she felt so sick proved finally to her that what they said was true. She was going to have a baby. She was going to have a baby. She was going to have a . . .

Fear is the unexpected shape in the dark, the face across a room, the voice behind one's back. It was all these things to Vinny, who shrivelled inwardly to something smaller than nothing at all – at least that was how it felt. The thing was true, proven. She was to be a mother. In her body now she carried another that was growing inexorably every minute, every hour, bigger and bigger. She pulled her stomach muscles in with hatred and anger as she shuffled with the rest of the class into school and, edging to her desk, stumbled and almost fell. She knew Mr. Moller was watching her as they all stood until he gave the order to be seated. Momentarily her face raised its pallid disc to his, and he was shocked by the deadness of the expression.

"Are you all right, Vinny?" he asked.

Two desks away Betty Klee's amusement burst from her in a giggle, but Moller quietened her with a glance. He noticed that there were a number of grinning faces as he repeated his question.

The child replied with lowered head.

"Yes, sir," she said.

"Very well. Sit, everybody," Moller ordered. The policy of England in her colonization programme in eastern America continued uninterrupted for twenty minutes through degrees of boredom and clock-watching and stifled yawns. Moller was reading a note from a supplementary text when he heard a scuffle at the back of the room. He looked up in time to see Vinny Lalor flop sideways as the girl on her left tried to raise her from the desk where she had fallen. She was diving into deepness, into nothingness, into the whole heart of the world, tumbling round and down like a stone. Moller strode forward into a startled quiet and put his arm round the girl's shoulders. She stirred slightly, and half-dragging her, he edged down the corridor between the desks and then carried her out of the class into the staff-room. There he laid her gently on the sofa.

Helen had been sitting in a centre of grief, unable to work, and unwilling as well. She jumped up to help, but her grief went with her like a garment, and her eyes met Moller's with other queries in them than the one she asked.

"What's wrong?"

"I don't know, Helen. She looked pretty sick at the beginning of class but said she was all right. Do what you can, will you? I can hear that bloody mob starting to buzz already." He kissed Helen quickly. "Buck up," he said. "*Sursum corda.*" And raced out of the door.

Helen gazed down at the quiet face under its mop of red hair. The forehead and mouth were shining with perspiration. Helen quickly loosened the neck of Vinny's blouse, and then sat her up, swinging the child's legs down over the side of the settee. Then she pushed Vinny forward until her head drooped between her knees.

After a while a faint colour stained the girl's cheeks and she slowly raised her head. The rocking walls steadied down, the dreadful heat and nausea receded, and the centre of her world was Mrs. Striebel seated beside her, a look of anxiety on her face and one arm round her body.

"Feel better now?" Helen asked.

"Yes, thanks," Vinny whispered. Her voice crept from her mouth, the untrue whisper of the sea that lives in a shell.

"Lie back," Helen said, "and put your feet up. I'll get you a cup of tea."

She prepared the tea, saying nothing more until it was ready and she had poured both cups, setting one on a chair by the child. For two days she had been unable to work, her whole person sick with the wretchedness of leaving; and her body and her mind travelled a monotonous plain of spiritual hopelessness that vanished before her into further miles of unrelieved flatness. After the first unavoidable discussion with Findlay, she had tried not to see him, had spoken to no one but Moller of her approaching transfer and awaited the oncoming-never-coming, too-soon-here week-end. This diversion in her afternoon was welcome because of the hiatus it created between this pain and that, because it gave her something to think of other than loving and being loved and the cessation of both those things.

Vinny's eyes had closed. Now and then, Helen noticed, a small muscle twitched in her cheek, but apart from that she lay perfectly still.

"Here's your tea," she said gently. "Think you can manage it?"

Vinny opened her tired eyes and squeezed out a tired smile.

"I'll try." She sat up and reached for the cup, held it between both hands and sipped. The heat made her jump back slightly and then she sipped at the tea again.

"Better? You'll be able to stay here the rest of the afternoon in comparative privacy. I'm off until last and there won't be anyone else in here."

"Thank you, Mrs. Striebel," Vinny said.

Clumsily she placed her cup back on the saucer, spilling some tea, and stared at the window, the coats, the briefcases. To have been here alone with Mrs. Striebel last week would have been an unplumbable ecstasy. She hardly cared now. Worship was failing her. Involuntarily she sighed.

"What do you think made you faint?" Helen asked, swung in by the sound of the sigh from the roadways of her own pain to those of another. "Tummy upset?"

Vinny looked up quickly, wondering why she should ask just that.

"No," she said emphatically. "No. I guess it was the heat."

"Probably," Helen agreed. She hesitated, then said, "Would you rather go home? It is too far to your place, you know, and I think you'd really be better off here."

"I think I'll wait a bit." Vinny found herself moving through the groves of conversation as cautiously as a cat. "I don't think I could walk that far, anyhow."

Sipping some more tea, she lay back. All the indecision of the past few days, the frightening worry, seemed to have been climbing towards this period of time when the emotional whirligig took respite in this quiet, safe corner of the school with her last friend beside her. The resolve taking shape in her mind was tiny now as a figure seen at the far end of a long avenue, moving towards her, increasing in size and hope and bearing with it the tremendousness of her own request. For a long while she lay silently, her eyes closed, hearing the soft sounds made by Mrs. Striebel's pencil as it made correction marks on the pile of books in front of her. Resolve flung its giant shadow down the avenue of trees on her face, her resting body.

The period bell rang.

Miss Rowan clattered in from the infants' department to get a song-book from her locker. She stopped short on seeing Vinny.

"What's up, lovey? Sick?" She did not wait for an answer, merely rattled on to her locker and rummaged for the music.

"Culture next step for the little souls," she said over her shoulder to Helen, and sang ironically:

"Swish, swish, I'm a tree,
Sway–ing, sway–ing."

At this point she found the book and went out of the room still singing, and with exaggerated actions:

"Swish, swish, I'm a tree,
Swaying in the wind.."

Helen did not feel like laughing, but she could not help herself at the sound of Miss Rowan's unhappy voice. She glanced at Vinny, who had watched the scene indifferently. That is how I really feel, Helen told herself. Yet this child receives the impression with no visible emotion, but I, who am experiencing the worst week the years have given me, laugh. Perhaps because she is a child she misses the humour. Perhaps she is worried as I am. Perhaps. Perhaps. She had no wish, either, to continue marking books that after tomorrow she would never see again. All of those twenty samples of handwriting, the full, the flowing, the meanly cramped, the backhand, the semi-print, the really irritating style of Howard's with the curlicues on the capitals and final g's and y's, would become by some form of retroactive inhibition as if they had never existed. From the next room she could hear Moller's voice explaining a point, soft and rich – and male. Oh God, it was the maleness of it that made it hardest to listen. Quickly she closed her mind to its sound and flung a question at Vinny. Any question.

"Did you enjoy the dance?"

Vinny was still in the long avenue of her fancy and she stared back at her questioner through the leaves of worry and hope.

"It was all right," she answered carelessly.

"Only all right?"

"Well . . . pretty nice, I s'pose."

Helen smiled kindly. She was grateful to Vinny for involving her thoughts.

"I think you had a good time, Vinny," she joked pleasantly. "I saw you dancing."

Vinny said nothing. A memory struck at Helen's mind of Vinny awkward in Saturday morning sunlight, grinning past her in the gardens.

"That photograph," she said. "Remember the one you had taken in Brisbane? We never did anything about that ticket, did we?"

"No," Vinny said, thinking. That will be the last time anyone will see me as thin as that. "No," she said again. "And I don't want to either."

Helen was startled. As far as her emotional state would allow her to notice such things, she had thought that the girl had seemed upset and withdrawn for the last few days, but sullen rudeness was most unlike her. She put out a tentative hand and patted Vinny's arm.

"Tell me," she said, "is something the matter?"

Vinny turned her head away to conceal her agony. Now at this very point of help she felt her resolution fail in floods of tears of wretchedness that ran unchecked down her face. She gulped and rubbed the back of her hand across her streaming eyes and fumbled uselessly in the front of her tunic for a handkerchief.

"Here," Helen smiled kindly. "Take mine."

She laid her hand once more on Vinny's arm and perhaps it was the happiest moment the child ever had. After a while her sobs were less shaken, her eyes glanced shyly from under their red puffed lids at Mrs. Striebel, and gathering all her courage like a diver, feeling the warmth of the hand on her arm and the warmth in the eyes watching her, she said, "Please, Mrs. Striebel –" then she stopped.

"Yes?" Helen questioned gently.

"I – I don't know how to ask this, but . . . ."

"But what?"

"Have you any books you could lend me about babies?" The plunge taken, the body striking water that was not terrifying after all, to vanish into depths of release.

The puppet that was Helen's mind jerked convulsively

at the end of the verbal string. She knew she must be careful or she would frighten whatever shy gazelle of fear lurked in Vinny's mind by her next question. One thing she was quite sure about and that was that here was not the moment for asking why. So she said, as casually as she could, "You mean about having them?"

The answer came faintly and effortfully: "Yes."

Helen hesitated for a minute. Vinny was staring down at her lap, at her freckled fingers knotted across her tunic. Putting forward words was delicate as web-spinning. Remembering her own adolescence Helen felt certain that what Vinny really wanted to know was the origin of the baby, how it came to the mother's womb, not how it grew in that nine months of confinement. But she was discreet enough not to ask further.

"Being thirteen can be very difficult," she said. "I didn't like it much myself, I remember. All sorts of ups and downs and feeling out of everything. I think I can get you a book or two you might like to read. I know they'll help. Only I'll have to ring my sister and get her to send them if she can get hold of them."

Vinny raised her eyes for a moment.

"Thank you, Mrs. Striebel," she said. But more than "thank you" was in her heart.

Helen patted Vinny reassuringly. "Don't worry. How about coming down to the hotel on Saturday morning? I might have them by then. Anyway," she added, "we can have a little talk."

The tears had stopped flowing, and Vinny's face shone mildly, redly, but less unhappily. Here was the plank for the tired swimmer. Her friend, her last, only, dearest and best, had promised her help. Today was Thursday, and tomorrow would be Friday, and Saturday was so close it was almost here. Once and for all her worry would be solved like a problem in algebra. She smiled her gratitude.

The staff-room door flung open after the most perfunctory of knocks, the sound and the opening of the door coming in the same movement and Findlay cast his importance before him like a shadow.

He looked at them both curiously and then said, "One moment, Mrs. Striebel, if you'll excuse me. I'd be glad if you'd come to the office for a moment."

Helen's face twisted wryly and she rose. "Don't forget," she said softly to Vinny.

Findlay fidgeted in an embarrassed way. Since he had met Vinny over the notices he was always conscious of the moral lapses of those who should be in authority; it undermined all the things he taught the children to believe about the importance of adults.

"Not well, girlie?"

"No, sir."

"You should be quite all right there," he said, "without Mrs. Striebel's ministrations. Come along, Mrs. Striebel. There's a little matter concerning the monthly return I must fix up."

Eleven

"I have never dreaded a day ending so much, nor longed for it to end so fiercely at the same time," Helen said.

"This isn't the end."

"But I go tomorrow. I have to go in the morning. I made a mistake about the train."

"That's ten hours yet."

"But, Robert, I can't see you in the dark."

"We'll write."

"And then we'll stop writing."

"I say you're wrong."

"As you like."

"Whatever you like," Ruth Lunbeck said to the long unhappy body at her side. "But I say they deserved it."

"You judge like God," her husband grunted into his pillow. "Judge me," he reproved in a moment of compassion for the victims, "if you dare."

"December and June dey come along da bays, fat as figs and t'ousands of t'em. Absolutely t'ousands!" Szamos stirred salt into the supper coffee. "And vill I be glad, momma, to get avay from dis dirty little shop and town. Ven dey ask for a milk-shake today, I fill like saying all da time, 'Vot flavour is it, lady? Moller or Striebel?' "

"Silly coots," Sweeney said, cuddling Rose Jarman in the front of her father's car. "They were bound to get caught. It's crazy to fool around when you're married. That's one thing I'd never do, honey. You can be sure of that."

"Oh, Greg!"

"Marry me, Rose." It was more an order than a question.

"Yes, I do dare judge you. Playing around for years and I've taken it. What do I get out of this rotten marriage?"

"Clothes, cold creams, permanents. The lot," Harold said.

"Poppa, I can hardly vait, me also, to get that little house at the sea. Maybe next summer, eh?"

"Helen, you know I love you more than anything on God's earth. Don't be so hopeless about it all."

"I'm going to be a realist, Robert. If it goes on – well, it goes on. But no matter what happens we've had our – forgive me – fun."

"You sound rather like me."

"You've been a good teacher."

"My dear, you've been the most apt of pupils."

"You've talked all through the Bach. Now what?"

"I said she was rather an over-confident person, anyway. The jolt will do her ego good. I really cannot bear people who are so cocksure with so little basis."

"Really, Jess, be fair. She wasn't an unintelligent person, you know."

"I grant a certain text-book cleverness. But she had no sensibility. Alec, lower that just a little. And in addition, think of the benefit to the school."

"There is that, of course."

"Of course I was right to tell Findlay, Sam. You have no thought for our girls."

"You're a bloody interfering bitch," Welch said. "And right now I lump the kids with you, see?"

"You're drunk."

"Not as drunk as I'm going to be, Mary Ann. Not nearly as drunk. When I've pushed this bottle over I got a couple more lined up. Stick around and see me really tick."

"Allie can do her room out tomorrow afternoon after she's gone. I think I'll change the furniture round in there."

"Kind of superstition, is it?" Farrelly lay contented in sheets like bank-notes. "We'll keep it for C.T.s. if you like, instead of permanents. Make a bit more on it."

"Put that phone down, Cecily. It's time for the news."

"Just a minute, Freda. What was that, Garth?"

"I said put the damn' phone down."

"Garth's getting mad, darling. I'll see you tomorrow. 'Bye."

"Happy?" he asked. "Busy spreading it round?"

"Last patient, thank God." Rankin closed the door between the surgery and the hall. He could see his wife in the living-room still reading one of the glossy magazines she seemed to need monthly. Like a shot, he reflected.

"Who was it?"

"Perce Westerman. Had a flint in his eye."

"Hear the news?"

"You mean Helen Striebel's leaving?"

"M'm."

"Vaguely. Where did you get it?"

"Cecily Cantwell rang me a while back. She ran into Ma Findlay. It's all fearfully confidential till she goes."

"That means everybody knows, then."

"Did you say good-bye to anyone, Helen?"

"I had to see Farrelly, of course. And just before I left school this afternoon I said good-bye to the few who were still around. Rowie and Rose and Millington. They were surprised, but you could see the zest for the situation all over their poor dear faces."

"Kiss me."

"I'm not staying!" Marian shouted. "Not with you. If necessary I'll ring Cecily and ask can I spend the night with her. See how you like that."

Welch smacked the table hard with his palm. "You'll do no such thing," he roared. "Do you hear? No such bloody thing! There's been enough mischief done with all the yackety-yacketing in this joint. From now on you'll lay bloody well off."

"You dirty drunk! You couldn't stop me if you wanted."

"Couldn't I! Try that." He lurched over to her, across the carpet on which their marriage was founded, and hit her hard, twice, on the face.

"We'll be without a substitute for two days," Findlay murmured, "but everything should be right by Wednesday. They're sending me a man this time. We've saved the ship, my dear."

"Have we?" his wife said with a rare scepticism, remembering "Sweetie" Russell. "How old?"

"Well he's a one-one man, so he can't be too young."

"Mrs. Striebel did teach well. You often said so."

"Maybe. But other factors must be considered."

"I always like to feel, Alec, that where I can have acted for moral good, I have done so."

"Jess, please. I missed the announcement. What did the man say?"

"A concerto in D major for 'cello and piano by Vivaldi."

"How do you do it? Talk and listen at once?"

"I'm brilliant, darling."

"Are you crying, Robert?"

"A little. How did you know?"

"Your face was all wet when I kissed you."

"This is all back to front, Helen. You're the one who should be weeping. Hard wench!"

"I am inside. It rains in my heart . . . *il pleut dans mon coeur comme il pleut dans la ville*. Is that right?"

"You know," he said, "this will be all right. I feel it. Holidays soon. We'll have time together."

"The thing is complete in itself, though, isn't it? Like a wave breaking. Rise, sweep, fall, backwash."

"It's the after-effects that could matter, of course," Findlay said, slipping into his pyjamas. "Even now I feel there's been something going on in the senior school. Poor tone, there, you know. Poor tone."

"You haven't had your bismuth," his wife said.

"Oh Greg!"

"Will you? Will you marry me, Rose?"

"Oh yes . . . oh, stop it, Greg!"

"Why? We're engaged, aren't we?"

"I suppose . . . oh no, Greg!"

Subsiding into the scuffling darks of acquiescence.

"No more gingerbread, momma. I vil be op arf da night. Is lovely, t'ough. Yiss. I liked t'em real vell vot I knew, dat is to say. A nice lady. Always 'allo. Not passing me as if I vos dirt. And 'im, on O.K. fellow."

"Go on, Szammie. Joost a liddle piece. She sent me a big bonch of flowers, vunce, remember, the time I vos so ill. Sorry also, she is going."

"You're being very moral all of a sudden," Cecily Cantwell said. She looked with near-hatred at the slumped, flabby figure of her husband.

The man glanced up quickly at the half-pretty, near-neurotic face.

"Morals!" he said. "I've known about you and Lunbeck for weeks."

Welch steadied himself against the table (genuine walnut veneer) and nodded slowly over his words. "Now get to bed. Leave me alone, see."

"You hit me," Marian sobbed. "I'll never let you forget that. Never."

"I bet you won't. Go on. Beat it, before I do it again."

"How did you hear, Frank?"

"Oh, Findlay dropped a hint yesterday. Asked me not to mention it."

"You beast! You might have told me!"

"My dear, in that case I might as well have rigged up a loudspeaker system at the top of the hill and done the thing with *éclat*."

"That's not kind."

"I know you women," Rankin said contentedly, sure that he did.

"Everything except what I got married for," Ruth Lunbeck said bitterly.

"But that's how you like it, isn't it?" Harold said. "I always thought that was how you liked it."

"I'll tell you something," his wife said, propping her venom on one elbow. "It's the job, really. I married you for your job."

"There's no need to tell me that."

"And all I've got out of it is a stinking little country town brimful of fornication."

"That's a big word for you. You're full of philosophy tonight, darling."

"Don't darling me."

"When will it be?"

"What?"

"Come on. No kidding. The marriage. When will it be, eh?"

"Oh, Greg! Soon."

"I'll say soon." He looked lovingly at the car and thought of the spanking big beach week-ender. "Soon as you like, kiddo."

"I just thought of something, Robert."

"What's that?"

"Young Vinny. Remember I told you yesterday about her request. I haven't had a chance to see her. She was away today, and I'm going early tomorrow."

"What of it?"

"Well, I asked her to come down to the hotel after lunch to see if the book I phoned Margaret to send me had come in the midday mail. It's one of those very good sex-instruction booklets we used to use at that private school I was at. Anyway, I wanted to have a talk to her."

"Think something's the matter?"

"Certain. But I can't imagine what."

Mrs. Farrelly sighed on the edge of sleep. "Has she left a sending address, dear?"

"Yes. Everything's to go on to Camooweal, but Bert'll get it up at the post office before it reaches us."

"It's good to know in case."

"Wonder if Herc will come to badminton any more?" Freda pondered. She poured herself a brandy and settled back.

"Probably. Hide enough for anything, that sort."

"Bet the Welches are tickled."

"Marian might be. Old Sam's a queer fish. Don't understand him, I'm afraid. Pour us a snifter, Freda."

"Fonny, poppa, 'ow ve saw them that Sunday also, ven you took me for a run to the Bay. I 'ope you never told 'im."

"Vot you t'ink me, momma? Vot dey call 'ere a no-good bastard? No so, my dear."

"Come on, Szammie. Vot talk for 'eaven's sake! Let's go to bed."

"You are brilliant, my dear. But you do talk through my music. You seem very pleased Helen Striebel is going?" Alec Talbot said.

"Why? Aren't you?"

"I'm glad the situation between Moller and her was brought to Findlay's notice. I suppose her going does solve everything."

"You don't sound certain." Her jealousy nagged her.

"Goodness, Jess," mildly, "you seem suddenly annoyed. You must admit she was decorative." He was punishing her in his own special way for interrupting his evening's culture.

"All right, all right," Findlay said testily. "You've made me lose track of what I wanted to say next . . . ah yes! It's the innocence of the other pupils that must be guarded. The freshness and the innocence."

"Whom are you thinking of particularly?" his wife asked acidly.

"Why, all of them. They're all a nice lot of kids really."

"Don't forget that one of them was nice enough to scribble knowing and obscene messages all over the road."

Findlay's speech stopped in its tracks. Sometimes he resented Marcia's criticism. In a wife he expected a bulwark of confirmation.

"Where's that bottle?" he snapped. "I'll take the stuff now."

"You're probably imagining things, Helen."

"Probably. Anyway, do me a favour and collect any mail that comes to the pub. If that book comes after I've gone, give it to Vinny for me."

"Shall I give her the little talk, too?"

"Oh, darling! Still, the poor kid! I feel someone needs to do something for her."

"We need to do something for us, too, you know."

"Yes. But she's so helpless. We're not. I've never seen anyone so alone."

"Haven't you, my dear? Wait until we're parted."

"Will we tell the others?" Rose Jarman asked hopefully, longing for the boasting, the flashing of the engagement ring.

"Why not?" he agreed, thinking of the wedding gifts they would receive. His mind trickled through green valleys of acquisition, around islands of possession.

"Oh, Greg! I can't believe it's true."

"Neither can I," he said, looking at the car.

"One thing about her," Farrelly suggested charitably. "She always paid on the dot. Never had to wait."

"Wassmatter?" His wife rolled away from his voice.

"I said one thing she always paid on the dot."

"Glad to see her go. Gives us a bad name having men up."

"She's got some pretty rude friends, too. I never told you. . . ."

Lunbeck sighed. "Well, if you don't want to be darling'd please shut up and let me get to sleep."

"Now you won't even talk to me. I suppose you condone that pair."

"What if I do? Helen Striebel's a very good-looking woman."

"Yes, I'm sure you think she is, and I bet you wouldn't have minded being in Moller's shoes."

"Hardly his shoes, dear. And, seeing you mention it, no, I wouldn't have minded at all."

"I hate you!"

"All right, Ruth, think of that next time you pass Nev's and book up lots and lots of cosmetics. Have a wallow. And I swear I'm not going to argue any further or answer one more damned question."

"It's rather squalid, isn't it, Frank? I mean being caught up at the Bay like that. And don't forget Harold saw them together in Brisbane."

Frank Rankin heaved his feet on to another chair. "Poor show, with his wife ill, too."

"Think she'll get better?" Freda asked. She didn't really care one way or another except as the fact affected the scandal.

"No hope." Rankin loved definite diagnosis. "The paralysis is too advanced. Three months maybe, if she's lucky." He called it being lucky in spite of knowing the whole progress of her illness. "Certainly no more."

"I suppose Herc's really laying in stock for the lean times."

"Oh, I think the whole business – between Herc and Striebel, that is – has been going on longer than we suspect."

"Frank, you know we make a point of suspecting back further even than that."

"Witty old thing," he said admiringly. "Pour another for yourself, darling."

"Do you think so?" Jess Talbot countered. "Alec, did you ever notice her hands? And so often had half an inch of slip dangling. That's unforgivable, in my opinion."

"Couldn't I please hear the Vivaldi? Please?"

"Well, they're reaping their reward."

"Please, Jess."

"They might have been interesting to a Bohemian clique, but they certainly weren't the type I'd ever have chosen as friends."

Alec Talbot snapped the radio switch down. "There," he said. "Satisfied?"

"You're being bad-tempered and inconsiderate, Alec," his wife said. "And you know I like Vivaldi."

"That's what I said a while back, Robert. I can hardly wait for our separation because the waiting itself is so painful."

Moller had not let her go once as they lay in the darkness. He spoke with his lips placing words like kisses in the hollow between jaw and ear.

"Aloneness. A very special problem," he said. "No carrion comfort until we met. Ah, my dear. The aloneness is going to make our togetherness an extreme of pleasure."

No answer in the dark; in the dream within shadow and the warmth in his arms.

"Who's crying now?" he asked, suspecting. "Don't let's talk any more, Helen. Not for a while."

Twelve

Road into town once more on a Saturday of sunlight; and hope was the straw clutched at, the ticket in the lottery, the six chances for a shilling with the bamboo hoops. Hope kept the head raised and the eyes observant of the town-dwellers shopping and post-lolling, restored the senses of sight and hearing and taste and smell, sweetly, temporarily until hope secured the prize for itself, the fact in the pocket for the homeward journey.

Vinny had lived since Thursday hope-buoyed and fed, waiting for Saturday with an impatience that was almost pleasant. She had not gone to school on Friday, the fact that she had fainted the previous afternoon being sufficient argument for her mother, but had stayed in bed alternating moods of despondency with cheerfulness, picking at meals and dozing into calm from which she invariably awakened with a tug of apprehension. She tried not to worry. She tried to give herself respite from her panic by holding off all thought of her problem until Saturday should resolve it one way or another. She was only partly successful. Her hands kept creeping fearfully to her stomach and feeling it with a controlled dread. Friday was a no man's land, the time between despair and hope in their essence, the waiting hours that do not exist even in memory, once they have been crossed.

On Saturday morning she came to breakfast more nervous but happier than she had felt for days. It was only days, she had to keep assuring herself. It felt like weeks and months and years. Her mother looked at her closely as she turned the chops frying in the pan. They made a heavenly smell and sizzling noise and Vinny realized with surprise that it was the first time for nearly a week that the sight of cooking food had given her any pleasure – or that she had even noticed what she would be eating, for that matter.

Her mother drained the fat expertly into a tin.

"You look a whole lot better, Vin," she said. "There's no denying a day in bed sets you up when you feel no good."

Royce grinned as he spooned huge mouthfuls of cereal, and began to speak when a glare from his mother silenced him.

"I'm O.K., mum, thanks," Vinny said. She ate her breakfast without saying any more, wondering anxiously how she would be able to go to the township without her mother probing her with question upon question. Cunningly she decided not to mention it until that exact moment when she was preparing to leave, and then to give away nothing of her actual purpose. After she had finished her breakfast she filled in the morning doing her home-lessons, wrestling with the abstraction that was now an accustomed part of her. At half-past eleven she went to her bedroom to change into a clean dress. The quilt, the dressing-table, the wardrobe, and especially the stared-at ceiling and walls, all seemed to bear the imprint of her pain. She felt that never again would these four shabby walls hold her in quite the same innocent way, they would remind her again and again of the tears shed, the sleeplessness, the insanity of shame and guilt.

"Where are you off to," Mrs. Lalor asked when Vinny came back to the breakfast room, "all cleaned up and smart?"

Now the moment had arrived Vinny found that she had developed a glibness for her self-protection that amazed her. Persecution has peculiar off-shoots.

"I want a new homework book," she lied. The smoothness of her tongue gave her a feeling of pride. She had never lied deliberately to her mother before. "I want to get one before the shops close."

"Oh," her mother said. For the moment she could not put her finger on what gave her an impression of oddness in the girl's remark. She shook her head as if to shake off some of the worries nesting in her untidy hair. "You'll want some money then, won't you?"

"Yes, please."

"Well, here's two shillings. And don't be late back. We're having lunch soon."

Lunch soon can look after itself, Vinny thought. Lunch soon or now or never, and the excuses when I'm late can look after themselves, too. I'll say there was a crowd in the paper shop. Something. Something will come.

Casuarina, fig-tree ramparts along the hill and the rain-brimming creek curling cleanly under the footbridge were unseen landmarks as she hurried towards the morning's comfort. She came up by the hotel just as the rail-motor was pulling in at the station, emptying the bumped and rattled bodies with their stiff legs on to the platform. She did not notice. Purpose propelled her single-mindedly to the hotel where it squatted, roaring like a lion with the morning drinkers, packed with starting-price punters and farmers in for the Saturday beer while their wives did the shopping, under the shelter of the upstairs balcony that projected over the footpath the earth had been beaten flat by at least a quarter of the town. Cars and trucks fringed the road like boats along a jetty, and the patrons spilled their packed numbers out on the path, where they stood clutching their schooners and testing their geniality.

Vinny felt nervous about going into the hotel. The

ranks of red faces frightened her in their sacred, packed male preserve. She had never entered the hotel before, though sometimes when the bar was empty she had stopped for a minute to gaze in at the wide dark stairs marching upwards, and turning on the landing and then marching up again. The sombreness of the brown linoleum in the hall, the grey air, and behind the stairs, on the ground floor, the number of doors closed or half-open, impressed her as a kind of magnificence. The majestic backdrop of sin. That was how she saw it.

She hesitated at the door, afraid to enter but longing to achieve her purpose. Mrs. Striebel would be waiting for her with kindness wrapped like a gift for her to take away. Two men standing near the bar entrance were watching her curiously and she turned her head quickly when she noticed them.

"Hey, girlie, watcha want?" one of them asked kindly.

Vinny looked round unsmilingly. "I want to see someone," she answered.

"Hey, Joe!" The man stuck his head in the door and roared down the length of the bar, his voice hurtling over the long room of wedged voices and bodies. "Hey, Joe! Girl here wants to see yuh!"

Farrelly bustled down the bar, wiping automatically the splashes and wet rings from the wooden counter. He handed the damp rag to the yardman, who always helped out on Saturdays. "Keep it going," he said, "and watch that change. I'll be back in a minute."

He went outside, puzzled when he found a thin, red-headed girl waiting timidly on the footpath. For a moment he couldn't place her, and then he remembered she was one of old George Lalor's brood. Youngest, she must be, he reflected. It's years since George left town. There went a special part of the Railway Hotel income. Ah, well.

"Yes?" he asked, trying to smile kindly, and not succeeding. He had been a publican too long. "What's the trouble?"

"Please," Vinny said. "Please, I want to see Mrs. Striebel. She asked me to come and see her."

"Mrs. Striebel," Farrelly said. He looked hard at her. "Didn't you know? She's gone."

"She's gone?" Vinny said, automatically repeating his words.

"Yes," he said. "Gone. Went first thing this morning on the rail-motor. Thought you'd know. You're up at the school, aren't you?"

Vinny didn't answer. The whole morning, the bright, the golden, had turned black as pain, was the straw floating away, the lottery drawn and lost, the hoops flung uselessly with the prizes tantalizingly close and unattainable. She felt nothing but a numbness as the shock of the words spread an aching cold over her body. She became nothing, whirling and spinning round foolishly as a dandelion ball in the wind. She opened her mouth to ask a question and the words squeezed out thin as a dream-cry.

"Where to?"

Farrelly was startled by the sudden whiteness of her face. She looked as if she might fall over.

"Are you all right?" he asked, hating her for delaying him, wanting to get back to the bar.

"Where to?" Vinny repeated.

"Camooweal. She's been transferred. Didn't you kids know?"

Vinny could not answer him. It would be public admission of Mrs. Striebel's treachery in not telling them. She couldn't understand why they hadn't been told. Everyone liked her. She shook her head silently. Funnily, it wouldn't stop shaking for nearly a minute. She had to make a very strong effort to control its spastic jerks. Farrelly watched her, wondering what was the matter and feeling unexpectedly sorry for her in spite of his impatience.

Vinny raised her pale eyes and looked at his, at the face fatigued with its own striving after money, after the swift deal, the cut here and the gain there.

"She had a book for me," she said. "I came to get the book. Did she give it to you to give me?"

"No," Farrelly said, shifting his feet impatiently. "What sort of book was it?"

"Just a book" – becoming once more as cautious as a cat.

A flush of irritability prickled right through Farrelly's being. He really couldn't stay here chattering with kids. "Look," he said, "I haven't been up to her room. She only went a couple of hours ago. Would you like to go up and see if she's left it for you?"

Hope flared. Another ticket was pressed miraculously into the hand, the hoops were handed round again.

"All right," she said.

Farrelly turned away, relieved at getting the business out of his hands and into someone else's. That was the way he had run his whole life when things were proceeding unprofitably for him. Going inside to the foot of the stairs, he called Allie.

"Come on," he said to Vinny. "Come on in. I'll get Allie to take you up. You can have a look round Mrs. Striebel's room and see if she's left it for you."

Allie clumped towards them from the upper storey and stood resentfully on the landing.

"What is it?" she asked. "I was jus' goin' to start the polisher, Mr. Farrelly."

"It won't take more than a minute," Farrelly said apologetically. It wasn't easy to get maids these days. Girls were getting above themselves. "I want you to take young – what's your name, girl?"

"Vinny Lalor."

"Here's young Vinny Lalor wants to go up and see if Mrs. Striebel left a book for her in her room. You haven't found anything, have you?"

"Me?" Allie said. Her fat, normally good-natured face was oily with sweat, and annoyance pouted her mouth. "I haven't been in yet. Too busy."

"Well, take her up and have a look," Farrelly said. "I've got to get back to the bar."

He rushed off thankfully. Saturday serving was a divine office.

Vinny and Allie stared at each other. This was the one, Vinny recalled, who had got into trouble last year. She knew because she had overhead her mother and Mrs. Gilham talking about her going to Brisbane. Superstitiously Vinny decided that some external force had brought them suitably together for this last humiliation.

"C'mon," Allie said abruptly. "I got too much to do here as it is."

Wearily Vinny followed her up the stairs, hopelessly hoping. Here was the corridor along which Mrs. Striebel had moved. It meant nothing. It was merely a dim passage running away from her to left and right with lots of little brown rectangles for doors stamped on it. Allie opened one of them – it did not matter which, and inside in the shadow they both gazed at the bare furniture, the bed with its mattress rolled back, and on it a pile of used bed linen all neatly folded. The wardrobe door swung open on three dangling coat-hangers that underlined the emptiness of the room. Everything spelt departure.

"Have a look inside," Allie said. "It might be inside."

Vinny moved hopelessly across the room, opened the wardrobe door fully and peered in. Nothing. Nothing but a sheet of newspaper on the floor and some mothballs rolled into the corners.

"Nothing," Vinny said. "There's nothing there."

She looked across at the wash-stand, but there was only a soiled runner on it, and on the shelf below a water-jug with a broken handle. She stood dazedly in the centre of the room, tasting a despair so dreadful she did not care how foolish she might appear.

Allie looked at her oddly.

"What sorta book, love?"

"Just a book."

"Maybe she forgot an' took it with her."

"No," Vinny said. And it was worse remembering this, because it was so true. "No, she never forgot anything. She always used to do what she said."

"You haven' tried the dressing-table," Allie said. "Try the dressing-table, love. You never know. She might have jus' popped it in one of them drawers."

Hope flickered like a match and lit Vinny's search in the top drawer. It was empty. So was the middle one, and Vinny had difficulty putting it back in position because the wood was warped. She pulled the bottom drawer out and her heart leapt convulsively, for at one end there was a heap of things shoved to one side. She squatted on the floor and pulled the drawer right out to see better. There was a pile of unmarked geometry papers, a belt, an odd glove, and the china basket of flowers she had given Mrs. Striebel.

Vinny's thoughts were tumbled every way in a sickening incoherence as she looked at it, as she swung in a mental fun-fair razzle-dazzle. Something in her throat seemed to be hitting her violently, bringing her to the point of choking. Her lovely gift – it was more than that – it was herself – had been left behind as a thing of no value, equal with test papers and bits of unwanted clothing. The basket shimmered in the light from the hotel veranda as she and Allie looked into the drawer, and Allie ravished by the gilt cried out with pleasure.

"Ooh!" she exclaimed. "Mrs. S. musta lef' that behind. Fancy leaving a pretty thing like that! Lemme see."

She edged Vinny aside and bent down to pick up the basket and set it on the dressing-table where it wobbled and fell over.

"Gee, it's brummy," she said, but she picked it up again and examined with her head on one side and her eyes taking in every detail like a bird. "It's pretty, though. Gee, it's pretty!"

This was the final agony of a week that had been unbearable. Nothing more, she thought, could hurt her like this – that her gift, chosen with such love and gratitude, could be now as forgotten and unwanted as old examination papers. The day had been reduced to its lowest common multiple. She wished she could cry but there was such a dreadful, hard, tight feeling in her chest, as if all the tears of the last four days had finally dried up, leaving nothing but this pain, solid as rock in her heart, in her mind.

The heat in the room closed about her, its warm unfriendly arms squeezing tightly so that they would hurt. Fearing she might faint, she sat on the edge of the bed, dizzy in the clutch of the hot air. Allie did not look round. She was still admiring the basket, running a loving finger over the involved flower clusters.

"S'pose we'll have to send it on to her. I coulda fixed it with a bit of gum." She patted her stomach, now curving ever so slightly over the new life it was bearing tenderly within. She glanced over at the girl sitting miserably on the bed and staring unseeingly ahead. Allie thought she looked funny, kinda dazed as if she'd had a shock or something.

"Well," she said hesitantly, "your book don't seem to be here."

Vinny, blanketed by thicknesses of air, heard nothing, said nothing, had lost touch with meanings and places and people.

Allie repeated her statement with a doubtful expression on her plump face. "I said your book doesn't seem to be here."

"No," Vinny said. "No."

She stood up with an effort and walked to the open door, past the large girl whose generosity with lovers was the talk of the town. Here we are, a small voice said far away in Vinny's mind, both of us here in the same room at last. There is a meaning in that. A proof.

"Thanks," she said without irony. "Thanks for showing me."

She went out into the corridor and she did not look back. The dimness of the building was inseparable from her feelings, as empty. Down the stairs, through the dinning, sweating hall-way beside the bar into sunlight that hit her like a blow.

Her fear was definite now, resolved at last into its final terrifying shape, pointing nine months ahead to the worst shame she could imagine. She wished desperately that she were dead, and when the word in the thought slipped across her mind, at first without meaning, as often happens in impulsive desires, she chased after it and caught it and held on to the wish with a cornered fierceness. She wanted to melt into no time and no trouble as rain-water vanishes in a pool.

She turned towards home automatically. Where else was there to go? Along the roads the women were coming from the shops, loaded with vegetables and groceries and meat to pile into the backs of old sedans and trucks. Vinny pushed past them, her eyes staring blindly at the curve of road by the bridge and the long hill that took her home. There was nothing at all left for her now. Her worship was unwanted, her affection, her gift.

A figure swung on to the bridge from the side road. Betty Klee, swollen and red in the sun, moved past her without a glance and then, struck by an idea, stopped at the far end of the bridge and called back, "When are you going to start knitting?"

Vinny lowered her head against the words. Words were weapons. Her feet raced the laughter that chased the words and then Betty Klee's voice, smooth as oil, said, "Let me knit you something."

Let me die, Vinny prayed, her feet stumbling in the dust-filled car ruts. Let me die quickly. I only had one thing and now it's gone. I never really had it. Maybe she never even liked me. She guessed what I wanted to ask her and she was too ashamed to help, too frightened to give me the truth I didn't want.

She felt desolate as a beach at dusk pounded only by the monotonous theme of the sea. Here finally was the point of isolation, so perfect, so complete, there could be neither a going forward nor backward. Here was the occasion when it is better to remain still and allow the forces outside the central situation – but compelling it nevertheless – to take charge.

The hill home, down which she had walked that morning, less than an hour ago, in the tolerance of hope, was more huge and terrible than she could believe. Her legs dragged in leaden fashion and her whole body felt as if she were pushing enormous weights up the powdery stretch of road. Sky was still blue. Sunlight was still yellow. Trees were still green. She saw none of it. The primary colours escaped a mind absorbed like Sisyphus with its primary task of attaining the top of this impossible hill. Her pain was the boulder she rolled before her. Sweat damped her hair, but her eyes were dry as sand, and her mind, her heart were dry, too, and bent on securing for her the road-crest that seemed to shimmer now in waves of unendurable heat. I hope I die, she said aloud.

There was the casuarina wilting in the midday sun, sad across the picket fence with its unpainted wooden slats, the lantana hedge dotted with hundreds-and-thousands of colour, thorny and overgrown. She looked back down the hill and saw the township's hundred houses, the red roads, the railway-line with its shunting goods train. On the far side of the tracks Betty Klee's dumpy figure was still visible trudging up the slope towards the school.

Vinny pushed open the front gate and went cat-soft along the side of the house on the uncut grass. She could hear the thudding of the iron in the laundry and then the tiny splashing noise of the water in the jam jar as her mother damped down the clothes. Ducking her head instinctively as she passed the window, she ran on round the corner of the house to the toolshed where it leant drunken against the bright green cassias, its roof spattered with brilliant yellow buds and flowers. Vinny stood inside the door, staring outside at the blue and gold air, and was a column of anger and pride and hurt and fear all at once, but mainly anger; and for the first time in her life, she felt a rebellion of egotism that made her want to be noticed. She wanted to punish someone, cause another person pain and thereby transform her own, be a tragic heroine, a centre of a huge pity, a public martyr.

She looked all round the walls, at the junk, the bottles matted with dust and cobwebs along the bench, at the heaps of dried cassia leaves and seed-pods blown in by the wind. There were rake and mattock handles jumbled in corners and across and against the packing cases and the tea chests that they once used for storing old clothes, and there were a dozen chipped flower-pots that her mother had used before she lost her husband and her enthusiasm. Along the shelf behind the door were the tins of fertilizer and the packets of lime and bottles of lye and weed-killer that they used from time to time.

When Vinny saw these her whole body stopped moving for a second, became as still as death which she suddenly knew as her purpose, was the intention of anger that had carried her cat-footed past the house to the toolshed. It was an impulse of resentment that first kept her eyes fixed steadily on the bottles of poison, innocent as the grail, in shadow and under dust. Her intention was shaping itself less with despair than with a fury of desire for attention, for notice, prominence ultimately in school and out of school; even among the adults she would be talked about with awe and pity and perhaps sorrow. She would punish them all. Later Mrs. Striebel would hear and would be sorry too late.

She felt a spasm of heroic elation, and her freckled hands, no longer those of a child, reached untremblingly for a bottle on which, years before, her mother had printed the warning word. The ink had run, was faded. She took the cork off and looked down into her fame that lay still and dangerous and for her, devoid of any fear.

It became so desirable she smiled, a quiet thin little smile, while the cassias trembled and shook their flowers against the rotting timber of the shed. No more fear, her mind rejoiced, no baby, no shame, no voices nagging and pestering and tormenting, no empty lunch-hours, no longer the nothingness of everything, the gift unwanted, the person. She wondered if it would hurt, but she didn't really care. Fame was worth any pain, fame and revenge; and this was her ultimate and most special way of getting even. It wouldn't be hard to do at all. When she was small she had made herself do things like jumping from the steps or the veranda or swinging off trees by counting to three and accusing herself of cowardice if she didn't act on the last number.

She lifted up the bottle and rubbed the dust from its wide rim with the palm of her hand.

In this moment before glory, everything had an amazing clarity. Outside, the grass stood in millions of separate blades, green and sharp, so plainly she could see the shadow of one blade on another, and by the door the image of leaf stamped on leaf. The house sat in shade purple as a grape. Vinny heard the radio bellow suddenly and then the click of the switch snapped down and Royce's feet thudding like hooves across the uncarpeted floor of the back sitting-room.

They would come looking for her soon for lunch. That would be her moment. Hatred, not love, was the last emotion of her heart, and despair was somewhere at the back of this, was everywhere like air, like sounds too high to be heard.

In the gentlest of breezes blowing across the doorway she looked down the lawn at the bloody flags of the acalyphas, and raising the bottle, counted to three. It might hurt a bit, her mind said, but she would never have to be hurt again. That was the main thing.